So Much For Walls

So Much For Walls

A Novel By

Lynn Gregory

So Much For Walls
A novel
By Lynn Gregory

Copyright 2022 by Lynn Gregory
Cover design by Blueline Marketing LLC

Published by Woods Pond Publishing Group

ISBN: 978-0-578-28320-3
Printed in the United States of America

Other fiction by Lynn Gregory:

The Other Side of a Tapestry (2020)

"The more enlightened our houses are, the more their walls ooze ghosts."
Italo Calvino

"Each person creates boundaries and walls around the self. This often keeps happiness at bay."
Govinda

"The walls between art and engineering exist only in our minds."
Theo Jansen

"Life for each man is a solitary cell whose walls are mirrors."
Eugene O'Neill

"What do you hang on the walls of your mind?"
Eve Arnold

"Spiderman can climb walls and he's got a cool outfit."
Rhona Mitra

Contents

PART 1: 1
February 1-April 26, 2002

PART 2: 67
June 8-September 10, 1973

PART 3: 163
April 26-June 30, 2002

EPILOGUE 239

Acknowledgements. 241

About the Author. 243

PART 1

February 1 – April 26, 2002

Chapter 1

February 1, 2002
Newark NJ Train Station

The first thing she noticed was the glare. It wasn't dark out, but it seemed like a lot of lights were directed at her face. A young girl was screaming. Sybil blinked and thought to herself. *What am I doing lying on the ground? What ground am I lying on?*

A worried face, a stranger's face, loomed over her. "Are you okay? Can you move your body? Can you see me?"

These words make no sense.

"I'm cold. My shoulder hurts." Sybil felt silly, but it was all she could think of to say. He looked vaguely familiar, a tall, dark-skinned man with kind eyes. Sybil blinked. *Who is he?*

A relieved expression crossed his face. He took his coat off and draped it over her. "Can you lie still for a minute? There's an ambulance on the way."

She heard the siren but remained confused. *What does this have to do with me?* Unable to come up with an answer, she decided to do as the stranger asked. With no desire to move, Sybil was primarily interested in her original questions. *Why am I lying on the ground? What ground am I lying on?*

The stranger studied her eyes. She found his voice comforting. It was forceful and quiet at the same time.

"There's been an accident. You're in the Newark Train Station parking lot. You may be injured, so it's best if you stay still until the ambulance EMTs show up. They'll know what to do. They'll make sure you don't hurt yourself more."

She didn't remember asking her questions out loud and was impressed with his ability to read her thoughts so well. *But who is he and why is he helping me and boy, he looks vaguely familiar, but I can't remember. I just want to sleep.*

An ambulance pulled up next to her and she was whisked into another confusing moment. The EMTs were sweet. Their arms were strong as they gently, but firmly, moved her onto a stretcher and into the back of the ambulance. She could tell they didn't want her to close her eyes. That could be why they kept asking questions.

"Can you tell me how many fingers I'm showing you? What's your name? Where do you live?"

Sybil saw three fingers and was clear her name was Sybil Morgenstern, but she wasn't able to get those words to come out of her mouth. She could visualize her apartment, but didn't have the words to identify its location. Her brain was singularly focused on wondering why she was there, what she was doing in the Newark Train Station parking lot.

"What happened to me? Why am I at the Newark Train Station? I can't remember."

The EMT responded in a soft tone. "We don't know. We're just trying to determine if you have a head injury—a concussion. We want to make sure you don't fall asleep before you arrive at the hospital."

Sybil nodded. That made sense to her. It was actually the first time she felt a little bit of clarity.

"Your friend said you were the victim of a carjacking."

"My friend?"

"The man who was with you when we arrived"

"I'm not sure I know him. He was very nice and stayed with me when I was lying on the ground, but I'm not sure I know him. Where is he? I want to say thank you. Did you give him back his coat?"

Chapter 2

Rocco had arrived at the Newark Train Station twenty minutes early. As he entered its main level, he heard loud activity in the parking lot. It sounded like someone was screaming. The lot was filled with people milling about as usual, but the screaming came from the entryway where cars lined up to drop off passengers. He quickly discovered its source was a hysterical teenage girl. She and a handful of bystanders were gathered around a woman who was lying on the ground. Someone said the woman had been thrown from a moving car, a carjacking victim. Local police were asking everyone what they had seen.

As he approached the fallen woman, Rocco did a quick assessment and came to the conclusion that she was alone. It was just the way people hovered, with concern and desire to be helpful, but no ownership. The teenager said she didn't know the woman, but had witnessed her being pushed out of a car. She thought the car was going to run her over.

Perhaps because he walked so purposefully, Rocco had no trouble getting through the crowd to kneel beside the woman. From the way she was positioned, he thought she had fallen on her right side. By the time he got there, someone had moved her onto her back. There was blood seeping from an injury on her forehead. The victim was a pretty young woman with large brown eyes and creamy café au lait skin. Rocco figured her to be in her early to mid-twenties. Her eyes were open, but she didn't seem to be registering what was happening. He decided to stay with her until she was safely delivered to an ambulance.

It felt as if all of this took place in a short period, just minutes, but it wasn't until the ambulance arrived and took the young woman away that Rocco's mind flipped back to his own reasons for being at the Newark Train Station. He was supposed to meet Gail by the information kiosk and was probably late. Hoping she was still there, he rushed to get back into the building and completely forgot that he left his coat behind. The intensity of the moment absorbed all of his attention and he had lost track of time. It had been twenty-nine years since he last saw Gail, but for some reason, they neglected to exchange photos or talk about what they would be wearing. Rocco had been surprised to hear from her. All she told him was that she was coming from Albuquerque, New Mexico and would be visiting Manhattan for the first time since 1973.

As it turned out, he arrived at their meeting place about fifteen minutes late, but there she was, the only person standing around looking as if she was looking for someone. Rocco couldn't take his eyes off her. Gail was as gorgeous as he remembered, still willowy, but shapely, and those amazing dancer's legs! Seeing her again reminded him how passionate she had been about dancing. And you could see all the parts of her complex genetic background in her face even though the Asian features dominated.

Reaching to give her a hug, Rocco thought about how much he may have aged. Although he rarely worried one way or the other about his appearance, he hoped she wouldn't be disappointed.

"Gail, I'm so glad you waited! I apologize for not being here when you arrived. A woman was injured in the parking lot so I went out to see if I could help."

If she was disappointed, Gail didn't show it. In fact, her smile signaled delight at seeing her old friend.

"No problem. I knew you would show up and when I heard about the accident, figured you'd be there to help."

Gail hugged Rocco back warmly, and then looked up. She hadn't forgotten how tall he was, but was still surprised. He had a bit of salt and pepper in his hair, but otherwise looked like she remembered him when they were in their early twenties. He still had magnetic eyes, deep pools of dark brown that smiled and conveyed the impression of constant thought at the same time. She was immediately reminded of how attracted she had been to him when they were young.

"Is she going to be alright?"

Trying not to stare, Rocco thought to himself, *of course she looks older but she could be even more elegant than I remember, and that magical smile! And that voice!* He had always found her Jamaican accent, somewhere between British and Caribbean, sexy as hell. Fearing he was staring rudely, Rocco quickly gathered himself and answered her question.

"Actually, it doesn't appear to have been an accident. It looks like she was a crime victim, a carjacking. I waited for the ambulance to take her. She seems to have been alone when this happened. I guess they'll find out when they check her out at the hospital. It looked to me like she had a head injury—there was a lot of blood from a wound above her forehead, but after that, I can't tell you."

"It seems like you learned a lot in a short period of time."

"I guess I never take off my attorney hat and we're trained to notice every little detail in case something turns out to be important. In fact, I'm curious about how this went down."

Turning his gaze toward the door to the parking lot, Rocco's expression changed. "Oh my God, I left my coat behind. I covered her with my coat while we were waiting for the ambulance. Do you mind going out there with me for a minute?"

"Of course not."

As they walked to the parking lot, Rocco and Gail joked that their twenty-nine-year reunion was starting off with a mystery, not unlike some of the adventures they and their friends were involved with when they were young.

Rocco approached a police officer who was still at the scene and asked whether anyone had seen what happened to his coat. The policeman smiled and went to his car where he retrieved the coat.

"We were going to drop it off at the station's lost and found."

"Thanks, it's too cold to be without this today! Even though she had a jacket and gloves on, the poor girl was shivering, probably in shock. Do you know what happened?"

"No-one is exactly sure, but it looks like she pulled over to park her car and was almost immediately thrown to the ground as the carjacker drove off."

"Does anyone know who she is?"

"Not yet. She had no identification on her body. She probably left it in the car. The only thing we found when we searched around where the car was stopped was a pair of busted glasses covered with blood."

Rocco reached into his pocket and gave the policeman his business card. The officer squinted and read the card.

"**John Rockman, Attorney at Law**; you're not one of them ambulance chasers, are you?"

Rocco laughed. "No, I specialize in real estate law and was only here to meet my friend. I work in Newark and live up the street in the Ironbound. Timing is everything; I guess I may qualify as a witness after the fact. If you think of any questions, feel free to contact me."

The policeman nodded abstractly. It was evident his mind had already moved on to other things.

Rocco turned to Gail, "Let's get out of here. Do you want to find some place we can get a cup of coffee or something to eat, a late breakfast? We're not far from the Ironbound."

Seeing a puzzled expression on Gail's face, Rocco continued. "It's a nice Newark neighborhood, primarily Portuguese. It's where I live."

"Sounds good, and, Rocco, it's wonderful to see you. I can't wait to hear all about your life."

"Same here--let's grab a cab."

As they walked towards the taxi stand, Rocco saw the girl who had been screaming. She was in the middle of a group of teenagers, telling the story of the fallen woman. Seeing Rocco walk by, the teenager said, "There's the guy who was taking care of her." Stepping away from the group, she called out to him, "I forgot to give this to the police. Can you do it for me? I found it on the ground where the lady fell."

Handing Rocco a glasses case, she ran off with her friends. Rocco looked closely at the case. It was a hard case covered with a fabric version of an Impressionist painting, perhaps a Monet. It had a flap that closed tightly with a clicking sound, as if there was a magnet holding it together. Inside, Rocco found an imprint giving a name and address advertising an optician located on Madison Avenue in New York City.

Rocco turned to Gail apologetically and said, "This might help the police identify the victim, especially if her head injury continues to cause her to be confused. I guess we'd better take it back to them. Do you mind?"

"Not at all Rocco; I've made no other plans for today."

Unfortunately, when Gail and Rocco reached the parking lot, the police were no longer there. Gail smiled at Rocco and said, "I think we're going to be involved with this for a while. Would you mind grabbing a cup of coffee at the little shop inside the station?"

They had made no plans about how they would spend their reunion, or even how much time they would be together, and Rocco was wondering what it was going to involve. He was happy to see Gail but still didn't know how she had located him or, more importantly, why she contacted him after all these years.

It was still early in the day, but thankfully past rush hour, so they were able to find a little table in the coffee shop where they sat down with their cups. Resting her feet, Gail sighed as she looked at the glasses case again. It was pretty unique. Then she saw a name and phone number hand printed on the inside of the cover.

"Look Rocco! It's a little smudged, but I think we may have the woman's name and phone number here. Let me get my reading glasses on—yes, the name is Sybil Morgenstern. Let's call the number and see if anyone answers."

Rocco pulled out his cell phone and dialed the number. There was a generic voicemail announcement, but no name. He left a message with little hope it would be received.

Gail had an idea. "I think we should take this to the hospital and return it to her. Any thoughts about what hospital they would have taken her to?"

"Actually, I do. Everyone around here goes to UMDNJ, the University Medical and Dental Hospital of New Jersey; it's a huge medical school. Do you want to get a bite to eat before we go?"

"No, this coffee has given me the boost I need. Hey Rocco, I love that we're reuniting with a little adventure. You know what I'm thinking?"

Rocco chuckled, "If you haven't changed, I'll never know what you're thinking Gail, but I'll bite, what are you thinking?"

"Isn't it weird her name is Sybil, the "stage" name of our friend who introduced us all those years ago? It's not a common name."

Rocco sat back and said thoughtfully, "I had forgotten Alice used that name, but wasn't it just when we were doing our thing in the park?"

"Yes, Alice called it her stage name, but I sometimes thought it was her alter ego, the all-powerful woman of Greek mythology."

Rocco thought about Alice Lyons. Of course she had been on his mind since he got the call from Gail. "Now I remember, she had read a novel called *The Sybil* that got her thinking about how names give you power. She was definitely into giving meaning to names. When we were in high school she went back and forth between Alice and Alicia, depending on her mood. I guess she figured she could change her name and be a Sybil when we were doing our alternative reality performances in the park."

"Funny about the stage name, I remember thinking about her when the television movie about the woman named Sybil with multiple personalities came out. That was a few years after we went our separate ways. It was such an unusual name. But I never thought of our happenings as alternative reality, just exercising free artistic expression. On the other hand, Alice was so different from me. I never really tried to understand her."

"I thought you two were close friends in college."

"I wouldn't say we were ever really close. In fact, at first I thought she was a stushface."

"Huh?"

"Oh I'm sorry, that's a Jamaican term for a snob. But as I got to know her, knew it wasn't that. She was a kind and caring person, just sort of a closed book. I met Alice in my freshmen year when we briefly dated two guys who were roommates. After that, we were friendly acquaintances, but never hung around in the same circles. Alice was politically active, super smart, and had a lot of friends, but she never seemed to let anyone get close. In retrospect, I think she was being self-protective. Remember how much she used to talk about walls and how important it was to conquer them, not just climb over them, but to go through them? It was like she was drawn to challenges as she simultaneously erected barriers. It must've been tough living in her head. I mean I understood wanting to get through barriers, but was never drawn to doing everything myself. Maybe I've always been lazy, but I wanted a smooth ride."

Gail stared at a corner of the room while she digested her thoughts. Then she looked back at Rocco and continued, "I guess I kept to myself too, but that was mostly because I was shy, and a foreigner. I was always pretty much of a nerd."

"That's really hard for me to imagine, Gail. When we met that summer, I thought you were the most glamorous, stylish girl I had run across. To be honest, you seemed so different from Alice, I wondered about you two being friends. I mean, she was cute, but never seemed to care about her appearance. There's no way you were ever a nerd! You were not only gorgeous, but a natural, fluid dancer. I've always thought of you as a dancer.

When I think about that summer, you're always in motion, dancing day and night."

Gail blushed. "Dance was definitely my passion, but I was a business major. My parents had very specific professional plans for me, to work in the family business. They saw no benefit to my learning about the arts or even the liberal arts. No, it was all about coming away with practical skills that would make money for them. Becoming a professional dancer was my personal dream, but it was always a long shot. Even as early as the summer of '73, I knew the difference between talent and genius. With a lot of work, I had talent, but genius just wasn't part of the picture. I guess that summer was the one moment I got to live in my dream world, yet, oddly, I probably learned more about life the summer of 1973 than in all of my college years combined."

"Me too, Gail, I have a hard time getting into my twenty-two-year- old head so it's almost impossible to put this in words; but those few months put me on a trajectory I wouldn't have been able to predict before that June. So how did you and Alice become roommates?"

"It was kind of an accident. I'm sure you remember that we were at Coral College in Southern California. It was a pretty liberal place for that time where they allowed upper classmen to live outside of the dorms. The summer before our junior year, Alice and I ran into each other and decided to find an off-campus place to share. We ended up doing that and stayed together until we graduated, but to be perfectly honest, I don't remember talking about deep subjects with Alice. That may have been why we got along as roommates; we didn't get into each other's business. I know I was pretty caught up in my own little world, and she always seemed to keep me at arm's length. When I think about it now, what we had in common, probably like a lot of girls at that age, was dreaming about the perfect lives we could have if everything worked out as it should."

Smiling as she thought about the innocence of that time in her life, Gail continued, "Alice and I shared a desire to be artists in the large sense of the word, to bring extraordinary creativity into whatever we cared to do. That was where we were mentally when we ran into you in New York. Remember her buzzword, 'Creative Authenticity'?"

Rocco nodded, "Yes, I really bought into that concept! I remember feeling like the three of us were uniquely in tune with each other creatively. That was what we were doing in Central Park, wasn't it, just letting go and allowing ourselves to let the creative juices flow. That part totally worked, at least for a while, but I agree with you about Alice. I don't believe Alice got really close to anyone back then. We were friends, I mean we shared our dreams of adventure, but I'm not sure I ever really knew what was going on in her head either. I always had the feeling she was holding something back. On the other hand, women's minds are mysterious to me in general."

Rocco stood up, stretched his legs and changed the subject. "Let's go to the hospital."

Chapter 3

February 1, 2002
Newark NJ

The emergency room waiting area was packed. It was Friday morning in an inner city hospital, a place many people used for their family's primary care needs. Nonetheless, Rocco and Gail were surprised to find it full, mostly with sick, unhappy children, frustrated parents, injured teenagers, wobbly adults who were high, drunk, or unbalanced, and a few quiet individuals with heads buried in books, magazines and newspapers who were simply trying to ignore the noisy chaos around them.

Yet, everyone in the room was primarily focused on the two swinging doors through which patients were escorted to get their current medical needs met. Each time they opened, all heads turned to see who the lucky patient would be; everyone except the woman sitting behind a computer screen who served as the gatekeeper. Her eyes did not leave the screen. She never looked at the doors but always seemed to know who was going next and who they would be met by. For this reason, she was viewed as an all-powerful Wizard of Oz who got to decide which of them would be considered a true medical emergency and which would have to wait.

The line wasn't long when Rocco and Gail entered, but the waiting room was full of people with immediate needs. Rocco and Gail didn't expect the computer lady to put their request to speak with someone about the young woman's identity on a front burner and figured they would be waiting for a long time for the brief conversation they wanted to have with her. Especially after seeing how busy the receptionist was, they decided if they were to achieve their goal of getting the glasses case to a doctor or nurse who could connect with Sybil Morgenstern, it was best not to leave it at the desk. It was going to be a long morning.

However, Gail and Rocco didn't really mind. Enjoying the idea of starting their reunion with a shared adventure, they both felt comfortable falling back on the playful way they had started games when they were young.

Rocco began, "I think that's a magic door. What would you guess is behind it?"

Gail chuckled and pointed to a corner of the room, "Do you see those two little boys fighting over who gets to use the water fountain first? I think this is about them."

"I agree Gail, I think they will go through those doors and immediately turn into sweet, but yippy puppies."

"So, does going through the doors change everyone who makes it through? Is that why they're here?

"Nah, no-one knows about the magic kingdom except you and me. People are here because they have medical emergencies or they're with people who have medical emergencies. Only special people are transformed into puppies when they go through those doors."

Gail laughed again. She had always loved hearing Rocco's playful imagination in action.

"Then, I have two questions. Is it a good or bad thing to be turned into a puppy? And what does it take to be chosen for such a transformation?"

"Now that's the big mystery, isn't it? No-one out here will ever know who decides. There may be people behind those doors who don't know either."

Just then, the doors opened to allow a man and a woman wearing dark pants with multiple pockets into the waiting room. Rocco immediately recognized them as the EMTs who had been in the ambulance with Sybil Morgenstern, and jumped up to tell them about the glasses case.

"It has a name handwritten on the inside. We weren't sure whether she had been identified, and thought this might be helpful."

The EMT recognized him. "Oh yes, you were the Good Samaritan who stayed by her until we came. I'm glad to see you got your coat back. She kept asking who you were and said she wanted to thank you. It's very kind of you to come to the hospital with the glasses case. Let me run and get the nurse who was working with her."

The EMTs went back through the doors and within a short time, returned with a harried-looking nurse.

Handing the glasses case to the nurse, Rocco asked if the young woman was going to be alright. Without answering his question, the nurse said thank you and turned to go back through the doors.

Rocco called out. "As you can see, there's a name and phone number hand-written inside the case. We tried the number, but there was no response. However, the imprint on the case gives a name and address of an optician on the Upper East Side of Manhattan. Maybe the optician has more contact information, perhaps an emergency contact, on file. I know it's a shot in the dark."

The nurse looked at the case, frowned, and then sighed. "As you can see, we're totally swamped here today."

Gail surprised Rocco with her next words. "I know it's probably not kosher to bring in strangers, but we might be able to help you identify her. I'm staying at a bed and breakfast that's not far from the optician's office. I can stop by and tell them what's going on and maybe, if they have emergency contact information, they can give you a call."

The nurse smiled for the first time. "That would be wonderful. Let me give you my cell number so they can reach me directly. Do you have a piece of paper?"

Rocco pulled out two business cards. He gave one to the nurse and wrote her cell number on the other.

Taking the card, the nurse looked up at Rocco, "Thank you, Mr. Rockman." She turned her head slightly to smile at Gail, "Thank you both."

Rocco's eyes followed the nurse as she rushed through the doors to her next emergency. Turning to Gail, he said, "I have so much admiration for the work these folks do. They have to be running on adrenalin much of the time. We were lucky to get a chance to speak with her. Thanks for coming up with the offer to check in with the optician. It's just possible they'll have a contact for Sybil Morgenstern. I know this is really inconvenient for you having just gotten off the train, but would you mind heading back to Manhattan now? We can have lunch there and maybe have a walk in Central Park. Then I'm afraid I will have to head back to Newark. I'm going to need to check in with my office later in the afternoon."

"Of course, how can we get across the Hudson quickly? There has to be a better way than waiting for Amtrak or New Jersey Transit to get us to Penn Station. I know some of the trains and stations were disabled by the 9-11 attacks. My God, Rocco, we haven't even talked about that! Were you anywhere near when the planes went into the World Trade Center towers?"

"I was in Newark meeting with a client and actually saw the second plane hit the tower. I had just arrived and saw it happen from a roof parking lot. Even being that close, it was unreal. It seemed like I was watching a movie. We do have a lot of catching up to do, Gail, but let's save that for later. Where's the B and B you're staying at?"

"It's on Second Avenue, somewhere around the low 70s."

"Then we're all set." Rocco pulled out his cell phone and called a cab.

Chapter 4

February 1, 2002
New York City

The trek into the City went as planned and, luckily, the optician was affiliated with an optometrist who had Sybil Morgenstern's records. Once they heard what had happened, the optometrist called the nurse and gave her Sybil's emergency contact information. As Gail and Rocco left the office, Rocco brought up the subject of lunch again.

"Interested in some deli food? I know a great place on Fifth Avenue, across from the Park."

"Sure Rocco. You know, I don't recall spending much time on the east side of the park back in 1973, do you?"

"No, we were mostly around Central Park West. Do you remember the apartment building? I believe it was somewhere in the 80s."

Gail looked at the ground, "I will never forget that apartment. The building itself had a personality that's forever etched in my mind. Isn't it odd that we never went to the east side to at least go to the Central Park Zoo or the Metropolitan Museum?"

"Maybe, but when you think about it, we were only together as a group for about three months—three jam-packed months, and we weren't exactly rolling in dough. Oh look, we're here."

As Rocco led her into a noisy delicatessen packed with people, all who seemed to be talking loudly at once, Gail felt overwhelmed and withdrew physically. Noticing her reaction, Rocco said, "This is Pan's Deli, one of the best in the City. The food is worth the craziness."

It had been a while since Gail had been in such a busy city. She had forgotten how much noise there was everywhere, and how quickly everyone moved around. They got into a fast-moving line along a long glass-enclosed counter. Everyone seemed to know exactly what they wanted and called out their orders loudly to multiple servers working behind the counter.

"Pastrami on rye with extra pickles on the side"

"Corned beef with spicy mustard on Kaiser"

The place reminded her of the old Saturday Night Live skit about a restaurant where they only sold cheeseburgers and Pepsi. But here there were many too many choices. *Don't they have a menu, for God's sake!*

Despite the unrelenting background noise, Gail's feeling of frustration was significantly relieved when she and Rocco were finally sitting across from one another at a small table.

Biting into her Reuben sandwich, Gail said, "You're right, Rocco, this food is worth the chaos."

Rocco smiled, "It's great to see you again Gail, but I guess we need to talk about why we're here, why you got in touch with me after all these years. How you found me? Are you in trouble? Are you looking for a lawyer? I haven't even asked how long you plan to be in town!"

"I'm sorry Rocco, I don't mean to be evasive, but it's so noisy in this deli. Do you have time to take a walk in the park before you head back to your office? Some of this is rather private."

"Sure."

As they walked into the park, passing by the Metropolitan Museum, Cleopatra's Needle and the Great Lawn, Gail thought about what to say. Once again, she was afraid of seeming foolish. *Why is that? He's an old friend and he's really being nice to me. Could I possibly have some unresolved feelings for him? I know I don't want to turn him off, but I have to say something.*

"I have to be honest, Rocco. I've enjoyed starting a new adventure and reliving my time in New York. I almost hate to change the subject, but I guess I have to. You are undoubtedly a busy man and I've taken you away from your office."

"Not a problem, Gail. I'm senior enough to decide how I spend my days. Talk to me."

"Okay, I guess I should start by answering the easy questions. I did some research to find you. There are a lot of John Rockmans out there, but I remembered you graduated from Gilmore University, so I contacted their alumni office and discovered you were an attorney working in Newark. Prior to that, I didn't know you had become a lawyer, but it turns out to be a happy coincidence. I could definitely use some legal advice. Before I go further, I honestly can't tell you which is the chicken and which the egg in this case. I'm not sure I would've contacted you without a legal excuse, but I was definitely interested in reconnecting no matter what. I apologize; this is probably much more information than you were looking for. I've been really confused lately. You came to mind because I remember trusting you. So the answer to your other question is that I think I need professional help."

"Legal help?"

"Yes"

Rocco felt himself adjusting his 'lawyer hat.'

"Why don't we start by you telling me exactly what is going on."

Gail shivered and took a deep breath.

"Are you cold, Gail? I forgot you just came here from the southwest. It has to be a major body temperature adjustment."

"Thanks for asking, Rocco, but I'm fine. Knowing I would be here in February, I came prepared. I was just shivering because I need to tell you some painful things. It's been so nice to be with you and away from all of that."

Rocco nodded, "I understand, but it might help to give it some air. You're safe here. I've learned as an attorney that people usually try to say uncomfortable things in as few words as possible, but they often leave the important parts out. Lawyers want to hear everything and make their own decisions about what's important and what isn't. I know you haven't hired me to represent you at this point, but you can presume that everything you say to me will remain completely confidential. You're speaking to me as a friend who can turn what you say into a lawyer-client relationship on a dime."

Gail took another deep breath, "Okay. My husband died and left everything to me."

Rocco didn't know what he had expected her to say, it certainly wasn't that; but he put on an objective professional face and responded, "I'm sorry to hear of your loss, Gail, but the rest sounds like the beginning of a happy problem. I didn't know you were married, of course. How long were you together? Who was this lucky guy?"

"I'll slow down, I've just thrown a lot of new information at you. My husband is, sorry, was, Mike Lucas. We live in New Mexico. You may have heard of his father Ed Lucas. He's a well-known physicist who was involved in the Los Alamos Project way back when."

"You mean the folks who created the atomic bomb that ended World War Two in Hiroshima?"

"That's the one."

"Why do I know that name? It's not because of the history. I was never much of a history buff."

"Do you mind if we sit down on that bench? This is going to take a few minutes to explain."

"No problem."

"Mike was in college with me and Alice. She and I rode as far as Albuquerque with him and his friend Joey Knox when we came east after we graduated, just before we ran into you in Manhattan all those years ago. Alice and I stayed at Mike's parents' house for a few days before heading to New York. You probably heard us talk about him when we met up in the City that summer."

"Oh yes, now I remember. He had a thing for you, didn't he? And you were pushing back. Did he come to New York at one point?"

"No, he never came to New York. He talked about it, but was busy with his new job working for his father. I liked him, but I wasn't ready to commit and was very confused about what I wanted to do. There had been sparks between us in Albuquerque but I wanted the New York adventure with Alice, and to be honest, my family was expecting me in Jamaica. I had already lied to them about what I was doing that summer and was feeling guilty."

Gail decided to stay away from the elephant in the room; that she had lost interest in Mike when she met Rocco that summer. She thought he had been aware of her feelings, but there was no sense in bringing that up at this point. Gail was also trying to keep her personal needs in check. She was aware it was common for widows and widowers to make stupid relationship moves in the wake of their losses. While it was possible she had come in search of Rocco, in part, to find out how she felt all these years later, her legal troubles were legitimate and had to be front and center.

Rocco was obviously not thinking about their past, and was all business as he asked more questions about her relationship with Mike.

"How did you end up together? When did you get together? Take your time Gail. I have no place to go, no promises to keep."

Gail smiled, recognizing the lyrics of a favorite oldie.

"I went back to Jamaica at the end of the summer of 1973. My parents never knew about my New York detour and I was feeling guilty enough to hunker down and help them with their business. I tried, I really tried; but my father was a gambler and had already run the business into the ground financially."

As if to illustrate her point, Gail paused, looked at her feet and continued, "To this day I wonder if things would've worked out better for them if they hadn't spent so much money sending me to college, but they didn't know how to run a business anyway. As I mentioned before, my father had a gambling addiction, so he had probably won big when I went away to school. Being able to afford to send me to a good college in the U.S. gave him a lot of prestige. I'm only guessing about this in retrospect. I didn't know what was going on at the time, only that I was expected to return from college with marketing expertise that would help to grow the business and make them a lot of money."

Looking up again, Gail added, "I was a kid."

"How long did you stay in Jamaica?"

"About fourteen years."

"That's a long time! What did you do there?"

"Well, besides help my parents dismantle the business, which took a few years following the couple of years we tried to make it work, I got a job doing marketing for a rival company. My college degree was actually worth something and I did pretty well there, but then my father fell apart. He ended up dying at an early age and I became the head of the family. I have three younger sisters who still had to be raised."

"I'm so sorry. This is too much loss. How's your mother doing?"

"Actually, my mother turned out fine. She's always been an attractive woman, and has a lot of charm, but very little business savvy. She ended up remarrying-- a German guy. They currently live in Switzerland."

"When did you leave Jamaica? Oh wait, were you and Mike in touch all that time?"

"No, that happened later. I was stuck in a rut in Jamaica. I never wanted to stay, and honestly, I only went back because of my family obligations. I know I never talked about this when we were in New York that summer, but I'm the oldest and was always made to feel responsible for my younger sisters. I paid the price for my college education, and the freedom I experienced in the States, with going back to being the family caregiver. I was very busy in Jamaica."

"So, when does Mike come into the picture?"

"To be perfectly honest, I wasn't thinking about Mike. I was in Jamaica for fourteen years and sort of expected to spend the rest of my life there, so I tried. I mean I dated and met more than one guy I liked, but ultimately the thought of spending my life there just wasn't working for me. So when my youngest sister was finally settled into her own adult life, I lifted myself up and went to Albuquerque."

"That was an interesting decision. Did Mike know you were coming?"

"This may seem strange, but I didn't even know if he would be there. All I knew was that I had happy memories of the few days I spent in Albuquerque and visiting other places in the Southwest on the way to New York with Alice. I had just graduated from college and everything felt possible. I associated good memories with Mike, so when I was looking for a place to start my new life, I just up and went there. It was probably bizarre given that fourteen years had passed, but I did it anyway. It was definitely an impulsive move for someone who always liked her ducks in a row before taking any steps."

"And?"

"I was really nervous when I got there, and questioned my sanity a million times. I kept telling myself I just liked the place and it wouldn't matter if I ran into him one way or the other. But, I kind of disproved that when I arrived and instead of looking him up, I looked for his friend Joey Knox."

"That name also sounds familiar. Wasn't he a close friend of Alice's? I always thought she had a thing for him."

Gail looked at Rocco closely. *Was that more than just curiosity in his voice?*

"They did seem to connect, but she was always mysterious regarding relationships. It was like she became close to the men she was interested in, but always kept her wings ready to flit out of reach."

"Tell me about it!"

Gail couldn't help asking, "Did you see Alice after that summer? I always thought you two were in love with each other."

"I can only speak for myself Gail. I had a teenage crush on Alice in high school, but I don't think she ever thought of me that way. I know she thought of me as a friend, but in my high school at that time, interracial relationships were definitely not socially acceptable. Not just among the kids but the adults, our parents, would not have been at all amused; so it never came up. We did share, and found some commonalities in our personal dreams for the future, but we never once went to each other's houses. I didn't even know where she lived."

"What did you share?"

"I can't remember how it started, but somewhere along the way we discovered we were both obsessed with travel and adventure. I know a lot of people wanted to travel before they settled down, but Alice was the only person I knew who shared my desire to test boundaries. We were both seriously interested in experiencing extremes."

"I knew that about Alice, but only vaguely remember your talk about extremes, not the details. What extremes did you want to experience?"

"Probably just anything we hadn't done before, but at the time, we mostly talked about going places with really cold climates, like the north and south poles."

"Did you ever get to do that?"

"Yes and no, but we're getting way off topic now."

Gail nodded. She noticed he hadn't answered her question about whether he and Alice had been in touch since that summer, but decided to let it go.

"I always thought you were in love with her, but never knew what had gone down between you. As I said before, she didn't talk about her feelings and that summer was a time for all of us to try things out, to spread our wings." Gail looked closely at Rocco thinking, *it's now or never*. "I developed a big crush on you, you know."

"Ah yes, and I flirted back, but I always thought you were out of my league. You did know that every man who came near you fell madly in love, right? You were, still are, incredibly gorgeous. So yes, I guess I knew about the crush, but we were in our early twenties and you would be going to Jamaica soon, so it was fun and safe. That was one of the reasons I became convinced Alice just thought of me platonically. I was pretty sure she knew there was mutual attraction between you and me, but was taking it in stride. It seemed important to keep things simple among the three of us, but of course that turned out to be impossible."

Rocco stood up and stretched his legs. Watching him, Gail began to think that leg stretching was Rocco's tried and true method for changing the subject. She took a silent breath. *So that was how he thought about me. He knew I had feelings for him. Why did that still hurt?*

Chapter 5

February 1, 2002
New York City

"Rocco, are you married, have kids?"

Rocco laughed, "Nope, as far as I know not even once, or one. Hey, there's still time, I'm only fifty-one, not over the hill yet! So Gail, what can I do for you?"

"As I mentioned before we went off on one of our million tangents today, I reconnected with Mike about 15 years ago when I went to Albuquerque. He was in an unhappy marriage. His wife had been openly cheating on him for years and he was miserable. In a nutshell, we got involved and he got divorced. That was probably the only time in his life Mike rebelled against his father's wishes. Even though everyone knew about his wife's infidelities and how difficult it had been for him, they never accepted me. Mike figured they would get used to it and I quote, 'fall in love with me because how could they not'."

"From the tone of your voice, I gather that didn't happen."

"Nope, that didn't happen. The only people who ever stuck up for me were his younger sister and brothers. His mother liked me in the beginning. I guess she was impressed with my knowledge of the fashion biz, but his father always saw me as beneath them. He was/is a conservative Goldwater Republican."

Gail smiled at a memory, "But I have to say he liked me better than Alice. Oh, he disliked everything about her."

"I can only imagine Alice's liberal political opinions being hard for a Goldwater Republican to be around, especially that summer when the Watergate Hearings were in full flower."

"Yep, with her long hair and ragged clothes, she was the epitome of the dirty, anti-war, anti-establishment hippie. Alice was never shy about expressing her opinions and she was obsessed with Watergate. Anyway, both of Mike's parents were upset when his marriage to Lisa didn't work out. Her family is also wealthy, big shots in the community and the country club."

Rocco nodded and switched gears, "So Joey Knox helped you get in touch with Mike?"

"Nope, Joey was no longer living in Albuquerque and as it turned out, Mike and Joey had drifted apart. I ended up finding

Mike the old-fashioned way; I looked him up in a phone book."

"You and Mike stayed in Albuquerque?"

"Yes, and thereabouts. Mike worked for his father's consulting firm, a successful business he was expected to take over. I'm not sure he was ever thrilled with it, but felt obligated. He never shared his father's conservative political views. In college he was an activist, anti-war and pro-civil rights. That was how he and Alice knew each other. But he wasn't rebellious by nature; he was basically a laid back guy who avoided conflict. Marrying me was probably the most revolutionary thing he had ever done."

As she spoke, Gail couldn't help contrasting Mike's compliant nature with the strength of the man who stood before her now. She couldn't help remembering how being around Rocco made her feel all those years ago. And it was still there, the magnetism. Mike had been sweet, but Rocco was both sweet and strong.

Seeing Gail's eyes drift, Rocco thought she must be feeling sad. Of course she was sad, she just lost her husband. He decided to bring her back to the business at hand.

"He sounds like a great guy, Gail. I'm glad he brought you happiness."

Feeling guilty that she was actually thinking about Rocco, not Mike, Gail snapped her brain back. She was asking Rocco to help her in his professional capacity, not because she found him physically attractive!

"He did, and he made a ton of money, which brings me back to what's going on now. Mike and his first wife, Lisa, have a daughter."

"Oh, that makes the cheese more binding! How old is she?"

"Let me think, she was about ten when we got together, and that was fifteen years ago, so that would make her twenty-five."

"I almost hate to ask, what's your relationship with her?"

"Sadly, I've never had a relationship with her. She doesn't know me, but she hates my guts. Her mother has made sure of that. I can understand his ex-wife not liking me, but she also put a huge amount of energy into turning their daughter Cindy against her father."

"Mike and his daughter didn't have a relationship?"

"Not really; not in a long time. In the beginning the courts gave him visitation rights, but I wasn't allowed to participate.

Then she hit puberty and simply refused to see him. She always had other things to do and places to go. Mike's parents included Lisa and Cindy in family events we weren't invited to. I think Mike thought Cindy would come around when she was no longer under her mother's control, but I guess it was too late. It never happened."

Gail began to tear up, "It broke his heart. He was such a good person. It wouldn't surprise me to learn that it contributed to his heart failure."

"So, let me sum this up. Mike left you everything; nothing for his daughter?"

"I think he figured she would be wealthy anyway. Her mother's family is also rolling in dough."

"But they're fighting you for your inheritance."

"Yes, and they're also fighting to take our son Brian's rightful inheritance."

Rocco raised his eyebrows. "You have a son! Jesus Gail, you could've mentioned that earlier. I'm going to have to take notes. How old is Brian? Where is he now?"

"Brian's thirteen and at the moment he's in a boarding school in Colorado."

"Is there anything else you haven't mentioned to me?"

"No, I think that's it."

"Okay, I'm not an expert in inheritance law, but I believe relatives, especially children of the deceased, can challenge a will. However, unless it can be proven that it was written under duress or something of that nature, the will stands. What's worrying you? Why do you want an out-of-state attorney?"

Gail pushed a pebble with her foot and stared at the ground for what seemed like a long time, then looked up at Rocco and said, "I feel friendless in Albuquerque. Since Mike passed, I've become increasingly aware of how he protected me from his family's hostility, but even before that, I had learned to shut it out." Pausing for a minute, she sighed, "It's not like it was the first time in my life. I experienced racial hostility both here and in Jamaica. Even that summer; remember the slimy things that jerk Teddy, the apartment owner's son, used to say about me? I guess I decided a long time ago it's the price we pay for daring to integrate."

Rocco nodded, "Teddy Farrow; that asshole is still around. He's been making political waves in New Jersey these days, appealing to every white racist who's threatened by minority participation. He doesn't even try to disguise his racism. Unfortunately, he and his family have taken advantage of people's fears in the wake of the World Trade Center attacks on 9/11."

"What are they doing?"

"His family-owned real estate business, Farrow Holdings, the same one we rented from that summer, dominates the low-to-middle-income housing market in north Jersey and parts of New York City. The Farrows seem to be allowed to do whatever they want in their little world. So they've been systematically throwing people of color, especially Muslims, out of their rentals and successfully blackballing them in the sales market."

Gail sighed again, "I always thought there was something wrong with Teddy and could never understand why Alice allowed him to follow us around. The only time she drew the line was when he started being creepy with Melissa and Daphne. Remember the teenage sisters who hung out with us in the park? I never knew exactly what he did to them, but if I recall, Melissa stopped coming after that. I think Alice read him the riot act and he stopped coming too. When I think about it, though, Alice must have let him come back because I'm pretty sure he was there at the last happening before we went our separate ways."

"Yes, I remember you and I talked about our frustration with Alice on that very subject, but she was determined to find his 'inner artist.' She truly believed in the redemptive power of art and thought finding it in Teddy would prove her point. But as far as I can see, there was nothing there to begin with and he certainly hasn't changed. He's still living off his father's money but also has some position in the family business. I've even heard rumors that he's thinking about running for public office. That terrifies me. He may be an empty suit, but what a dangerous empty suit!"

Rocco looked at his watch, "We have a lot to talk about, Gail, and I hope we can get together again soon, but I'm going to have to get back to Newark. How long did you say you're staying in New York?"

"I hope I'm not taking up too much of your time, Rocco. I have no plans at the moment, so I guess the answer is, as long as I want. At some point, I need to go to Switzerland to visit my mother, but I'm pretty flexible, and as I mentioned before, money is not an issue. Can I finish my story so you can decide whether you want to help?"

"Of course"

"It seems like they all came after me with knives the minute Mike passed away. I now know that his parents, and Lisa's family, hate me for racial as well as personal reasons and they hate my kid because he's half me. No-one, not even Mike's sister and brothers have stood up for us. I honestly think they're afraid of his father. I've been showered with legal demands I don't understand and have honestly felt threatened for my life. I'm coming to believe that if I don't leave 'Dodge' quietly, with my son, but without my money, I will be harmed, or worse yet, he will be harmed."

"Have you gone to the police about the threats?"

"No, because I know I won't be believed. These folks are prominent members of the community. I'm an outsider with a funny accent who dared to marry one of their own. I know it sounds like a melodramatic soap opera, but I really need a friend!"

Rocco stood up, pulled Gail from the bench and put his arms around her. As he did that, she burst into the flood of tears that had been building up for a long time. After several minutes of standing together, Rocco pushed Gail away enough so she could see his face and said, "I'll do what I can to look into this for you. I may need some time to consult with people I know."

"Oh Rocco, I'm so grateful! I'll definitely stick around New York for a while. The folks at my son's school know what's going on and are protective of him and our privacy. I hate to admit this, but I came here with no plan B."

"It may take time to get your money when there's another claim on it. Do you have enough to cover your expenses? If not, I could probably help you out."

"That's really sweet, Rocco, but I'm fine. Mike always made sure I had my own pot of money, just in case."

"Great. That makes things easier. Let me walk you to your B and B; then I need to head back to Newark. I'll give you a call from my office tomorrow and may ask you to repeat some of the things you've told me. I will need names and contact information."

"I can't thank you enough, Rocco. I will sleep better tonight than I have for the past five months... since Mike died."

Chapter 6

February 1- 8, 2002
Toronto, Newark NJ, Jersey City NJ

Rick Morgenstern was in Toronto when he received a phone call from the Newark hospital with news that his wife Sybil was the victim of a violent crime. A popular science writer, Rick was on a book tour to promote his latest book, a study of prehistoric rock art. In the midst of a gathering, Rick had muted his cell phone but glanced at it briefly when he felt the vibration in his pocket. He didn't recognize the number and almost deleted it, then noticed there was a voicemail message and decided to have a listen when he was done with the meeting.

Rick had been in a good frame of mind. The room was filled with interested people, from both the academic and lay worlds, who asked intelligent questions about his work and its contributions to prehistory, art history, and art in general. Their questions and comments stimulated his imagination and he forgot about the phone message. Back in the hotel room making changes to his notes for the next presentation, he idly picked up the phone to call Sybil and once again noticed he had a message. This time he listened.

The news shook him to the core and as he fumbled with the phone, it took a while to reach the nurse from UMDNJ who had left the message. All she had said was that his wife had been injured at the Newark Train Station and was in the hospital. By the time he got a response to his return call, he had cancelled the remainder of his tour and made his way to the Toronto airport where his first stop was the airline desk. As soon as he told his story to the woman at the counter, she found him a seat on the next flight. He felt very fortunate. In the wake of the 9-11 attacks on the World Trade Center a few months previously, airports had yet to establish uniform improved safety procedures and just getting on a plane could be onerous. Although it added up to just a few hours, every step of his journey seemed to take forever. He had been unable to reach Sybil on her cell phone and had very little information about what happened and how she was faring.

Fortunately, he had parked his car in a long-term lot at the Newark Airport, but it seemed as if he had to jump through hoops to get there and when he finally got on the road, couldn't remember the best way to get to the hospital. His first reaction was to hop on the New Jersey Turnpike, but in his confused state, found that he was heading towards their home in Jersey City and the Holland Tunnel rather than Newark. He was too muddled to figure out how to get back on the turnpike to turn around, so he got off at the Jersey City exit, and traveled the familiar roads over the two bridges between Jersey City and Newark. Now he would just have to find the hospital. He knew its general location and figured once he reached downtown Newark there would be signs and it would be large enough not to miss; but in truth, he had never been there. It was getting dark and he was afraid he wouldn't arrive in time to be allowed to see Sybil.

By the time he made it to the hospital and parked in its indoor parking lot, Rick was on a fine edge. He rushed into the front lobby and begged to be allowed to go straight to her room. Seeing a man in distress, the receptionist contacted the nurse's station on Sybil's floor and asked if someone could meet him at the elevator. Everyone was kind and concerned that he would have a difficult time seeing her injuries.

Needless to say, Sybil was thrilled to see Rick. She was in obvious pain, but was able to explain that she had six broken ribs, one of which had resulted in a punctured lung. One side of her face was covered with wounds and she had stitches on her forehead where she had sustained a head injury. However, by the time he arrived, the pain killers had kicked in and she was much less confused than when she first arrived at the hospital.

While shocked by her appearance, hearing Sybil speak calmly went a long way towards easing Rick's fears. Once they were alone, he couldn't help asking why she was at the Newark train station.

"I was at a meeting in Newark with some folks from the Jaffe Anti-Racism Society. I was driving back to the office when my cell phone rang. I pulled into the train station parking lot to answer the phone. It's all blank after that."

"Have the police found the carjacker?"

"I don't think so, but they haven't been here to talk to me yet. I think they may have asked me some questions in the beginning, but I was too confused."

"I'll get in touch with them. Did they give you a card or tell you who to call there?"

"I don't think you're hearing me, Rick, I don't remember. I was too confused to register what they were saying."

"I'm sorry Sybil; I guess I'm still in shock. The most important thing is that you're okay."

"I'm not sure that's true. I'm only functioning because I'm full of pain meds. My lung may be permanently damaged. The puncture wound hasn't healed and it's affecting my breathing, and they seem to be worried about the concussion. I've been confused and can't remember what happened. They tell me I'll have to stay here until they're sure about my lung."

Rick didn't know what to say and was relieved when a nurse walked into the room. He asked the nurse if he could speak with the doctor. She nodded, and leading him towards the corridor, said, "Good time to give her a rest. Follow me and I'll try to catch the doc between patients."

Smiling at Sybil, the nurse pointed to a bag of clothes on the small table next to the bed and said to Rick, "I'll bet your wife would appreciate your coming back with her own underwear and toothbrush."

Reaching for the bag, Rick noticed the business card of a lawyer named John Rockman on the table. Puzzled, he asked, "Who's this lawyer?"

"This is the man who helped your wife when she was injured and later made the connection with the optometrist that enabled us to locate you. We thought you might like to be in touch with him, especially if Sybil has more questions about the carjacking."

Sybil looked up, "I definitely want to thank him. He was so kind to me." Then, shifting her position with a soft grunt, added, "He's a lawyer? I didn't know that."

Rick put the card in his pocket as he gathered her belongings. "Let's make a point of doing that once you're home and settled in."

Sybil spent a week in the hospital while her punctured lung healed. By the time Rick took her home to their apartment in Jersey City, she had spent much too much time blowing into a bag to measure the effect of the puncture wound on her breathing. She was also on large doses of pain medication for the broken ribs, but her other injuries were relatively minor. There had been concern that she had sprained her right wrist and left ankle as both were swollen, but the swelling was temporary. The right side of her face had been scraped from top to bottom and she feared there would be scarring. Then there was the head wound and concussion. No-one talked about the head wound. Sybil had the impression its effects weren't predictable but everything was expected to heal in time. For the time being, she was advised to avoid a lot of physical activity. That wasn't something she needed to be reminded of. Even with the pain meds, her body hurt all the time.

While Sybil was in the hospital, Rick tried to learn all he could about the event that had brought her there. He came away believing the police didn't try very hard. They repeatedly told him they hadn't located the car or the carjacker, but couldn't share any details about their efforts to do so. All they wanted was for him to sign off and accept their assumption that the car was a goner. They believed the carjacking was part of a gang initiation, not an uncommon crime in Newark. Rick contacted their automobile insurance company and started the reporting process, but, ultimately, couldn't give up needing to know. Fueled by anger that anyone could get away with almost killing Sybil, he vowed to persist. This would not be over for him until they closed the case with the bastard behind bars. Rick didn't care if it was a twelve year old or a ninety year old.

The trip home was both thrilling and terrifying to Sybil. Although relieved that her lung puncture hadn't caused permanent damage, Sybil was surprised by the terror she felt getting into and being in the car. It was almost a combination of claustrophobia, of feeling trapped and vulnerable at the same time. The car could not protect her. Rick could feel her fear and tried to make her feel safer by chatting about normal things.

"The cats are going to be so glad to see you. They don't believe I have the intelligence to choose the correct food for any of their meals."

Sybil laughed, "Well, of course they're right. You seem to think that just because they liked tuna last night, it's fine to give it to them for the next ten days and you never notice when they've gotten sick of the same old same old by the third day. Oh, I can't wait to see them and have them to snuggle up with in my chair and at night."

Thinking he had successfully distracted her, and happy to hear her sound normal, Rick said, "Well, I'm really looking forward to snuggling with you in our bed."

Sybil picked at a hangnail. "I don't know how that's going to work out, Rick. My body aches all the time and I know I didn't sleep at all at the hospital even with the pain meds. I suspect it's going to take a while before I can snuggle in bed."

"Not to worry, Syb, we'll figure out how to help you sleep comfortably, and hopefully as your ribs heal, you'll be increasingly able to sleep without the meds. Not sure I mentioned this before, but I picked up a body pillow for you. That might help you find a comfortable position on the bed. Oh, and Pam is coming over this afternoon."

Sybil looked up. "Massage therapist Pam?"

"Yes. When I called to cancel your appointment and told her what happened, she asked if she could come over to see if she could be of help."

"That's really sweet of her, but I don't think I could bear being touched. I know I can't lie down for a massage. We need to call her back and cancel."

As it turned out, they didn't reach Pam in time and she arrived at their apartment about a half hour after they got home. Pam looked relieved when she saw Sybil sitting up in a chair and brushed a tear away from her eye.

Sybil smiled at Pam, "You are wonderful and I really appreciate you coming here but I can't be touched right now. My whole body hurts."

"I know. What I want to do doesn't involve touching. It's a craniosacral treatment that's similar to Reiki. It's designed to get all of your parts back into alignment." Seeing the doubt and fear in Sybil's face, Pam continued, "Let me try, and if you want; I'll stop immediately."

Having had only good experiences with Pam's healing methods, Sybil decided to give it a go. While she remained seated in the chair, Pam stood behind her and worked her magic. Just being in Pam's presence calmed Sybil's entire body and for those moments, she felt better. After a few minutes, Pam walked around to face Sybil, and lightly touched the scabs that were draped along the right side of her face.

Sybil looked up. "I'm pretty sure I'm going to be left with scars on my face."

Pam took a small bottle of lavender essential oil from her handbag and said, "I think I can help you with that. This stuff is pretty powerful and you don't want to get it in your eyes. If you do, immediately rinse them with milk."

"Will it heal the scabs without scarring?"

"I think so. Do you want to give it a try?"

"Yes!"

Pam poured a small amount on her finger and dabbed it on the wounded areas. Its strong acrid odor irritated Sybil's eyes and nose, and it stung, but she could feel the healing almost immediately.

As Rick watched what seemed like a miracle happening, he thought about whether the psychological effects of the carjacking would ever be erased. He knew Sybil was a strong, independent woman who ultimately believed she could manage anything. In their conversations she told him more than once that it was just a matter of time before she got past her fears. He wasn't so sure, but knew she had to steer the ship. Meanwhile he would be her shelter.

Chapter 7

February 8-11, 2002
Jersey City NJ

By the time she arrived home from the hospital, everyone in Sybil's brownstone, and much of the neighborhood, had heard what happened. Many people called and offered to help, but Rick warded off visitors except a handful of their closest friends. This included their neighbors Carlos and Pablo, a couple from Barcelona who had moved into the third floor apartment at the same time Sybil and Rick first rented theirs on the second floor. Since each apartment comprised an entire floor of the brownstone, they spent a lot of time together. Carlos and Pablo were like family and Sybil and Rick knew they would make sure she had everything she needed throughout her convalescence.

The only other people Rick allowed in their apartment during the first few weeks of Sybil's recovery were her colleagues at Sussex Advocacy, her place of employment. Rick wasn't particularly happy about her getting involved in the difficult work they did during that time, but knew Sybil would draw the line at being excluded from staying on top of what was going on. Their work, advocating for people who were illegally discriminated against, was in a vulnerable place that required close attention. In the wake of the attacks on the World Trade Center the previous year, Muslim residents' legal rights were in jeopardy of being abused. Jersey City Muslims were particularly vulnerable to attack and prejudice because it was known that some Muslim terrorists had lived and met there.

Jersey City was also a hotspot because of its location directly across the Hudson River from the twin towers. What was left of the World Trade Center was clearly visible all along the river's shore, and the Jersey City Exchange Place PATH station was closed indefinitely while repairs were being made at the loop terminal at the very bottom of the six levels of shopping and parking below the twin towers. As the towers were being attacked, approximately four thousand New Jersey commuters' lives had been saved by quick thinking PATH employees who prevented five trainloads from entering the World Trade Center terminal, and bringing in a rescue train to evacuate people who were trapped in the terminal just after the second attack. Miraculously, there were no casualties or injuries. Nonetheless, many Jersey City residents had lost their lives when the towers collapsed as noted by a memorial that was quickly erected on the waterfront walkway. Jersey City was renowned for its multiculturalism and cross-cultural tolerance, but even there, the Muslim community was being targeted in negative ways.

On the day of her carjacking, Sybil had been attending a meeting with a counterpart Newark-based advocacy group, the Jaffe Anti-Racism Society. It was a preliminary meeting to explore whether the two agencies could work together on some of their projects. They had come together to discuss sharing what they had learned about the discriminatory activities of Farrow Holdings, a real estate company that owned several apartment buildings in low-to-middle- income communities throughout the region. While Farrow Holdings was historically known to discriminate against all people of color, they had always stayed within the boundaries of the law so it was difficult to identify and charge them with their violations. However, since 9/11, their discriminatory practices, towards Muslims in particular, had begun to cross legal lines. Taking advantage of the current negative racial climate, they had become increasingly blatant. In addition to finding ways to throw Muslim tenants out of existing rentals, they had begun to actively slander applicants to other realtors in the area.

As a junior member of Sussex Advocacy's staff, Sybil was proud to have been chosen to represent her company at this important meeting. Sybil had run into the Farrows more than once during her short professional life. They didn't hide their racist views, and whenever she was in a meeting with any of them, Teddy Farrow, who seemed happy to do the company's dirty work, would find ways to insult her. She learned that, behind her back, he referred to her as "that mulatto bitch" and other offensive, sexually explicit, epithets. It seemed to drive him crazy that she had been successful in challenging, and sometimes preventing him from the unethical and illegal practices he and his family engaged in. He, of course, disliked everyone involved in their efforts, but seemed to direct his hatred towards Sybil in particular and had recently begun to target her in personal and threatening ways. Although she found him annoying, Sybil was usually able to ignore the personal attacks because, for the most part, she won the battles. As a bi-racial woman, she had a lifetime of practice dealing with sexism and racism, yet couldn't help wondering why he directed so much of his animosity towards her in particular. After all, there were many people of color both at Sussex Advocacy, and in her field in general.

Rick stayed around to attend to Sybil during her first two days at home, but had to meet with his publisher in Manhattan on the morning of the third. Sybil appreciated his care, but was relieved when she found herself with a free morning and asked her fellow Sussex team members to come over to catch up with the project. Her colleagues, Stacy, Ed, and Les, were glad she was interested in talking. They were eager to hear what she had learned at the Jaffe meeting, but hadn't wanted to bother her until she was ready. On the other hand, they couldn't wait too long or they would lose their momentum. For her part, Sybil needed to have a clear head. She had dictated a few reminder notes on her cell phone but ended up losing the phone with the rest of her belongings in the carjacking. Even worse, the carjacker had driven off with her briefcase full of case files.

At the meeting, Sybil learned that the Farrows had been playing the same racist cards in Newark and Jersey City and managed to succeed at least half of the time. It was clear they were working with sympathetic lawyers and judges. Sybil wasn't authorized to create a partnership, but left the meeting determined to recommend a second, more senior level, meeting to explore options. She had felt comfortable with the folks she met from Jaffe and hoped they would be willing to share information and work together when possible. Sybil had walked out of the building with a woman named Angela Park, a Jaffe Society member who seemed to have an inside track on quickly collecting information about Teddy Farrow. On their way to the parking lot, Angela told Sybil they were close to having enough to take to the authorities, to take Farrow to court.

Sybil's colleagues were sensitive to her tentative state and made a point of keeping the meeting brief. They were primarily interested in learning what the Jaffe folks knew about the legality of Farrow's activities, and what they were doing about it. While Sybil felt constrained by the fact that she had lost the documents they'd shared, she was able to report what Angela Park told her.

After listening carefully to the details Sybil recalled, her team leader, Les, asked if she would share her impressions of the Newark group. This had been the first meeting with Jaffe staff and Sybil had been the only one to attend.

"We haven't had a chance to hear your impressions of those folks. Did you feel like we can work with them? Are we on the same wavelength?"

Although she didn't know Angela well, Sybil had been convinced they'd established a comfortable rapport and mutual trust. Yet, she hesitated as she gathered her thoughts and chose her words carefully.

"I didn't really get to speak one-on-one to anyone except Angela Park. We chatted briefly walking to the parking lot. But they definitely come off as serious advocates. I liked them."

Les asked, "Would you recommend that we follow up to find substantive ways to work together?"

"I think so, but I'd feel better with a second opinion. Can one of you meet with them? Maybe to ask for new copies of the documents I lost in the carjacking?"

Standing up, Les said. "Good idea. I'll make it a face-to-face visit. I totally trust your judgement, but it can't hurt to be sure we want to get in bed with these folks. Now it's time for me to get back to the office. Thanks for letting us stop by and interrupt your healing. We miss seeing you every day, but stay away until you're ready. Unfortunately, ours is not a calm workplace."

As everyone laughed, Les and Ed headed for the front door. Stacy asked if she could stick around for a little while. Sybil was happy for the company, and the opportunity to talk about things she cared about, but made it clear that with the medications she was taking, she could drop off on a dime. Stacy said no problem and got up to leave.

As she was turning the doorknob, Stacy looked back and said, "Do you think it's possible the carjacking was connected to your meeting?"

Taken aback, Sybil's first reaction was to reject that possibility. Stacy was known to be the pessimist, the 'Eeyore' of their group. She would always see the dark side, a trait that was sometimes helpful in balancing the rest of the Sussex team, who were basically optimists.

"What makes you think that, Stacy?"

Stacy closed the door and went back into the room. Settling in a chair across from Sybil, she finished her thoughts.

"It just seems like there are a lot of unanswered questions."

"Like what?"

"When the phone rang, was there anyone at the other end? Did you recognize the number? How close were you to the train station parking lot? Was there any place before that you could've pulled over?"

Sybil pulled at her earlobe nervously. Taking her back to those moments made her heart race. "I don't know, Stacy, I'm pretty sure the phone rang close to the time I pulled over, but I never had a chance to answer. It all happened really fast. The next thing I remember was lying on the ground, seeing that kind man's face. Do you think the Farrows could've had something to do with this?"

The implications of that being the case floored Sybil and her face drained of color. She knew Teddy Farrow hated her, and wouldn't put anything past him, but how would he know where she was?

Just at that moment, Carlos opened the apartment door and called out, "Hey Sybil, just checking to see if there's anything I can pick up for you at the deli; oh, hi Stacy."

Then looking at Sybil's pale face, "Oh my God, Sybil, are you okay?"

Getting up to leave once again, Stacy began to worry she had picked at a scab much too soon and apologized. "I'm sorry Sybil, I hope I didn't make things worse. It's just a theory."

Carlos interjected, "What theory? What's going on here?"

Sybil smiled wanly at Carlos. "We were just talking business and I do believe it's time for my mid-morning nap."

Turning back to Stacy, she said, "Thanks for coming by, I'll give you a call later."

As Stacy walked out the door, Sybil accepted Carlo's offer of deli food.

"I would love some of their pasta salad, the one with sun-dried tomatoes and Kalamata olives. But I need to nap first. When you come back can you tiptoe by me and stick it on the kitchen counter?"

"No problema."

Rick returned from his meeting just as Sybil was waking up from her nap. They ate lunch while she told him about the Sussex staff meeting, and then, hesitatingly, shared what Stacy had suggested about there being a connection between her work and the carjacking. Rick was concerned. He couldn't decide whether he was more worried about Sybil's physical safety or mental and emotional well-being.

Chapter 8

February 12-April 24, 2002
Jersey City NJ

For the next few weeks, Sybil was content to sit in front of the television in an overstuffed living room chair. She had outfitted the chair with soft pillows on three sides and a hassock for her feet and legs. During the day, with one or another cat on her lap, she either read novels or watched DVDs of her favorite movies, interspersed with naps in the same position. Although she tried, she was never able to find a comfortable position lying prone on the bed, so she also slept in the chair at night. The only times she got up from the chair were to use the bathroom and brush her teeth.

While Rick offered to help, she shrank from being touched in any way and even avoided showering. At first, he figured she was taking care of herself and needed to do what she was doing to heal. Then he began to worry that she was crawling into herself both physically and mentally. It was almost as if she was starting to bury her painful memories even deeper. So he came up with an idea. "Would you have any objection to speaking with a therapist? I know you're totally capable of handling anything, but I'm wondering about a couple of things."

Sybil was wary. "What couple of things?"

"I'm wondering about your memory; your kneejerk reactions and fears."

"Aren't they normal reactions? I don't know if I want to relive this."

"If you find it painful, we'll stop. I just want to bring in someone with expertise because it doesn't seem as if you're getting better or learning what happened. I know your ribs still hurt, but it's not good for you to spend night and day curled up in that chair. It's almost as if you're afraid to leave it and if you don't start moving around more…I don't know, it might affect your body more permanently."

Sybil laughed uncomfortably, "Okay, do you know of someone local who will come to our apartment? I really don't feel ready to go out yet."

Relieved, Rick said he would ask around and hit gold with the first ask. Pablo had a close friend who lived a few blocks away, whose next door neighbor, Carmela Cortez, was a trauma specialist. Carmela had a thriving private practice in Jersey City in the wake of the 9-11 attacks, but was free to help a friend of a friend as early as the following evening.

Sybil surprised herself by enjoying the therapy session. During their initial visit, Carmela asked Sybil to tell her story with very little interruption. Taking notes, she figured out where the emotional hotspots were but was careful not to poke at them. She obviously wanted time to decide how to approach the tender issues in nonthreatening ways. From Sybil's point of view, just telling the story felt easy. At the end of the first visit, they set up a second appointment for the following week.

Carmela began the second session with a different, business-like tone. Opening her notebook, she said, "You may not have noticed the other night that I took notes while you described your experience, but here they are. I will be happy to share what I wrote with you if you want, but first I want to tell you what I think."

"What do you think?"

"I believe you have a classic case of post-traumatic stress. It would take more digging to label it further as either a disorder or a syndrome, but whatever the fine words are, your brain has been chemically altered by this experience and I believe I can help you."

"With talk therapy?"

"That and I believe you would benefit from a course of anti-depressants."

"Wouldn't that alter my brain chemistry? Why would I want to screw it up further?"

Carmela smiled. "Believe me when I tell you this. Your brain chemistry has been scrambled by the trauma. While an anti-depressant isn't the cure-all for what ails you, it can calm those nerves so you can begin to heal. Right now, well, let me ask you; do you feel like you know how to begin?"

"I admit it's all a jumble. I don't sleep well and even when I'm relaxed, it's hard for me to concentrate. I think that's why I'm happiest watching predictable happy old sitcoms. I'm not being challenged mentally at all and that feels okay."

"And when you're not sleeping, what's happening in your mind?"

Sybil laughed uncomfortably. "To be honest, I spend a lot of time beating myself up. Not for the carjacking—I don't blame myself for that—just for everything I've ever done wrong in my life—and that's a long list!"

Carmela nodded, "So this is what I'm thinking. Let's get you sleeping again. Let's get you a prescription for a mild anti-depressant and see if it helps you to relax. If it does, we can start at square one and unpack your trauma with talk therapy. Do you have a medical doctor I can speak with about your situation? It will obviously be up to them to decide if medication is warranted. I'm not qualified to write prescriptions. Would you be willing to go that route?"

"Sure, that would be Dr. Woodward. I'm sure her number is in my address book." Sybil sighed, "I know it was in my cell phone, but that's gone. That reminds me, I need to get a new cell phone."

Dr. Woodward concurred with Carmela's diagnoses, and, once established, the anti-depressant went a long way towards helping Sybil to sleep, which, in turn, contributed significantly to her mental and physical healing. Each time they met, Carmela took Sybil through baby steps to engage her mind and body in that process. By the end of the month, she was walking around the neighborhood and occasionally getting into the car without panicking. Yet, while her understanding of what happened was clarified, she remained incapable of bringing up specific memories. It was as if her brain had blocked the worst of them.

Carmela wasn't sure remembering every detail was necessary for healing, but both she and Sybil had come to believe she needed to remember more to successfully deal with the trauma. Feeling that talk therapy alone was hitting a wall, Carmela suggested Sybil might want to try hypnosis or EMDR. "I'm not trained in either of these methods, but there are people who swear by them for treating trauma victims. With EMDR, you don't have to remember to heal; it's more a way to release the trauma from your body cells."

Sybil thought for a minute and made a decision. "I think I'm ready to take a break from therapy, and honestly don't want to work with anyone but you. I'm starting physical therapy in a few weeks. Maybe I should step back from our sessions for a bit." Carmela agreed.

Rick had been pleased with Sybil's progress and was surprised at the decision to take a break from therapy. "What happened? I thought it was going well."

Sybil answered thoughtfully, "It has gone really well. I feel a ton better now than when we started. It's just that I still can't remember what happened that day. It's not that I don't know what happened; I just can't actually remember it. Carmela says there are some specific techniques designed to work with trauma victims that might help, but she's not trained in them and is happy to refer me. I guess I just need to take a break. Maybe when I stop working at it, I'll be able to remember better."

"What about the other symptoms, the sleeplessness, the beating up on yourself?"

"I'm going to keep taking the antidepressants. You know, Rick, I'm not giving up on it, just giving my brain and body a break. Maybe at least until I get into the physical therapy." Sybil smiled. "This has affected everything—if I didn't believe in holistic medicine before, I'm sure of it now!"

Rick really missed hugging Sybil, especially in times like this. Instead he squeezed her arm lightly and said, "I love you." Then he interrupted her response, "Hey, what about that lawyer who was at the scene; maybe he could tell you something that would trigger your memory. I keep moving his business card around my desk."

"That's a great idea, Rick. Seeing his face was my first real memory. He was so kind, and then he went out of his way to help the folks at the hospital find out who I was. I really want to thank him. I'm ashamed I didn't do this sooner. It's been almost two months."

"You have nothing to be ashamed of. I sometimes think you've never recognized how injured you were."

"Do you think it's too late to call him now?"

"It can't hurt to try. If it's an office number we can leave a voicemail message."

Rick retrieved the card and gave it to Sybil.

Rocco answered right away. He was glad to hear from her. "Thank you for calling. My friend Gail and I have wondered how you are."

"I'm the one who needs to do the thanking. I can't tell you how much I appreciate how you went out of your way to help. I see from your card that you work in Newark. We're not too far away in Jersey City. We'd love to have you come over for an official thank you drink if that's at all possible." Sybil paused and added, "I really do want to thank you in person, but I also have an ulterior motive I hope you don't mind. I've been having trouble remembering and wanted to pick your brain a little— about what you saw."

"I'll be happy to oblige, but I have to tell you, I wasn't there when it happened. I think I showed up just afterwards, but I'll be glad to share what I know."

"Can you come over Friday evening?"

"Sure, what time? Can I bring Gail along? She was with me most of that day, at the hospital and the eye doctor's. I think she would enjoy meeting you."

"Absolutely, would seven work for you? What do you like to drink?"

"I believe Gail is partial to red wine; I'm a beer drinker. Now all we need is your address."

"We're in the Paulus Hook neighborhood, a couple of blocks from the Hudson-- 69 Sherlock Street, second floor."

Chapter 9

April 26, 2002
Jersey City NJ

Rocco and Gail hadn't spent a lot of time together over the past few weeks. He kept in touch but was frustrated with his attempts to reach the lawyers in Albuquerque. From what she told him, he wasn't surprised they were dragging their feet, but the worst part was not getting past the assistants who were obviously screening their calls. He had yet to connect with anyone on the ground. He also had a lot of his own work taking up quality time.

Gail didn't seem to mind. She was enjoying being in New York and having the opportunity to go to theaters, museums, and dance performances she could now afford. She had even discovered an authentic Jamaican restaurant in the neighborhood which brought back fond memories of home cooking. It was all diverting, but ultimately, she would have preferred spending more time with Rocco, so she jumped at the chance to go with him to meet with the Morgensterns.

Traveling to the ferry terminal at the Jersey City waterfront walkway gave Gail the opportunity to have a new adventure, a ferry ride across the Hudson River from Manhattan to Jersey City. Gail found the ride delightful. It was a beautiful day and fun being on the water. From the river, she could see the wreck of the twin towers close up, as well as how close Jersey City and lower Manhattan were to one another. As the ferry approached New Jersey, she could see New York Harbor, and the emblematic Statue of Liberty and Ellis Island. She had boarded the ferry at Battery Park City, the luxurious riverside neighborhood that was created from the deep hole that formed the foundation of the World Trade Center. The dirt from that excavation had actually enabled the creation of 92 acres of extremely valuable Manhattan real estate. It was interesting to see how close all these important icons were to one another. On the Jersey City side, there was the famous Coca Cola Clock, and Liberty State Park, the location of the original train terminal where immigrants who had been processed through Ellis Island boarded trains to other parts of the country one hundred years ago.

When Rocco met her at the ferry terminal, Gail was bubbling with information she got from chatting with a fellow passenger. "Did you know the Morris Canal, that inlet that divides Liberty State Park, is the tail end of a canal that was built in the early eighteen hundreds to transport coal to New York through New Jersey from Easton, Pennsylvania and the bed of the canal was used to create the current Newark subway system?"

Rocco laughed, "And now it ends up as a marina for luxury boats. I actually hadn't heard the part about the Newark subway tunnel."

"I was talking to a woman who belongs to a New Jersey historical society. There sure is a lot of history in this area."

As they walked along the waterway boardwalk, Gail couldn't stop talking about the sites she had just experienced.

"Yes, this place has a lot of American history going back to pre-Revolutionary War times" Rocco said. "The little neighborhood these folks live in, which is called Paulus Hook, was never won by the colonists during the American Revolution. I think the British army was camped there."

"Wow, how do you know that?"

"I wish I could say I carry these historical tidbits around in my head, but the truth is, I just read it on a sign in a small park I came up on as I was walking to the ferry. I do know that after the Revolution, Alexander Hamilton owned all of this land. Anyway, I can give you the nickel tour another time. We can stop to take a look at the 9-11 Memorial on this side of the river, but then we should head back through the parking lot. Their brownstone is on the other side of this lot."

While the neighborhood was mostly residential, there was a deli or small restaurant on every corner. Gail was impressed with how multi-cultural the neighborhood seemed. As they walked to the building, she heard more than one language and saw a variety of people with different skin shades, many of whom were walking dogs. It was like a residential neighborhood in Manhattan, but the pace and sound volumes were slower and softer. Gail thought she could live happily in a place like this.

Rick answered the door. He was medium-sized and muscular with bright blue eyes, dirty blond hair and a huge welcoming smile. Shaking hands with Rocco and Gail, he thanked them for all they had done for Sybil. As he spoke, he led them into a living room decorated in bright reds and oranges where Sybil was seated in an oversized chair surrounded by bed pillows. When she looked up, a large orange tabby cat jumped off her lap and ran into another room.

Rick laughed, "That orange streak is our cat Billy, and this is, of course, Sybil."

Reaching out her hand, Sybil remained seated, "I apologize for not standing up. My ribs are still healing and getting out of this chair, where I've been living the past several weeks, can be complicated. But, I'm so glad you've come." She looked at Rocco with a broad smile. "I have dreamt about your face since that day. It was honestly the only part of the experience that was real for me for a long time. You were so nice, and when I learned about what you did later, I knew we had to thank you in person."

Rocco smiled back at her. "It's a pleasure to meet you in much better circumstances, Sybil, but I can only take credit for sitting by you until the emergency folks showed up. Gail was the one who made sure we got your information to the hospital."

Turning to Gail, Sybil said, "Thank you very much as well. I'm looking forward to hearing how this all happened; but first, can we offer you folks something to drink?"

Before they could respond, a strange expression crossed Sybil's face and she cried out, "Oh my God, now I know why you looked so familiar! Rick, can you get the framed photo of Mom and Daphne's theater group, the one that's hanging over my dresser?"

Looking at a puzzled Rocco, Sybil said, "I think you're both in that picture. I thought your face looked familiar in the parking lot. I just couldn't focus."

Rick went to the bedroom and brought back a framed photograph, and sure enough, it was a picture of a group of people posing in front of a large weeping willow tree that included a younger Rocco and Gail standing next to each other, Rocco's arm draped casually across her shoulders. Memories flooded through Gail and Rocco's minds as they looked at the photograph that included their friend Alice and a handful of other people they had been acquainted with in the summer of 1973. And, they were standing in front of the magic wall tree, the place where their adventures, their happenings, all began.

Sybil continued to talk excitedly.

"I remember asking my mother what the photograph was about. She told me it was a group of people who had performed what she called "happenings" in Central Park. She said the photograph wasn't connected with a particular performance, but when I asked her why they had kept it, she looked a little sad and said it was a group of people she and my Aunt Daphne met when they were teenagers and that meeting them had changed their lives. And look, both of you were there. I always remembered you, Rocco. You stood at least a head and a half taller than everyone else."

Rocco and Gail were dumbfounded as Sybil explained how she had grown up hearing stories about what her mother and Aunt Daphne described as "that magical summer" when they first met the woman she was named for.

Gail searched her memory and spoke first, "You were named for our friend Alice? Sybil was her stage name for the happenings in the park. Daphne's is your aunt? So you must be Melissa's daughter."

"You remember my mother, Melissa? Yes, I think she took the picture. She's going to be so excited when I tell her we've met!"

"And you're the spitting image of your mother!"

"Everyone says that. I guess you knew her when she was even younger than me."

Rocco and Gail remembered Melissa as the slightly older teenager who always seemed to be trying to keep her feisty younger sister in line. Both were so lithe, they seemed to fly when they danced so everyone had nicknamed them "the floating dancers." But of the two, Daphne was the natural talent, the sprite who oozed creativity. No-one knew exactly how old the sisters were, but it was obvious they were still in high school.

Somewhat shaken by the coincidence, Rocco looked at Sybil. "This is amazing. Why didn't you mention it before?"

"I didn't because I couldn't remember where I had seen you. The photo always struck me because you stood out. You're so much taller than everyone else. I think that's why you stuck in my mind."

"And, I'm blacker than everyone else."

Sybil didn't flinch. "That's true; the other people are white except for my Aunt Daphne, but she's smaller and a different shade of brown, more like caramel."

Rocco liked how this young woman was so comfortable with racial differences, talking about skin tones. He saw it as a generational evolution that had gone right.

Gail piped in, "I'm also part black and in any case, no-one sees me as white or black."

This surprised Sybil, who had simply seen Gail as Asian, even though she was tall, but when she looked closely, thought she might have looked Filipina. There was definitely something else in her background. Sybil was ashamed to have made such a quick assessment, especially given her own mixed racial make-up. When she thought of it, why would someone with Asian features be automatically labeled as white?

"You know Gail, being mixed race, I should be more sensitive to making snap judgements. People often assume I'm Hispanic. I didn't really think about it but figured you to be Asian, even though you're tall for a stereotypical Asian woman, at least in my experience."

"Don't worry about it Sybil, I'm used to being stereotyped. There's a lot of racial mixing in the Caribbean where I come from. I was born in Suriname, the United Nations of racial diversity. My father and grandfather were Chinese; my grandmother was a black-white mix; and my mother was half Chinese and half black-white. So I'm three-quarters Chinese, one eighth black and one-eighth white. Confusing enough for you?"

"I hope you can stay for a few hours at least, I really want to hear about your life, and have a ton of questions about the photograph and the people who are in it. Just to begin, what you were all doing together that summer and what you were doing at the Newark Train Station last month?"

Gail responded, "I, for one, have all night."

Rocco nodded. "I don't have all night but I can at least visit for an hour or two."

Sybil let out a breath. "This is awesome. Before we start, is anyone interested in having a bite to eat? There isn't much in the house, but we have several takeout places within two blocks where they know us well. What's your preference, Thai, Italian, vegetarian, or deli?"

Gail answered. "They all sound great, hmmm, maybe Italian. What about you Rocco?"

"Italian works for me too."

Rick went to a kitchen drawer and pulled out a pile of menus. He chose one and passed it to Rocco. Smiling at Sybil, he said, "I know what you'll be getting, but do you want to add garlic bread and a large antipasto we can all share?"

Studying the menu, Rocco asked, "What's good here? What do you always have, Sybil?"

"I always get their eggplant parmesan. It's excellent."

Gail asked, "Do they make the outside crispy and get all the slime out of the eggplant?"

"Exactly, that's what makes theirs so good. And I think they use some special herbs and spices in their batter. I dream about their eggplant parm!"

Gail smiled, "Then, I'm in!"

Rick headed to the door as he put on his jacket. "Okay, two eggplant parmesans and a large antipasto; what about you, Rocco?"

"Do you mind if I go with you Rick? I want to smell the flavors before I decide."

Chapter 10

April 26, 2002
Jersey City NJ

As Rick and Rocco walked out the door, Sybil asked Gail, "Do you remember Daphne?"

"Oh yes, she was adorable, and an amazing dancer. I always wanted to be a professional dancer but even with training, could never capture her natural grace. And when she sang, I was in awe. She was amazing, almost otherworldly." Gail looked at the floor as if to recalibrate the direction of her thoughts. Then she looked at Sybil directly, "I left New York at the end of that summer and never really looked back, so I wasn't in the loop of following up on people's lives. Did Daphne become a professional dancer, or singer for that matter?"

"You didn't know about her accident? The terrible fall that left her crippled for the rest of her life? I thought it happened that summer, when she was a teenager."

"Oh no, how terrible; the last time I saw her, she was dancing through the park! That can't be. What a tragedy!"

"Then you obviously didn't know that she died from those injuries later, in 1985. She was only twenty-eight years old."

"Oh Sybil, I'm so sorry. She was such a sweetheart. How old were you when you lost her?"

"I was seven years old. It was devastating."

Looking at the photo, Sybil continued sadly, "After I lost my Aunt Daphne, we moved to Canada. My dad is Canadian so we had family there too, but no-one has ever taken Daphne's place in my heart." She looked up and smiled wistfully, "But we did stay in touch with Daphne's guardian angel Alice for a short time. I know her real name is Alice, but Daphne always called her Sybil."

Gail was stunned, "You know her?"

"I did a long time ago. I haven't seen her in years. She used to come to our house sometimes and tell me stories about places she visited and places she wanted to visit. She was always on the go, but came back to see Daphne. They definitely had a special relationship. She was great. I know my mother and aunt were very fond of her."

"When was the last time you saw her?"

"I can't tell you exactly. I know it wasn't long after Aunt Daphne died. It was devastating to lose Daphne. She was like a fairy princess to me. So when the people came to our house, I hid in a closet. That's where Alice found me. I couldn't deal with all the people, all the mourners. I guess I sort of believed that if we didn't acknowledge her death, she wouldn't be dead... the power of magical thinking, hah."

Sybil paused as the sad memory took over her face.

"I was in the closet with the door closed. I could hear people wondering out loud where I was, but then the house filled up and I was left alone. I don't know how long actually, but there was a knock on the door and it was Alice. She asked if she could join me. It was funny because I was pretty small and I was crowded in the closet, but somehow, she found a way to join me, and to sit on the floor."

"What a wonderful memory for you, Sybil. Can I ask what she said to you? Did it help?"

"She told me two things I've never forgotten. The first one blew me away. She said she could figure out a way to go through the wall if she wanted to. I've been inspired by that all my life, what it said about her self-confidence. It made me want to be like her. That was also the day she told me why she had called herself Sybil. She said sybils were powerful women in Greek mythology and just having that name would give me special powers. She said that since it was my given name, no-one could ever take those powers away. I was so proud!"

Gail couldn't help thinking, *Holy Shit, that permeable wall.*

"Was that the last time you saw her?"

"I think so, but she did come by one more time to give me something. I wasn't home, so she left it with my mom."

"What was that?"

"Actually it was two things. She gave me a copy of the book *Alice in Wonderland*. I still have it. She wrote something inside the cover, and I quote, 'This is my inspiration and the reason I've always liked my given name, Alice. Alices aren't necessarily wise, but they are always curious and adventurous.'"

"That must have made you feel very special."

"It did, as did the other gift she left for me. Although I have to admit, I wasn't that thrilled when I first saw it."

"Now you have me curious."

"Believe it or not, it was a kachina doll. It wasn't soft like my other dolls, you know, the kind you could cuddle up in bed with. It was more like a decoration, so I wasn't a big fan but I kept it because she gave it to me. I learned later it was a Pueblo Indian treasure that was traditionally used as part of a growing up ceremony for girls. I think they're valuable artifacts in the tourist market."

Gail was surprised to hear Alice had given away a kachina doll. She remembered how much they intrigued her that summer when they were in Albuquerque. If she had purchased one later, it had to have cost a pretty penny. This young woman as a child must have meant a great deal to her. Gail decided to keep her thoughts to herself. There was already an awful lot to digest and she wasn't sure how to feel about the memories, both good and bad, this encounter was bringing up.

Her thoughts interrupted by the sound of footsteps climbing the stairs, Gail got up and went to open the apartment door. "I think I hear dinner outside."

As they ate with their guests, Rick, once again noticed how good it was for Sybil to be engaged. She had been eating like a bird and lost about ten pounds since leaving the hospital. Yet here she was, actively participating in conversation and obviously enjoying the food. After dinner, while they drank coffee, Sybil brought out the photograph again and asked Rocco and Gail to tell her who was who in the group.

Rocco started, "Let me see if I can remember. We've already identified Gail, me, and Daphne."

Then, pointing to a young man wearing granny glasses and a funny smile, said, "This guy is my friend Phil Trotter. We went to college together and I was staying with his family on Long Island when I first moved to New York. You may have heard of him, he's made a successful living as a character actor, mostly on stage. The rest, I don't remember. There were a lot of people who joined in when we were performing who didn't stick around past the day." He handed the photo to Gail, "Have I missed anyone?"

Sybil pointed to a slightly chubby baby-faced young man who looked prematurely bald. "Is it possible this is Teddy Farrow?"

Rocco sighed, "Yep, how could I forget that idiot? It looks like he hasn't changed his hairstyle all these years."

Gail pointed to a dark-eyed woman with a mass of curly auburn hair holding a guitar and wearing a tee shirt with a picture of Richard Nixon that said, "Would You Buy a Used Car from this Man?"

"Did you really forget Alice?"

Rocco replied thoughtfully, "Of course not, Alice Lyons, AKA Sybil. I remember that tee shirt, she was obsessed with Watergate. Who could forget her?"

He turned to Sybil, "When we discovered you had the same name, Gail and I had flashbacks about the summer of 1973. Alice was the one who brought us together."

Gail interrupted, "Rocco, Sybil just told me Daphne passed away seventeen years ago. She was injured in a terrible accident when she was a teenager that affected her for the rest of her life. Did you know she had injured herself? I know it didn't happen when I was around."

"No, I would have remembered that. I left New York shortly after the last time I saw her. How sad to hear she passed away at such a young age. I only knew her that summer, and even then, I can't say I got to know her well at all. Gail and Daphne were the best dancers in our little group, but none of us really stayed in touch after the summer."

Sybil asked, "Why was that?"

Rocco was silent, giving Sybil the impression he wasn't comfortable with her question, so she quickly switched gears. "I'm sorry, that was a rude question."

Rocco was silent for another moment before he answered Sybil's other question. It seemed to her that he was about to choose his words carefully, like a lawyer. Then he spoke slowly, "I'm sorry to hear of your loss. I do remember Daphne was an amazing dancer. She was so lithe and seemed to fly instead of touching the ground and I think she was a natural musician and vocalist too; the kind who can harmonize almost effortlessly. I have a strong memory of her magical voice. But to be honest, I didn't know her well. She was very young and didn't share much with us. We believed she was sneaking out to come to the park. She and her sister, your mother, seemed to enjoy participating in our happenings."

Chapter 11

April 26, 2002
Jersey City NJ

Sybil smiled, "I know it will be a while before I feel at all normal, but you two have brought some excitement into my currently quiet life. Before we go on to something else, I want to apologize again about the racial stuff. This part of the country is such a mixed bag, but racism and the negative stereotyping and labeling never go away. Where I come from, the focus is on white racism towards Blacks."

Gail nodded, "If I recall, Daphne and your mom lived in Harlem or Inwood, or was it Washington Heights? Is that where you grew up?"

"Until I was eight, then we moved to Canada. As I mentioned before, my father is Canadian. He's also white. Despite my parent's efforts, I never felt completely accepted in either world. I think racism aimed at black people in this country is directly related to the deep down guilt white people feel about the fact that they embraced slavery—in fact, the most insidious form of slavery."

"Isn't all slavery terrible?"

"Of course, but slaves have traditionally been war bounty. I'm not saying they haven't always been treated like shit, but ultimately, there was recognition of their humanity in other cultures. Here they were completely dehumanized as property. Plantation slavery was a lifetime and multi-generational evil. Especially after the African slave trade was abolished, they had to keep their workforce growing so everyone was born into slavery, slavery defined by skin color."

Sybil began to fidget and idly twisted a lock of hair around her finger. "No matter what people said to me when I was a child, I always knew I didn't belong in either world completely."

Recognizing the emotions around this subject, Gail nodded, "I understand that feeling. We moved from Suriname when I was eleven. I think although Suriname was very mixed—the dominant culture was Dutch, but there are a lot of people from India and Pakistan in addition to Blacks, Chinese, and Native American Indians and we were all kept in our place by profession and other things. It seems like everyone wants to have someone to look down on. My grandmother, my mother's mother, was my grandfather's concubine. They had eight children together. He had another "legitimate" family in China at the same time."

"How did you end up in Jamaica?"

"My father was a merchant. That was also a Chinese stereotype, by the way. He was a gambler who more than once during my life made large pots of money. I was only a kid so I can't tell you exactly what was going on when we moved to Jamaica, but I do remember going from rags to riches. When we got to Jamaica, I was turned into a good Catholic girl, dressed up in a uniform and sent to a Catholic girl's academy where I got an excellent high school education. Everyone in my school was Chinese."

Sybil was intrigued. It always amazed her to learn how complex relationships among different racial and ethnic groups could be, and how different they were in different countries. "I didn't even know there were Asians in Jamaica. I've always thought everyone there was black, beginning with Harry Belafonte."

"We were in the minority there too and my parents didn't approve of me hanging around with the street "riff raff" so they encouraged me to do well in school and made sure I was successful enough to get into an American university, which is how I ended up here. But, I have to admit, I've never lost the deep down fear that I could be poor again. It comes to me in dreams and I wake up shaking."

"I could listen to your stories all night. I hope we can get together another time soon, but I know you and Rocco want to get going. Can I ask one more question before you go?"

"Of course."

"I guess it's not exactly a question, but can you tell me more about Alice? Even though she was an important part of my early life, she's always been a bit of a mystery to me."

Rocco answered, "Don't feel like the Lone Ranger. She was a mystery to all of us. She was oddly both uniquely reachable and remote at the same time. What do you want to know?"

"You said she brought you together, but what was she like? How was she different? How did you know her to begin with?"

"Well, for me, it started in high school. We were lab partners in our junior year chemistry class. I think we bonded because we were both placed in an advanced chemistry class completely peopled by the brains of the school. They were super smart and way ahead of us in both math and science. I never figured out why we were placed in that class. We stood out for other reasons too—I was the only black kid and she was the only female."

Pausing to explain, Rocco continued. "You have to remember it was the early 1960s when there weren't many mixed race friendships let alone mixed gender and race friendships, but we really liked and understood each other at what felt like a deep level. Although it never went further than that, we both knew that was how we felt. Being one of the few minority students in the school, and just about the only one on the college track, I appreciated having a friend who understood me."

"You two stayed in touch after high school?"

"No, not at first; our colleges were in different parts of the country—she went west and I stayed east. We reconnected accidentally in New York after college. That's when I first met Gail."

"That was the famous summer of '73?"

"Yep, we had all just graduated from college and headed for the Big Apple to make our fortunes."

"And you just happened to run into each other in New York City. What are the odds?"

Rocco laughed, "Just like the odds of running into you at the Newark Train Station. Amazing isn't it? We first saw each other across the tracks at the 14th Street subway station. Gail can vouch for me, she was there. I had been in the City for a couple of weeks, commuting in from my friend Phil's house on Long Island. I was dying to get out of there and find a place I could afford in Manhattan. Alice and Gail had arrived from the West Coast around the same time and had scored a sublet in an apartment building on the Upper West Side. They invited me to crash with them while I searched for my own place."

"What a lucky coincidence! What about you, Gail, how did you know Alice?"

"I met Alice in California where she and I went to college. We dated two guys who were roommates in our freshman year and ended up sharing an apartment during our junior and senior years. When we graduated, Alice decided to move to NYC and I went along for the ride, I guess. I met Rocco through Alice."

"Were you planning to settle in New York? What were you doing there then, why New York?"

"Why New York?" she repeated, "Because that's where Alice wanted to go. She said she wanted to be in the cultural center of the world. I was definitely a follower, but also felt going back to Jamaica and my family's business, which was what was expected of me, was the end of life as I wanted to live it. I lied to my parents and followed Alice hoping for a last great adventure. I guess what some people call a 'gap year' these days, except this would be a gap summer."

Sybil returned to her original question, "What was she like? What made her so special?"

"It's hard to describe in words. Alice was just Alice. She always seemed open-ended; I think that's the best way to describe her."

"Do you mean open-minded?"

"Maybe that's what I mean, but to the nth degree, like a missing word at the end of the sentence. She wanted to see what would happen and didn't shrink from controversy even when everyone else saw trouble. She was always challenging herself to see how much she could manage. I sometimes thought she saw herself as being invulnerable." Gail smiled at Sybil and continued her thought, "that she really could go through walls."

Chapter 12

April 26, 2002
Jersey City NJ

"One more question."

Hearing Rick groan, Sybil laughed and said, "This one's easier, I promise. How did you two end up at the Newark Train Station that day? It's funny, that was all I was planning to ask you about and we haven't even touched on the subject."

Rocco smiled. "We're old friends who hadn't seen each other for twenty-nine years, so we decided to meet at the Newark Train station. I live in Newark and Gail was visiting Manhattan. I won't bore you with the details. Anyway, I got to the station a few minutes before her train was scheduled to arrive and was ambling along when I heard the commotion in the parking lot. I went out to see what was going on. As it turned out, what was going on was you lying on the ground. There were a lot of people milling about, but it didn't look like any of them was with you, so I decided to hang around until the ambulance showed up. That was about it."

Gail picked up the story. "When I arrived at the station, Rocco was nowhere to be seen but I heard the buzz about the so-called accident. No-one knew what had actually happened at that point, so I think they assumed you had been hit by a car walking through the parking lot or something. Remembering the kind of guy Rocco was twenty-nine years ago, I assumed he'd been drawn to the scene, and I was right. I waited and he showed up and told me what had happened. Then he remembered he had left his coat so we went back to the parking lot to see if we could find it."

"And did you?"

"Yes, we ran into the policeman who was about to take it to the Lost and Found. So, of course we asked him if anything further had been learned about what happened. He said all they knew so far was that you had been pulled out of a car that was being carjacked and had no identification."

Rick stepped in for the first time, "Here we are two months later and they have yet to even locate the stolen car. I don't think they really care to go any further with this so-called investigation.

They seem to be sure the carjacking was part of a common gang initiation so the car has probably been stripped of all identifiable parts. They tell us we should take our insurance money and let it go."

Sybil added with a smile, "But Rick isn't letting go. They're really getting to know him at the Newark Police Station."

Gail said, "Good for you Rick. The police officer we spoke with didn't seem particularly interested in talking with us, but Rocco gave him a business card and offered to be available to answer about the little he knew. Then, we ran into a girl who was at the scene who gave Rocco the glasses case, and the rest is history." She paused, "You know Rocco is an attorney?"

"Yes, we saw that on his card, but honestly, until a short while ago, Rick and I didn't know his name was Rocco instead of John."

At that moment, a long-haired brown tabby cat with a large fluffy tail walked into the room and jumped with one smooth movement onto Rocco's lap. Rocco immediately began to scratch under its chin and everyone laughed.

Rick said, "This is Sasha, our Norwegian Forest Cat. She thinks she's honoring you, and to be perfectly honest, she usually shies away from strangers, so I guess you have a good kitty vibe. I can take her out of here if you don't want her."

"No, it's fine. I've never thought of myself as a cat person, but they seem to like me. This one is really soft. So, that's two, is this it or do you have more cats?"

"Just two, but they are our children. Both of us have work that takes up a lot of time and energy. Cats are easier than people kids."

Gail laughed, "That's for sure."

"Do you have children, Gail?"

"I have a son. He's in boarding school at the moment."

Smiling at Sybil, Gail changed the subject. "We've been here for over an hour and I still don't know much about your life. What kind of work do you do?"

"Rick is a famous author. You may have heard of his new book, *Prehistoric Rock Art around the World and its Commonalities*."

Rocco said, "I think I read a review in the Times recently; sounds like it's doing very well."

Rick nodded, "Yes, so far, so good. I'm a popular science writer so I make no academic claims, but I was able to include some great color photographs as well as drawings, and of course, the book is full of information I got through interviews with experts in the field. Even if it doesn't wow the world, it was fun collecting the data. Sybil and I got to do a lot of traveling to exotic places to photograph the art."

Gail was interested, "Did you get out to the Southwest? There are some prehistoric rock art sites in New Mexico and Arizona."

"Yes, but nowhere near as much as I would've liked. Sybil's work kept her here a lot of the time so I ended up doing some of those trips alone. That was the hard part."

Rocco turned to Sybil. "What kind of work do you do, Sybil?"

"Nothing as exciting as Rick; I work for a local advocacy organization."

"Now you're talking about my world. Does your group specialize?"

"Lately our work has focused on advocating for people who are being discriminated against in housing, and a little bit in employment. As a matter of fact, the morning of the carjacking, I was coming back from a meeting with a sister group in Newark. Are you familiar with the Jaffe Anti-Racist Society?"

"I've heard of them, they have a good reputation."

Sybil looked at Rocco with new interest. "As a matter of fact, our meeting was focused on Teddy Farrow, no doubt the same Teddy Farrow you knew when you were younger. He's our biggest problem these days. Farrow Holdings have been blatantly, and I might add, criminally, discriminating against Muslims since 9-11. They had a history of racist policies even before 9-11, but since then they seem to be taking advantage and loudly stoking people's fears of anyone with brown skin. The folks at Jaffe told us they're on the brink of taking them to court. That was actually the last conversation I had, with a woman named Angela Park. We walked to our cars together." Sybil paused, "Did you say you've crossed paths with the Farrows in your work?"

"Yes, indeed. I specialize in real estate law and have faced these folks in court more than once. They're a bunch of hucksters and we're pretty sure, have mob connections. Of course in Newark, a lot of business is political so you can't always figure out who's who, but we know that if our mayor is involved and likes them, people get what they want."

Sybil sighed, "It's all about machine politics and I guess slimebuckets like the Farrows are good at greasing palms."

Gail said, "We were just talking about him the other day. Teddy Farrow's father owned the building we were living in that summer. Teddy called himself the building manager and always seemed to be following us around, even when we were doing our little performances in Central Park. What an annoying person!"

Rocco added, "I ran up against him pretty soon after I showed up in Newark. He has yet to acknowledge we knew each other back then, but I haven't brought it up either. It's not like I have fond memories. In fact my first memory of him was when he tried to keep me from even being in that apartment building."

Gail sighed, "He was pretty horrible to me too."

Rick cleared his throat, "So this is getting weird, but one of Sybil's colleagues has been wondering if Teddy had something to do with the carjacking. The more I hear about his mean-spiritedness, the more I wonder too."

Sybil shivered. "It's just a theory Rick. I'm not ready to believe someone was out to murder me."

"I don't want to upset you, Sweetheart. I just want to point out he could've been threatened by your meeting with the folks in Newark, potentially sharing stories of the things he was doing in Jersey City that could build on the evidence they already have."

Sybil thought it best to change the subject and turned back to Rocco and Gail, "Please tell us more about that summer. You were all just out of college, but what were your plans? What were you actually doing in New York? How did you make money to live on?"

Gail laughed, "We all found low-paying jobs, but what bonded us was a love of the performing arts. I don't think any of us believed we had the talent or perseverance to make it as performers, but it was definitely a shared passion. We were young so we had the energy to do both. I was in love with dance-especially expressive jazz. All of us had something we loved to do like that."

"What about you Rocco?"

"Mostly music, but we all loved playing around with expression—in addition to playing instruments, I liked writing and acting and even directing—mostly the stuff I wrote, but honestly, it was such a great group of people, it was fun to be creative together. Alice played the guitar and sang mostly folkie sounding music she made up. She had a nice singing voice, but I think her greatest love was writing and composing. She talked a lot about traveling the world and collecting stories. I figured someday I would walk into a bookstore or an airport and read a story about a fictional character that sounds a lot like me." Rocco laughed out loud.

Gail added, "At the time it felt like the sky was the limit for all of us. Don't let Rocco's humility fool you. He's a very talented musician. He can play anything. We were here to have fun and to feel free to express our creativity. I think we knew our lives would change and become more restricted, but that summer, we basically lived for the day. That was probably what drew us to doing the happenings."

"That word keeps coming up, what exactly is a happening?"

"What we did was a sort of bastardization of official happenings and I would probably mischaracterize them, but I can tell you what we did. It was pretty simple. We would go in to Central Park, stop somewhere, and start a spontaneous performance. We almost always started at a particular tree, the willow tree that's in that photo."

"Why that tree?"

"It's hard to say except it felt magical, or maybe we just agreed to attribute magical power to it. I later read that weeping willow trees are supposed to symbolize hope, a sense of belonging, and safety. Whether that was true of our tree or not, I do remember that we were really drawn to it. We'd go there and ask permission to penetrate a wall; maybe it was an imaginary wall that felt real. Nine times out of ten, permission was granted and the minute we got through, our creativity, our imaginations, began to flow. Sometimes someone would say something like, 'that tree just kicked me and buried its roots'; and it would go on from there. Alice carried her guitar everywhere she went, and Rocco played whatever he had on hand. I almost always got to dance along with your mother and Aunt Daphne. People who walked by often stopped to watch or participate. That's why we couldn't identify all the people in the photograph. We probably never saw them again."

"That sounds like fun, but I have to ask, what did Teddy Farrow do? I can't imagine him even having a sense of humor, let alone a single creative bone in his body. How did he get into the group?"

Frowning, Rocco said, "It was my fault. He knew my friend Phil, the guy whose house I was staying at when I first lived in New York. They had grown up in the same social circle on Long Island, but even Phil described him as soulless …the kind of sadistic, entitled kid who tore wings off of butterflies. No-one liked him much. He was out-and-out racist and openly offensive to women, but Alice felt sorry for him and believed everyone, especially in the arts world, had something to contribute. His father owned the apartment building and Teddy was always there. There was no getting away from him."

"That must have been a real downer, having him around when you were trying to do something so joyful. Why do you think Alice defended him? Why did you let her?"

Gail answered. "When Alice was determined, it was really hard to argue. She was a true believer in the redemptive power of art and that everyone is an artist deep down. And, she was really convincing; I think we all wanted it to be true. I sometimes thought she believed if everyone could connect with their inner artist, the world would be rid of basic evils like intolerance, prejudice, racism—all of that nastiness. In retrospect, she was playing God with Teddy. He was so offensive. I think she saw him as a test case for redemption through art."

"So, he was allowed to participate even when he was being offensive?"

"For the most part, but if I recall, Alice called him on it one time towards the end of the summer. I think it was because your mother told Alice that Teddy was scaring her and Daphne with sexual innuendo; that he was violating their personal space and making crude remarks about their bodies. I'm pretty sure that was the only time Alice drew the line but I never knew exactly what he had done to push her over the edge."

"What did Alice do?"

"She told Teddy he couldn't be with us if he was going to do shit like that. Unfortunately, he only stayed away for a week or two. I always did my best to ignore him, but by the end of the summer, he was definitely affecting morale."

"Is that why the group broke up? My mom never wanted to talk about that."

Rocco answered, "It was the end of the summer and we all had to get on with our lives, so we went our separate ways. It was probably time anyway; things were starting to get complicated."

Gail looked at the ground and said nothing.

Sybil decided to shift back to Teddy. "What did Teddy do in the group? Did he sing or dance or play an instrument?" Gail and Rocco burst into uncomfortable laughter. Then Gail said, "He really wasn't good at anything so he got to be the guy in the crowd who mumbled—you know, like in movie crowd scenes when all the extras repeat the words 'rutabaga rutabaga'. We even started referring him as 'Rute' behind his back, of course.

"Your happenings had crowd scenes?" Sybil asked incredulously.

"Not really, but if we had, he would've been the one saying 'rutabaga rutabaga.' Although we never called him that to his face, he knew what we thought of him and he didn't seem to care. There didn't seem any way to get rid of him."

Sybil felt her toe tapping spontaneously, "That's an interesting way to think about him. As far as I can tell, he doesn't have any skills now either, but he definitely has the ability to get himself into the middle of things. I guess his one skill is not caring what other people think. The guy's a total attention whore and, probably, a narcissist."

Rocco looked at his watch and said, "This has been fun, but I need to get going; I'm afraid I have an early morning meeting. Maybe next time we can have dinner at a restaurant, my treat."

Sybil got up from her chair and said goodbye at the apartment door. Turning to Rick as they watched their guests walk down the stairs, she said, "I think there's more to this summer of '73 story. I need to call my mom. Maybe she can fill in some of the gaps."

"I totally agree. Why don't you give her a ring now? I'll be right back. I need to run downstairs to make sure the outside door is locked."

As Gail and Rocco walked towards the ferry dock, Rocco said, "Boy, what a trip down memory lane! I remember a lot of it, but find it hard to answer questions about what I was thinking. Maybe I knew then, but can't for the life of me remember how it all started. Do you remember what you and Alice had in mind by going to New York that summer? Was it really as serendipitous as it seems in my foggy old memory?"

Gail smiled, "All I can tell you, in retrospect, it feels like the minute I graduated from college, I got picked up by a gentle, but forceful breeze named Alice. She had the power to make me believe in possibilities. So I followed her and I met you."

PART 2

June 8 - September 10, 1973

Chapter 13

June 8, 1973
Southern California

For different reasons, neither Alice nor Gail's parents attended their college graduation ceremony.

Alice's parents were overseas someplace and she hadn't given them the graduation date in time to change their plans. They had paid little attention to her since she started college and she had been fairly certain they didn't even know she was graduating this year, so Alice was pleasantly surprised to receive a graduation gift, an American Express Card in her name and her father's business address. Her father had always sent money when she asked, but this gave her the freedom to spend without asking. It was oddly satisfying to feel she was being trusted with an adult privilege. It felt like an acknowledgement of sort. However, she wasn't ready to share with them her dreams of being an artist. Throughout her life, whenever she had tried to share her enthusiasms with her parents, they patted her on the head and said things like, "isn't that cute?" No, this was a major moment for her. She needed to figure out how she would be successful on her own terms. It was not a good time to be deflated and she had dreams of trying things out, spreading her creative wings.

Gail's parents said they were too busy with work obligations, but she knew they were struggling financially and would have a hard time scraping up enough to cover the roundtrip flight to LA from Jamaica. She also knew they were eager to have her return to Kingston and begin their dream job (for her) of expanding their export clothing business. She appreciated the sacrifices they had made to enable her to obtain a degree from a well-respected American university, but her strongest emotions were a combination of guilt for what it had cost them, and dread for the obligation she had earned as part of the deal. She had simply wanted to get away and spend her college years in the United States. Now she had to pay the piper.

Alice and Gail shared an apartment during their final two years of college. While their personalities were at odds some of the time, they liked each other and found ways to accommodate their conflicting tendencies. Generally speaking, Alice found Gail oppressively organized, while Gail saw Alice as being much too laid back and lacking rules and boundaries. Gail was a business major with a practical streak and Alice was all about the liberal arts, so they tended to hang out with different sets of people while on campus. Despite their differences, they were mutually respectful, and shared a love for the performing arts.

For Alice, it was folk music, a passion she wore comfortably as it fit her persona as an anti-war and human rights activist. Well-known around the campus, she was rarely seen without her guitar and was always willing to lead protest marches with song. She enjoyed singing but in the end, was most passionate about the creative process, writing stories with both lyrics and music.

Gail kept her mouth shut, but had little interest in political issues. Growing up with financial insecurity where survival took center stage, she saw the current protest movement as belonging to the children of wealthy white people with leisure time. But Gail was passionate about dance, a fact she tried to keep close to the vest. It didn't fit the practical business woman mold she was destined to fill, but in the end, just about all of her electives in college were dance classes. In the process, she had become quite proficient as a jazz dancer and had even performed with some local dance troupes.

The last few weeks of May were dominated by enjoyable graduation-related events including honors ceremonies, the matriculation itself, and many beach parties, but for Gail, it was also a sad time. As per her parents' plans, she had to return to Jamaica and her family's business. In contrast, Alice saw herself as "going with the flow," heading into the unknown to do something neither she nor anyone else could predict. She had always been drawn to people who were different from her, and although she had no specific plans, decided to start in New York City to be "where the action is."

Gail was envious and found herself living vicariously as Alice flitted through the possibilities. The one-way airline ticket to Kingston weighed heavily in Gail's bag as she watched Alice do nothing to even begin the next stage of her life's journey. Meanwhile, Gail longed for a break, a little time to just be. As they went through the motions of saying goodbye to their college life, just about all their conversations centered on Alice's journey and the adventures she would have. In some ways, this allowed them to avoid talking about the inevitability of going their separate ways, but as Gail's departure time approached, they knew they were unlikely to see each other again.

Gail was scheduled to fly out on June 12th, three days before their apartment lease was up, and Alice had yet to decide when and exactly where she would begin her journey. The apartment came furnished and neither Gail nor Alice had many possessions they were interested in taking with them. They donated school books and their well-loved secondhand Selectric typewriter to a graduate student who lived in their building. Alice was determined to travel as lightly as possible because she wanted the freedom to walk and hike in addition to traveling by car, bus or train. And, she had her guitar, which would always take up one of her shoulders.

On June eighth, they spent a mellow day at the beach, soaking up the sun and reminiscing about the many times they had both counted on the ocean's magical properties to get them through difficult moments. Alice decided it was a good time to have a conversation.

"How do you want to spend our last few days here, Gail?"

Gail sat up and began brushing sand off her legs. Then she turned to Alice and said, "I've been thinking a lot about this, so hear me out."

"Okay"

"I'm going to go with you."

"That would be awesome Gail, but how can you? What will you tell your parents? Aren't they expecting you to be home, like next week?"

"Well, yes, and you know I will end up there, but I really want the summer off, to have fun and adventures and be free with you. So I'm going to tell them I got a miraculous temporary job opportunity, like an internship, that will give me great experience working with budgets and running a business in the fashion world."

"Do you think they'll buy that story?"

"I'm going to have to do some research, but I know they're counting on me to use my experience as a young woman with a marketing degree who has been living as an American college co-ed." Gail chuckled, "They still seem to think that because I've been living in Southern California, I'm on top of what's going on in the current fashion world. Little do they know that I mostly wear jeans and t-shirts. Anyway, I'm going to tell them I was offered a summer internship with a local fashion house through my school connections that will provide me with, not only great experience, but also valuable networking in the fashion business."

"This is wonderful for me, Gail. As you know, I haven't had much luck taking my first step, but doing this together will get me off my ass. How should we start? I guess the first thing is to work it out with your parents." Alice was happy for herself, but worried about Gail, so she added, "I'm really sorry you have to lie to them."

"I've thought a lot about it, Alice. I've been so unhappy with the prospect of returning to Jamaica and having my life planned out by my family. I mean, next thing I know, they will have found me a suitable husband and that will be it. I need this summer to figure out whether I'm ultimately okay with that, or whether there's something I would prefer to do with my life. I'll deal with my family one way or the other."

"Okay, you do that and I'll do some research on how we can travel. Will you be turning in your airline ticket, getting a refund?"

"I guess. I haven't thought through any details. I know I want to see a bit of the country along the way. Maybe I'm being melodramatic, but I'm afraid this will be my only chance."

Alice sighed, "I confess I was little nervous about doing the cross-country trip by myself. Maybe that's why I haven't started to plan, but traveling with you changes everything."

A warm feeling came over Gail as she listened to Alice thinking out loud. "We could try different modes of transportation along the way. I mean, there's no-one expecting us anywhere at a particular time; and going by car or bus would surely be cheaper than flying anyway. I haven't seen much of the country either, so this trip could be our first adventure. Oh, this is going to be so much fun!"

Gail, who had been drinking a Coke, lifted the can and made a toast, "to our first adventure as college graduates." Putting the can down, she looked at Alice and said, "I know you're going to see this as my trying to structure things, but don't rebel just yet. Can we start with a plan of action? I don't need to have every little detail down, but a general outline?"

"Okay Gail, but you need to be the leader in this planning part. You know I'm really bad at that. I also need to feel like I can comfortably tell you when it's getting on my nerves. Deal?"

"Okay, let's start by picking out a route east that includes seeing places we want to see. I know there are a number of interstate highways in California. What part of the country do you want to start with?"

Alice scratched her chin. "I guess the Southwest, maybe start in Arizona and New Mexico. I've always wanted to see the Grand Canyon and the Petrified Forest and Navajo and Pueblo villages."

"Me too, Alice, I have no idea where they are exactly or whether they're on the same route. Let's check out the map room at the college library. Do you want to go now?"

Alice looked at her watch. "It's only six, we have plenty of time. Even in the summer, the library stays open until 11.Want to walk to the campus? We can stop at a Pup and Taco, or Der Weinerschnitzel for a celebratory dinner on the way."

Even though she was caught up in the moment, Gail stepped back; this was starting to feel real. "Can we do it tomorrow? I need to call my parents. I want to start our journey without any noise!"

As Gail stood up and gathered her towel and beach bag, Alice continued talking. "Sounds good, Gail. I think I'll stay here for a while so you can have the apartment to yourself. I'll meet you back there in about an hour, and if you want, I'll pick up some takeout. Which would you prefer: hot dogs or tacos?"

"Both sound fine."

Chapter 14

June 8, 1973
Southern California

As she watched Gail leave the beach, a restless Alice also got up and walked around the neighborhood she had called home for the past two years. She was genuinely happy Gail wanted to join her for the first leg of the next chapter in her life. *Even if Gail ends up back in Jamaica after the summer, we'll have the luxury of sharing a transition from student to adult. Is that the correct title of where we're headed?*

Switching mental gears, Alice looked at the palm trees lining her path and thought about how different the landscape would be in New York City. *I don't know if I'll miss palm trees. I like green grass and trees and have never been a big fan of the omnipresent oil wells of Southern California, but I know I'll miss living within blocks of the ocean.* With that thought, she headed back to the beach where she took off her sandals and walked along the surf. As usual, she found herself hypnotized by the movement of the waves and comforted by the feel of the water and drifting sand as it moved rhythmically in and out along her feet. Caught up in meditation, she didn't notice that her friend Mike had been running to catch up with her and calling her name.

"Hey Alice, I didn't know you were still on campus. When will you be leaving?"

"As a matter of fact, I can actually answer that question as of an hour ago. My roommate Gail and I are going to travel across the country beginning next week."

"Flying to New York?"

"No, we aren't exactly sure yet, but we're talking about crossing the country in a more leisurely fashion so we can stop along the way to see a few sights. Neither of us has seen much of the U S of A and thought this might be a good opportunity."

"That sounds really cool, Alice. I'm jealous."

Alice looked at Mike with interest. She had always liked him, but knew little about his background, or even where his family lived. They had taken a few classes together and seen each other at parties and political demonstrations, but that was the extent of their relationship. "Will you be sticking around this area, Mike?"

"Oh no, I have to get home and start working."

"Where do you live?"

"Albuquerque, New Mexico."

"Oh cool, maybe you can help me and Gail figure out our travels through the Southwest. The one thing we know at this point is that we want to start out through Arizona and New Mexico."

"I'd be happy to consult. Have you decided how you're going to go through the area?"

"Nope. I think we have it in our heads to do a mix of bus, train, and maybe even hitching, but we literally just decided to take this trip together."

Mike smiled, "If you're ready to take off in a couple of days, my friend Joey Knox and I are driving to Albuquerque. He has a van so there's room."

"That would be awesome, at least for part of the way. We haven't talked details, but I think we want to stop in Arizona and see a few sights. Maybe we can go that far with you and you could drop us at a bus station somewhere. Of course we'll help pay for gas."

"Let me talk with Joey and I'll get back with you. Will you be on campus tomorrow morning? We can meet for coffee."

"That would be great. Tell me about Joey, I'm not sure I've met him."

"That's probably because he's just finishing his freshman year here. You two would be unlikely to have any of the same classes."

Mike explained that although he and Joey graduated from high school together in 1968, Joey had decided to take a break from school and ended up being caught up in the military draft. He served in the army for the next two years, part of which involved combat in Vietnam. They had run into each other accidently at a bar after which Mike stayed in touch and eventually convinced Joey to come to California and join him at Coral U.

"He was pretty messed up by the war and was sitting around doing nothing but being depressed. I still worry about him sticking it out and finishing school, especially without me there to stay on top of things."

Alice thought about other people she knew who had returned from Vietnam in shock, not only because they had the surreal experience of living in a place where combat was the norm. In addition to feeling unwelcome because of strong anti-war feelings among their peers, they also returned to a country that had changed dramatically in other ways. It was as if they had missed a decade instead of a year. She recalled overhearing a recent vet commenting on seeing women wearing mini-skirts for the first time. He said he felt like he had entered a cheesy science fiction movie based on the 1950s television show, *Rocky Jones, Space Ranger.*

Mike continued. "So he tends to be quiet a lot of the time. I think it would be great for us both to hang out with you and your friend."

"I would like that, Mike. Gail and I will already be on campus in the morning. We're woefully ignorant about our country's geography and want to get a sense of where things we might want to see are located, so we've decided to check out the big U.S. wall map at the library. What time do you want to meet?"

"Let's meet at the cafeteria at 10."

Alice nodded again and looked at her watch. "Whoops, I need to get back to the apartment. See you in the morning!"

Alice waved to Mike and walked back to the apartment, stopping briefly at the local Der Weinerschnitzel to pick up a chili cheese dog for Gail and a kraut dog with mustard for herself. She wasn't sure what to expect in the wake of Gail's conversation with her parents, but figured a hot dog in her belly might be of some help.

Gail was sitting in the living room staring out the window when Alice arrived and handed her the hot dog.

"Thanks Alice, I'm starving."

"How'd the call go?"

"I don't know. I already feel guilty for lying to them, and, when I heard the disappointment in my mother's voice, I almost changed my mind. Then I thought about how much I need to step away and get some clarity. So I did it, and they accepted that I would just be putting off my return for a few months. Please don't say anything like what if I decide to stay in the States? I'm going to take this one day at a time."

Alice said, "I might have good news. I think we've scored a ride as far as Arizona."

Gail cheered up as she listened to Alice describe her conversation with Mike and heard they had made plans to meet for coffee on campus in the morning.

"Is that Mike Lucas, the cute guy with blond hair and a ponytail? I know him a little too. This is great. Having a ride with people we know for the first leg of our trip would be awesome. Do you know this Joey guy?"

Alice shook her head. "No, but I do know Mike. He's a nice guy. I met him a couple of years ago and have run into him in a number of classes and anti-war demonstrations. In fact, I think we first met protesting in the wake of the Kent State and Jackson State massacres in 1970. We definitely share political views. But getting back to your question, Mike said he and Joey were friends in high school in Albuquerque and he's just finished his freshman year here."

Chapter 15

Gail and Alice stayed up late. Too excited to sleep, they decided that even if the ride didn't come through, they would begin their journey in Arizona with a visit to the Grand Canyon.

Arriving on the campus at nine the following morning, they went straight to the library and its map room where they located the Grand Canyon in northern Arizona and other places they might want to see along the way to New York. They agreed that, at this point, they were simply dreaming. Financial and travel constraints could be dealt with later. While the new American Express Card provided a safety net, Alice was determined to begin her post-college life by making it on her own instead of depending on her father's money. She had never shared the fact of her family's wealth with anyone, and had no intention of starting now.

Gail made a list of places they were interested in visiting so they decided to go to the campus bookstore in search of a roadmap. The roadmap showed the quickest, most direct route to Albuquerque was via Interstate 40, but 40 was south of the Grand Canyon. It would take around nine hours without stopping to drive to Albuquerque, but the Grand Canyon would require a detour. They wondered if the guys could give them a lift as far as Flagstaff or one of the towns along the highway where they could catch a bus to the Grand Canyon.

At ten o'clock, Gail and Alice met with Mike and Joey at the college cafeteria. Joey seemed very different from Mike, who was outgoing and wore the ragged clothes of a sixties guy. No-one called themselves hippies anymore, but there was a clear distinction between 'freaks' and 'straights'. Just by virtue of the way he presented, Mike came across as a 'freak', while Joey appeared to be a 'straight.' He was quiet and wore a clean shirt with a button-down collar and while not cut short, his hair was neatly combed. Everything about him seemed neat. Alice gave him a pass because he was Mike's friend. It didn't hurt that he had amazing dark brown eyes and was extremely good-looking.

Following greetings and introductions, Alice began by describing their tentative plans. "We know we want to end up in New York City and we want to start in the Southwest; but after that, we've made no specific decisions. We're hoping to hitch a ride with you, at least as far as Arizona. Do you plan to drive along I-40?"

Mike answered, "Yep, it's an eight to nine hour drive, which should be pretty direct with four of us driving."

"I'm happy to take a turn driving, but Gail and I want to see the Grand Canyon, and since it's not on your way, we thought you could drop us off someplace along Rte. 40 where we can catch a bus north."

Mike looked at Joey. Alice was beginning to wonder if Joey might not want them along. He had been quiet and his face was a blank sheet, so she was surprised when he said,

"I'd like to see the Grand Canyon myself. I've never been and I hear it's pretty awesome. Would you mind if we tagged along? What do you think Mike?"

"That makes it a two to three-day ride, but I'm up for it. I was hoping to take a little time off before starting work, so a detour like that would be great. I saw the Grand Canyon once when I was a little kid. It blew me away."

The decision to visit the Grand Canyon contributed to a collective feeling of comfort and all four began to anticipate the trip with a sense of adventure. The next few days went by quickly and they finally took off at seven in the morning on June fifteenth.

Since it was his car, Joey drove the first leg of the journey, through Barstow and the Mojave Desert. Alice sat in the front with him while Gail and Mike chatted happily in the back seat. For the first hour, Alice's efforts to engage Joey in conversation were met with polite one-word answers to what she considered her increasingly inane questions. She finally gave up and after what seemed like an endless period of uncomfortable silence, asked if they could turn on the radio to listen to what was going on with the Watergate Hearings. She had become a self-described Watergate "junkie" for the past year, beginning with the almost daily revelations Bob Woodward and Carl Bernstein had been reporting in the Washington Post since the break-in to the Democratic Party's National Committee's office in June 1972. As it turned out, Joey was also interested in following the day-to-day changes in what was being learned about the break-in at the Watergate Complex, and the Nixon administration's role in the break-in and cover-up.

There wasn't much news on the radio, which was just as well because the minute they hit Barstow, they lost access to radio reception. Instead, they spent the next few hours sharing their views. Mike and Gail also piped in every once in a while, but the conversation mostly took place in the front as both Alice and Joey had spent a lot of time paying attention to the details of news reports. They had both also watched the Senate Select Committee Hearings that had been broadcast from 'gavel to gavel,' every weekday since May 18th.

Alice was convinced that President Nixon, his administration, and his Committee to Re-Elect the President, appropriately nicknamed "CREEP," were complicit in all of the crimes. She also thought Nixon had been at the helm. "I don't trust Nixon in the slightest. I think he's totally driven by his ambition and need for power. He may know the truth, but would never let it get in the way of winning."

Although not a Nixon fan, Joey found it hard to accept the idea that the US government could be so corrupt. He wanted desperately to believe this was the behavior of a few bad apples, maybe zealous rogue actors. After all, the guys who broke into the offices were rabid anti-Castro Bay of Pigs veterans. Still struggling with the role he played as a soldier fighting in Vietnam, he wanted to believe that his government did things, even clandestine things, for the good of the country.

"I want to keep my mind open Alice, but doesn't it seem more likely that somebody else, maybe someone who thought it would make Nixon happy to get the goods on the Democrats' plans for the election, would do something this stupid? I mean, the guy's the president of the United States. He has to be too busy running the country to have time for that petty shit."

"So, who do you think is behind the burglary? John Mitchell, the former attorney general who ran the re-election campaign? Could he have done this without Nixon knowing?"

"Mitchell was clearly in the middle of it. I guess he was pretty effective at running the campaign. I mean, look at the landslide victory."

"Maybe some of the slimy stuff they did contributed to Nixon winning re-election, but he was also running against a flawed candidate in George McGovern. McGovern is a decent guy, in my opinion, but not good at running for president."

Alice held back from going further. McGovern ran on an anti-war platform and she didn't want to get into a conversation about the Vietnam War with Joey. "You know, Joey, I find it interesting that the Watergate Hearings have been about the cover-up. It's almost as if no-one is interested in who was behind the break-in itself."

Joey smiled. "I got hooked on this soap opera fairly recently when the big guns in the White House started dropping like flies: Haldeman, Ehrlichman, John Dean, even the Attorney General, Richard Kleindienst. Then when John Dean started talking, wow, you can't make this stuff up!"

"Do you still think there's a possibility Nixon wasn't behind the break-in?"

"I honestly don't know. I guess I still hope it's not true. He has obviously been directing, or at least giving support to the cover-up, if what Dean says is true. At this point it's Dean's word against Nixon's and the rest of his cronies."

"Did you read about the memo addressed to John Ehrlichman describing the plans to burglarize the office of Daniel Ellsberg's psychiatrist back in 1971?"

"No, what's that got to do with this?"

"Same people, the so-called 'plumbers.'"

Joey sighed, "A lot of circumstantial evidence that wouldn't hold up in a court of law; and most of these people are lawyers. I assume they know how to be careful, to cover their tracks."

"And we're left with a shifty president whose closest advisors are either in prison, or likely to end up there, while he's protected, watching the bodies build up."

Gail stuck her head up between Joey and Alice. "This has been fascinating, guys, but do you think we could stop for a bathroom break?"

Joey responded, "Of course, we're almost out of the desert, how long have we been on the road would you guess?"

Mike answered. "Believe it or not, time flies when you're having fun. It's noon, I'm hungry, and we've been on the road for about five hours. Needles has to be coming up pretty soon. I vote we stop there for lunch. Then we only have a couple of hours before we get to our Grand Canyon jumping-off spot, a town called Williams. I need to stretch my legs and I'll bet the car is ready for some giddy-up go juice. By the way, I have a trivia question for you that involves the town of Needles. Ready?"

They all laughed and Gail said, "Okay, what's the trivia question, Mike?"

"What famous cartoon character lives in Needles?

Chapter 16

June 15-16, 1973
California, Arizona, New Mexico

It was an old-fashioned diner with a small juke box in every booth. Alice immediately started flipping through the choices and put a quarter into the slot. The list included both popular oldies and current hits.

"We get three songs for this quarter, what shall they be? I'll start. I choose Carol King's *You've Got a Friend.*"

After much discussion, they all agreed on Johnny Cash's *I Walk the Line* and Bill Haley and the Comet's *Rock and Roll is Here to Stay.*

As they listened to their first selection, Mike said, "Okay, your time is up. Who's the famous cartoon character who lives in Needles?" He was interrupted by a woman's laugh and the sound of her foot tapping on the floor. Embarrassed, they looked up and saw a smiling waitress. They immediately got to the business of ordering their burgers and fries. Alice asked if they had black and white shakes and was happily surprised the waitress knew they were made from vanilla ice cream blended with chocolate syrup.

"I've been in a few places where people never heard the term," Alice said, smiling at the waitress.

The waitress laughed, "Hey, we may be a small town but we're not in the boonies! By the way, I can answer the question."

Mike said, also laughing, "I would hope you know, after all he has to be your most famous neighbor."

"Oh he is, I hear him barking all the time. He's Snoopy's brother Spike. You know, from *Peanuts.*"

They all looked at Mike as Gail said, "You must be a major fan to know stuff like that!"

"Hey, I grew up with *Peanuts*. I had some friends in elementary school who were also into them, so we all took on a character and believe it or not, I chose Spike. I guess I felt knowing that kind of trivia would impress the other kids."

Alice turned to Joey, "Were you involved with that group, Joey?"

"No, we didn't move to Albuquerque until I was in high school. But it's funny, I don't remember you," looking at Mike, "as a goofy kid at all. You always seemed sort of serious, politically active. Weren't you a Goldwater supporter back then?"

Gail and Alice looked at Mike curiously. From college, they knew him to be politically active and definitely leaning towards liberal causes. It was hard to imagine him being a fan of the most conservative of Conservative Republicans, Barry Goldwater.

Mike's face took on a slightly pink tone. "It's a long story and it took me a while to see the light. Coming from the Southwest, Goldwater was somewhat of a native son. I paid no attention to politics at all until he ran for president in 1964 when I was a freshman in high school. And my dad was a major fan of Goldwater, so that's where I started. Yeah, I guess I changed as I got older and learned what was going on in the world."

Gail nodded, "I didn't have a clue about what was going on in the world until I came to college. My family are pretty much Royalists."

Alice thought to herself: *there's a lot I don't know about Gail, but this really comes out of left field. Being Chinese Jamaican is unusual enough, but being a Royalist! What does that mean in this day and age?* Stirring the ice cream into her milk shake, she looked around the table and said, "I think we're going to have a really interesting mini-vacation, guys. I just learned something about my roomie I never knew before."

Gail blushed. "Well, the subject never came up."

They all laughed and went back to eating. It was clear more would be learned about one another's lives over the next few days.

The remainder of the ride went as planned. The women were in awe of the scenery they encountered, beginning with crossing the Colorado River at the nexus of the three states in Needles. They had never seen such landscape as the deep canyons. They also enjoyed the fact that Interstate 40 intertwined with the historic Route 66, the old western road made famous by John Steinbeck's *The Grapes of Wrath* and the 1960s buddy television series, *Route 66*. There were places along the way that had been preserved to attract tourists interested in the old west, not to mention Native American cultural centers.

"You'll see a lot of Indians in Arizona and New Mexico." Mike announced when someone brought it up. "The Navajo

Reservation is on the other side of the Grand Canyon. It's the largest reservation in the U.S."

"How large is it?" Gail asked.

"I can't tell you exactly, but it's huge. It takes up the entire northeast corner of Arizona and goes into New Mexico and Colorado. And that's not the only Native American land around these parts."

Joey jumped in, "Yep, we have Pueblo Indians, Zuni and Hopi, Apache's, Utes. Just around this part of Arizona there are some of the lesser known reservations, the Hualapai, Kaibab, and Havasupai."

"Why are so many located here? Do you know?"

"Look around you. This is lousy land where you can't grow anything. The European settlers weren't interested in stealing something that was hard to work."

"And yet, is so beautiful!"

Joey smiled. "I've always been glad it was too hard to turn this beauty into parking lots."

They finally stopped in Williams, where they had no trouble finding a Motel 6 with its famous no-frills rooms for six dollars a night. As soon as Alice and Gail settled into their room, Alice put a quarter into the television slot to see what was going on with the Hearings. Gail went out to knock on Mike and Joey's door and found Joey also glued to the set. She and Mike made plans to meet at six to find a place to dine. She returned to the room and laid down on the semi-comfortable mattress thinking, *what should I expect for six bucks anyway?!*

The following day they headed up to the Grand Canyon, which did not disappoint. Leaving the van in a parking lot, they entered through the South Rim and hiked up to the North Rim and back where they absorbed the wonder of it all. It was noon by the time they got back, so after a quick walk through the Visitor's Center, they decided to head to Route 40 to find an affordable lunch.

Mike couldn't stop talking about what they had seen. "It's amazing how little I remembered about it from when I was a kid. I really want to go down to the river. I feel like I've seen a crater of the moon up close and personal. I used to think I would never have a chance to experience anything that meets the standards of a good acid or peyote hallucination. To think, it's just down the road from Albuquerque."

Gail laughed. "I think it's a little farther away than that."

"Not in Western U.S.A. terms. This is the vast frontier. It has to be super different from living on an island in the Caribbean."

Gail sighed. "That's for sure. I would love to spend more time in the American Southwest. This summer is already starting to feel much too short. I really don't want to go back to Jamaica."

Alice was beginning to wonder if Gail would end up staying in the States after all. "Hey, we have a lot of adventures to get through before you even have to think about going back."

A few hours later, they arrived in Albuquerque, a large sprawling city that felt like a shock after so much desert. Alice and Gail experienced another shock when Joey drove down a street populated by one mansion after another, and pulled into the circular driveway leading to an extensive single-story house. This was Mike's family's home.

Chapter 17

June 16, 1973
Albuquerque NM

Shortly after they arrived at Mike's house, a woman and three teenagers came out of the front door. All blond, they were soon joined by several dogs of various sizes. The woman, who was obviously Mike's mother, greeted them graciously, hugged Mike and Joey, and invited them into the house. If she was surprised by their being there, she didn't reveal it.

Mike made introductions. "Alice, Gail, this is my mom Lois, and these brats are Katie, Kurt and Tommy. Mom, Gail and Alice are on their way to New York but I invited them to stay here for a couple of days. They've never been in New Mexico. Joey and I want to show them some sites."

Lois took it all in stride, and smiling at Alice and Gail, said, "Great, let me show you the guest suite. I think there are clean sheets on the beds. Do you want to freshen up?"

Then she turned back to Mike. "I was wondering when we'd hear from you. I haven't seen you since your graduation, and even then, I hardly saw you. What have you been up to?"

"Oh this and that," Mike responded in the same casual tone.

Gail was fascinated. Mike hadn't mentioned he had seen his parents recently or that they had attended the graduation ceremony. She was astonished at how laid back they were with each other. It was like they were college buddies rather than parent and child. Her relationship with her parents was so different. And the house was huge and amazing. The walls and shelves were covered with colorful Native American art and artifacts, sand paintings and woven wall-hangings everywhere.

Lois picked up Gail's bag and turned to Mike. "I'll show the girls the way to the guest suite." She was definitely a take-charge person.

The guest suite was indeed a suite, somewhat like a private in-law attachment that was separated from the main part of the house by a long corridor with glass walls on both sides. It included three bedrooms, each with its own bathroom, along with a shared sitting room with a comfortable looking couch and chairs, and a large television set.

Alice said, "Thank you for your hospitality."

Lois smiled benevolently. "That's what it's here for. So, what are you planning to do in Albuquerque? Are you interested in Southwestern art?"

"I think I can speak for both Gail and myself. We're interested in visiting the artists' colonies in Taos or Santa Fe, but not to buy. The rest of our trip east is going to involve carrying our own bags. I know we'll be tempted, but that constraint will keep us from spending all of our travel funds."

"I understand. What about clothes? I know some great little shops in Santa Fe."

"I'm not much into fashion, but this is Gail's expertise. She just finished her degree in marketing and her family owns an export clothing business."

Lois looked at Gail. "Really? In the Philippines?"

Accustomed to being mislabeled, Gail smiled back, "Actually, my family's business is in Jamaica. I'm not Filipina, but have been mistaken for one before. That's what happens when you're Asian with a mixed background."

"Oh, I'm sorry," Lois flushed, "I didn't mean to, I mean, I just assumed because you're pretty tall and don't have the pure Asian look. Of course there isn't just one Asian look."

"It's not a problem, Mrs. Lucas. I'm used to people trying to figure out my origins. I know they are unusual in this part of the world, but in the Caribbean where I grew up, not so much. I grew up in Suriname and Jamaica. My father is Chinese and my mother is half Chinese—the rest is a mixed bag we've never quite figured out. I guess I get my height from the mixed bag part."

Recovering her grace, Lois continued to address Gail, "Call me Lois. We're very casual here. I hope you will come with me to some of my favorite clothing shops in Santa Fe. With your educated expertise, I'm sure I can learn from watching you assess the quality of the clothes."

Gail surprised Alice by sounding sincere when she responded, "I would love to go clothes shopping with you."

After dropping their bags in the guest suite, Gail and Alice followed Lois to the living room where Mike and Joey were chatting. Lois turned to Joey and asked politely, "Will you join us for dinner tonight?

His response was equally polite, making Alice wonder about their relationship and why there didn't seem to be much warmth between them.

"Thank you for inviting me, Lois, but I need to get home. My mom's expecting me."

"Of course, Joey, please give her my regards. Now I have to get to the kitchen and make dinner arrangements."

Alice said. "Can I help?"

"No, we're all set."

Mike laughed, "Nice of you to offer, Alice, but my mother does no food preparation here. She just gives orders to the kitchen staff, but you can count on the food being good. Hey Joey, do you want to make plans to show the ladies around tomorrow?"

Joey stood up and said, "Let's catch up in the morning. Meanwhile you can think about what you might want to see. I just need to put more gas in the van."

"Sounds good, I think the rest of this day is for chillin. Anyone want to take a swim in the pool with me?"

Gail nodded gratefully. Alice said she would join them later, but first wanted to see what was happening with the Watergate Hearings.

As they walked back towards the guest suite, Mike pointed to a sliding glass door and, said to Gail, "Just go through that door when you're ready and I'll meet you at the pool. I hope you don't mind the kids. They're very intrigued with my bringing two beautiful women home."

Gail laughed and said, "I'll be there in five minutes. I'm really ready for that swim!"

Alice was already watching the Hearings when Gail headed for the door, stopping only to ask if there was anything new since yesterday.

"There's nothing dramatic so far, but I'm totally addicted, and find that the news reporters, both in the papers and on TV news tend to miss a lot. I've been learning about how news is selected for the public by watching the hearings themselves. Even when I haven't been able to watch every day, I'm willing to bet I could win a trivia contest against any of these reporters—except Woodward and Bernstein, of course."

"I wouldn't dare try! I'm more into having a good time while we're here. Isn't this place amazing? I didn't know Mike's family was so rich, he's so down to earth and such a nice guy."

Alice looked at Gail. "I'm starting to get the impression your interest in Mike goes beyond friendship and watching you two together, it seems like he might feel the same."

"I don't know if either is true, Alice. I just know I like him a lot and I like his family."

Alice turned back to the Watergate Hearings and Gail left the room.

Gail returned an hour later looking refreshed and happy. "That was so much fun. Mike and his sister and brothers are adorable together. I'm going to take a shower and dress up a bit. What about you? Will you be changing for dinner?"

Alice, who was still attending closely to the Hearings, turned her head to face Gail and said, "Sure, I can put on my respectable clothes. Do you really think we need to dress up?"

Gail was serious. "I don't know, but the last thing I heard was cocktails will be served at six. That sounded kind of formal."

Alice returned to the television and said distractedly, "I'll see what I can find in my bag; cocktails, huh."

In the end, Alice found a pair of clean white bell bottoms to wear with a colorful peasant top. Gail was amazed that it looked like she might even be wearing a bra, but decided not to ask. Gail was wearing her favorite sundress, which was multi-colored and set off her tan nicely.

Finding their way to the living room, Gail and Alice discovered cocktails were being served on the patio. Everyone was already there, including Mike's father, Ed Lucas. He had evidently started drinking long before they arrived. He began by boisterously welcoming Alice and Gail to his "humble hacienda" and offering drinks. Pointing to several pitchers, he announced, "We're having margaritas, but we can scare up any drink you might like, perhaps a little plum wine or sake for you Gail. What about you, Alice, what's your pleasure? I'm afraid we don't serve marijuana here."

Clearly embarrassed, Mike's face turned bright red. "You're going to have to forgive my father; he's had a little too much to drink."

To Mike's relief, Gail and Alice handled his insults with grace. Alice replied that a margarita would be great and Gail smiled and said, "A common assumption, but I'm mostly Chinese, not Japanese."

Slurring his words, Ed went on to say, "Glad you're not a Nip. I don't need to hear about Hiroshima from people who don't know what we were up against. They started the war by bombing Pearl Harbor. I'm sick of people wanting to apologize for us saving our country."

Mike interrupted and said sarcastically, "And yeah, those damned Vietnamese attacking our shores, we need to kill them all."

Lois turned to Gail and Alice, "I was hoping we would get a night off from these two sniping at each other. This one," pointing to Ed, "is still fighting World War II and this one," pointing at Mike, "is ignoring the reasons for our current history. I think dinner is ready, follow me, and bring your drinks to the table if you want."

As promised, dinner was delicious and had a definite southwestern, Mexican-American flare. They had chiles relleños, chicken mole, and fresh avocado salad vinaigrette.

During the meal, Alice and Gail learned that Mike's father was a physicist who had worked on the atomic bomb at Los Alamos. Since then he had created, and continued to run, a consulting business with a great deal of financial success. They also learned he was a dedicated conservative Republican. Mike had previously told them his father had been a supporter of Arizona Senator Barry Goldwater, who had written *Conscience of a Conservative*, and run for president against Lyndon Johnson in 1964, but they were not prepared for his opinions about everything that was going on currently. And the more he drank, which he did more than eat, the more hostile he became. Alice tried to avoid him, but when he wasn't attacking Mike for his long hair and anti-war sentiments, he directed his rants at her.

"I hear you've been following these so-called Watergate Hearings. These people are traitors to our country, trying to undo our democracy by undoing our election system. Didn't they notice the people have spoken and re-elected President Nixon, giving him a landslide victory?"

Alice looked directly at him and said, "If Nixon is so secure that he serves at the will of the people, why did he have to break into the DNC headquarters?"

Just as he began to respond, Gail interrupted, acting as if this conversation wasn't taking place. "Everything is delicious, but I have to tell you, I have never tasted better avocados. Are they local?"

This provided Lois with an opportunity to shift gears and start to plan her "girls shopping expedition" for the following morning.

Chapter 18

June 17, 1973
New Mexico

As they were driving to Santa Fe the following morning, Lois thanked Gail for what she saw as skilled interference in redirecting the conversation from political to anything else. "As you can see, Mike's father is stuck in the past and when he has one too many, has even more trouble letting go."

Gail laughed and said, "Not a problem, Lois, I've had a lot of practice with my father."

Alice was fascinated watching Gail saying and doing just the right thing with Lois, to just the right effect. She had never seen her act this way, and for the life of her, couldn't remember a time when Gail described her father as anything like Ed Lucas. In fact, she had always made him sound like a quiet gentle soul who, besides being a fan of the British royal family, kept his views to himself.

To Alice, it was fun being in such a colorful town. She wasn't interested in shopping for clothes, but did enjoy looking at the western styles and colors. After a while, she drifted off and walked around the town by herself. Gail, Lois, and Mike's sister Katie were much more interested in the shopping part, so they made arrangements to meet her at a local café for lunch.

Wandering into a gift shop that featured Pueblo Indian art, Alice was drawn to a wall displaying kachina dolls. Seeing her interest, a saleswoman came over to ask if she needed help. Alice looked up apologetically and said, "These are wonderful but I'm only here to appreciate their beauty. I'm on my way across the country and have to travel light."

The woman smiled and said, "I completely understand. I love them too but can't afford anything in this shop. Do you know what they are?"

"I know they're kachinas and that they have cultural meaning for members of Pueblo Indian tribes, but that's about it. I also know they're a popular sale item for tourists."

"Actually, they're made by a particular Pueblo tribe, the Hopi. They do have cultural meaning and also have great appeal to art collectors of all stripes."

"What's their history, do you know?"

The saleswoman laughed, "Yep, it's a requirement of the job. They go back to the late 18th/early 19th Centuries and were created to be used in ceremonies to instruct young girls about the immortal beings that bring rain, control other aspects of the natural world and society, and act as messengers between humans and the spirit world. The dolls represent the spirits of deities, animals, natural elements or deceased Hopi ancestors. Like a lot of things around here, they became tourist souvenirs beginning in the early 1900s, and their look has changed to accommodate the tastes of the buying public. "

"How have they changed?"

"More moving parts and they no longer have to be hung up on walls. To be honest, authentic kachinas are extravagantly expensive these days. You can get miniature versions less expensively. That's become a tradecraft for some carvers. I can show you some if you're interested."

"I am, but not today. I don't even have room in my backpack for a miniature! One more question, are they still used in ceremonies to instruct young girls?"

"Yes, but those have also changed to accommodate the modern world."

Alice looked at her watch and realized she was late for lunch. She thanked the saleswoman and rushed out the door, then turned around abruptly and asked if she could have a business card. "I may be interested in buying at another time."

"Of course, are you interested in Pueblo culture?"

"I don't know much about it, but I do know I'm interested in anything that gives power to girls."

The rest of the group was at the cafe when Alice arrived, all three carrying packages of new clothes. They had obviously had a great time and Lois was bubbling about how Gail had contributed to the quality of their shopping trip. Smiling at Alice, Lois said, "I never paid much attention to the way things hang on my shoulders before. Gail showed me the difference in how it comes across with a good fit. She also taught me that I have a high waist that's pretty small. I always thought my waist was lower and huge."

Gail was beaming. She had obviously made a good impression on Lois and Katie. Growing up with three younger sisters, Gail was easy and comfortable with the young teenager.

Although they had been blessed with air conditioning in the stores and the car, by the time they returned to the house, everyone was complaining about the heat and decided to take a swim. Alice was eager to get back to watching the Watergate Hearings but joined the swimmers briefly before excusing herself to turn on the television to see what was happening. Mike had been in the pool when they arrived and, before Alice left, asked Gail and Alice if they would like to go to dinner with him and Joey later. Happy to avoid a second dinner with Ed Lucas, they both said yes enthusiastically.

Getting together for dinner with Joey and Mike felt like a reunion where they let their hair down and relaxed. Alice and Gail hadn't realized how attached they had become to their little group in such a short period of time.

Mike took them to a casual, family-style Mexican restaurant that was popular with local college students. As they sat down with bottles of Dos Equis beer, Gail said, "Your house is wonderful and your family has been very gracious, Mike. We couldn't have scripted a nicer start to our adventure."

"Thanks Gail, you seem to have made a big hit with my family too, but seriously, if either of you get sick of Mexican food, let me know. We do eat other stuff around here."

Alice laughed, "It's hard for me to imagine getting sick of Mexican food and I love that it's different here from Southern California. I mean, most of the dishes have the same names, but they seem to have regional flavor variations, except of course the beer."

Joey agreed. "I've noticed that too. I think it's about the spices, but, even drinks like Coke taste different in different countries because of the water they use. So, how long will you be staying around here? I was hoping to have at least one little expedition as a posse before you go."

Alice laughed out loud, "Posse—I like that—we're a posse. That sounds very western. To answer your question, Gail and I haven't talked about our next move. We need to do that soon, Gail. We can't impose on Mike's family much longer."

Gail said, "I agree Alice, but I'm having so much fun, I feel like I could stay here forever."

Mike looked at Gail with a serious expression. "I wish you could stay forever too, Gail, and I'm sure my mother and sister would be willing to adopt you, but I'm under a little pressure to start work."

Alice and Gail were surprised. "You already have a job?"

"Oh yes, working for my father. Anyway before I start, it would be great if the four of us could do some running around tomorrow and maybe the next day? Where do you want to go?"

Alice answered, "I know I want to go to Los Alamos and Taos. I don't know if Taos is a good place to go for this, but I'm interested in seeing authentic kachinas."

"Then you need to come to my house." Joey said quietly.

"Really, do you have a kachina doll?"

"My mother has some. Her grandmother was Hopi and some dolls have been passed down over the generations."

"I would love to see them. Do you think she'd mind showing them to me? I've been told they are sacred and very valuable."

"They are, but she's proud of her heritage and would probably enjoy talking your ear off. She can probably help you plan the next leg of your trip too. She runs a small travel agency."

Alice turned to Gail, "You see, if you don't worry or over plan, great opportunities fall into your lap."

Gail frowned, "I have a feeling it isn't in my nature to be as open-ended as you. My tendency is to be somewhere rather than be on my way to somewhere." Laughing and looking at Mike, she added, "I'm trying to learn to be more flexible and Alice is a great role model for that."

Chapter 19

June 17-18, 1973
New Mexico

Mike, Gail and Alice had met Joey at the restaurant and as they walked outside to their separate cars, Mike noted that no decisions had been made about the next day. "So posse, what do you all want to do tomorrow?"

Alice responded with a question, "Is Los Alamos near enough for a morning visit? If so, I vote for a tour. It's not up there with the Grand Canyon, but definitely a place I want to get a look at. So much of our history depends on what we did there."

Joey responded as he stepped into his van, "Los Alamos it is! I can drive. See you in the morning. Is nine a.m. too early?"

Mike stared after Joey with his mouth open. "I can't believe he wants to go up there!"

"Why is that?" Alice asked curiously.

"I always thought Joey blamed his father's cancer on Los Alamos. Like my father, he originally worked at the Los Alamos Science Laboratory where the atom bomb was developed, but he was incapacitated by cancer all through Joey's teen years and had been unable to work. It was a tough time for their family. Joey had to work all through high school and stayed home afterwards to help his family out. Then he was drafted and ended up in Vietnam. His dad passed away while Joey was in Vietnam."

Alice appreciated learning about Joey's life. She had sensed sadness in him since they first met. This helped her understand the choices he'd been making. Somewhat like, but also very different, from her, he had been forced to be an adult at an early age. "What a sad story, how did they manage while he was away?"

"It had always been tough money-wise because his mom had to stay home to care for his father a lot of the time, but with help from friends, his mom ended up getting a part-time job working at a travel agency. After his father passed, she became fulltime there. By the time Joey got out of the service determined to take care of his mother and sister, she was doing pretty well, making good commissions. That, along with her widow's pension was enough for them to make do. It took Joey a while to realize he didn't have to stick around to take care of everything, and his mother was really bugging him to use the GI Bill to get a college education. He dithered about it, but I got involved and practically filled out his application materials to come to Coral U. I must admit, I wanted to be close enough to keep an eye on the dude. He takes school seriously, but is hyper-responsible where his mother and sister are concerned."

"Joey said his mother runs a travel agency. Did she take that one over, the one she started in as a part-timer?"

"Yep, now she runs the place."

When Joey returned home after dinner, he sat with his mother to tell her about their plans to take a ride up to Los Alamos. She was as surprised as Mike to hear of his willingness to go there. He had always blamed the toxic work environment for his father's cancer. She couldn't help wondering what it was about these girls from the college that got him to change his mind.

The Los Alamos site was still dominated by a working research laboratory. It was small and while definitely of historical interest, limited in entertainment value. As they walked around the town, looked at the history and science museums, the famous Ranch School, and the bungalows where Oppenheimer and the rest of the people who had developed the first atomic bomb had lived, Alice was struck by the banality of its location.

"Both of your fathers worked in the laboratory here?" Alice asked curiously. "Did either of you live here as well?"

Joey was quiet, almost to the point of withdrawing. It was a mistake to view this as a nostalgia trip. He was beginning to regret coming, but recovered by telling himself he had at least discovered that it remained a sore spot.

Mike stepped in, "Nope, both our dads were commuters. Can we talk about something else, something more cheerful, like the Watergate Hearings?"

Alice laughed uncomfortably; it was clearly time to move on. "Thank you guys for bringing us up here. I feel like I'm vibrating and I have no family history here at all. But we do need to start planning our next move. What do you think, Gail, shall we stay one more day then head on to the East Coast?"

Gail nodded, "I agree, let's go to Taos tomorrow."

As they drove towards Albuquerque, Joey said they would be passing his mother's travel agency and asked Alice and Gail if they wanted to stop in. He was sure she'd find them a good deal no matter how they decided to travel.

Gail mumbled, "It had better be the cheapest way. I spent so much money on our shopping spree yesterday, I'm going to need every penny in New York."

Joey continued, "Oh, I forgot to mention, Alice, she said she would be happy to show you her kachina dolls."

Alice and Gail were impressed with Joey's mother Dora. Simultaneously warm and business-like, she asked how much they had to spend and whether they wanted to stop and see other places on their way to New York City.

The travelers admitted they wanted to save as much as possible for New York since they didn't know how long it would take to find jobs and an affordable place to live. Looking at the U.S. map, Alice said she was sure there were many wonders between Albuquerque and New York, but the only one she knew that sounded particularly interesting was the famous Gateway Arch in St. Louis; and of course, the Mississippi River. Dora smiled and turned to Gail, "And you?"

Gail answered that she was following Alice's lead on this trip.

"Okay, then I can get you discounted bus tickets between here and Harrisburg Pennsylvania. You can pick up an Amtrak train to New York City there. The bus route takes you through St. Louis, where you go through the Arch as you cross the Mississippi River. If you want, you can stop along the way, but it will cost more. You're leaving day after tomorrow? Think about it but let me know as soon as you can, this is what's available right now."

She told them what it would cost.

Alice looked at Gail. "That sounds reasonable. We can do a Simon and Garfunkel type bus tour of America. I say we go for it. If we see something through the window that makes us want to stop for a while, we stop for a while."

Gail said, "Sounds good to me too. I've been worried about money and this feels do-able."

Alice turned to Dora, "It's a deal. What do you need from us?"

"Do you have a credit card I can put this on? If not, I can do the guaranteeing."

Alice surprised her friends by pulling out her American Express Card and saying, "Will this do?"

Dora smiled at Alice. She liked everything about her.

"Joey tells me you're interested in taking a look at my kachina dolls. I would love to show them to you. Can you come by the house later this afternoon or early evening? I have to do some juggling here with coupons and other things which may take a while, but I promise I will have your tickets ready by then as well."

Joey turned to Mike, "If your family has something going on, I can come get her."

Even though he enjoyed being with the whole "posse," Joey knew it was unlikely he would see Alice again once they headed to New York and liked the idea of having a little alone time with her. He had come to feel they had some common interests, but more than that, there was something special about her and he found her to be an intriguing puzzle.

Mike looked at Joey and thought to himself, *is he falling for Alice? I've never seen him show this much interest in anyone, let alone a woman. He's always seemed withdrawn and depressed and now he's positively bubbly. Well, bubbly is probably an exaggeration.* Smiling, he answered, "Sure Joey. I'm not sure what they have planned, but I imagine my mother and sister will want more time with Gail before she and Alice take off for New York."

Chapter 20

June 18, 1973
New Mexico

As it turned out, Lois and Katie had plans for Gail, so Alice went to Joey and Dora's house alone. On the ride over, they talked about the Watergate Hearings and their increasing mutual belief that they would result in the end of the Nixon presidency. Alice told him how uncomfortable she felt being around Ed Lucas, "He looks at me as if I'm the devil incarnate who's intent on destroying the world and humanity."

"That doesn't surprise me. He's a drunk and he's living in a make believe past. I feel really bad for Mike. I think he wants to make it on his own but if he stays around here, his father's world is going to gobble him up and spit him out."

"Do you think he'll stay in Albuquerque?"

"Yes. The plan has always been for him to inherit his father's consulting business. I think he might be too laid back and lazy to fight his father's will, and there's the money. You may have noticed, the Lucas's are rolling in it and Mike is used to a certain lifestyle."

"That might turn out to be a good thing for Gail. I've had the feeling there are vibes between her and Mike and it seems like Lois is crazy about her."

"I've noticed that too, but it could that cause issues with Ed Lucas! He does not like people who aren't WASPs, especially Asians." Joey paused and said with a serious tone, "Pearl Harbor and all; people who worked at Los Alamos to develop the bomb had to believe the Japanese were devils who needed to be destroyed to save humanity from fascism."

Alice sighed, "Why does such hatred persist? This is so unfair to Gail. She doesn't have a single drop of Japanese blood. Besides, although it doesn't seem to have affected her recent life, the Japanese and Chinese have a long history of antagonism. Poor Gail seems to be hit with a ridiculous amount of stereotyping wherever she goes. Anyway, before we get to your house, I want to make sure I don't make a stupid political remark. What does your mother think about Watergate?"

Joey laughed, "You have nothing to worry about there, she's a Democrat through and through She hates Nixon and is super proud to have our Senator Joseph Montoya on the committee. She has also liked the good things he's done for the state—he got the money to fund an irrigation system for the Navajo Reservation back in 1962 and it doesn't hurt that he's Hispanic."

Alice wasn't surprised to find Dora and Joey's house to be quite different from the Lucas sprawl. Like most of the homes she had seen in the southwest, it was a modest single-story stucco with a roof made of brick-like tiles. Alice knew nothing about roofs, but figured there was a reason these were so common, and liked the contrast between the red tiles and pastel external walls.

Dora greeted them at the door with a big smile. "I just got home from work. Do you mind if I change into more comfortable clothes before I show you the kachinas?" Kicking off her heels, she headed into a short hallway. A few minutes later, she returned to the living room barefoot, wearing jeans and a loose sleeveless blouse. In the office, her long brown hair had been pulled back and contained by a large hair clip. That too was allowed to flow. Alice thought Dora was beautiful and couldn't help contrasting her comfortable home with the Lucas' house, which had felt to her like a showplace, not unlike the house she grew up in. She loved the colorful native art, but for some reason, in the Lucas's house, it felt staged as if it were set up for color coordination. Dora's house was more like a home where you could sit comfortably anywhere without disturbing the plan.

As she led them back down the hallway, Dora said, "My kachinas are in a back room I've been using as a sort of home office. Please excuse the mess."

Joey laughed and looked at Alice. "The rest of this room could be a mess, but the dolls are her most revered possessions. I grew up knowing this was one part of the house I had better not disturb."

He pointed to a glass enclosed case hanging on a wall where six kachina dolls were displayed in upright positions. All were carved cottonwood, but they varied in character, which apparently reflected when they were made. Alice loved the personal family connection they had for Dora and Joey, "These are awesome. You can feel their power!"

Dora smiled. "My grandmother would have loved you! These have been passed down through the family for several generations. You see this one? This was the one that was given to her as part of the ceremony, which was basically her coming of age ceremony where she was taught how to be a woman in her family and tribe."

"What about your mother, and you? Did you have the ceremony?"

"Unfortunately no, she was my father's mother and the Hopi are matrilineal, which basically means that things are passed down from mother to daughter. My father married a non-Hopi, an Anglo, as did I. The only reason I have them is because my grandmother had no daughters or granddaughters from that side, but I'm happy to say she always knew I treasured them. I know they are very valuable, but I would never sell them for money, never!"

"Thank you for showing your treasures to me. I feel honored."

Dora reached over and gave Alice a hug, and whispered, "I haven't seen Joey so happy in a long time. I'm glad you have entered his life." Then in a normal voice, she added, "Have a great trip to New York. I hope it provides you with the adventures you seek. But please come back and see me someday."

Alice smiled, "I would love that, and thank you so much for helping us with our travel arrangements."

Dora handed a manila envelope to Alice. "I think this includes everything you will need. It's been a pleasure doing business with you."

As they walked to the car, Joey said, "You've obviously made a big hit with my mother. And Alice, this may be the last time we'll be alone before you set sail for you next adventure, but I'd like to stay in touch."

"Me too."

Joey hesitated, "Are you hungry? Would you like to grab a bite to eat and maybe take a ride around and see Albuquerque at night? Take the nickel tour as my father used to say?"

"I can't think of anything I would rather do."

Joey looked at his watch. "Hey, I think if we hurry, we can make it in time."

"Make what in time?"

"The Sandia Peak Tramway; it's the best view of the city in one fell swoop."

They arrived at the tramway at 7:45, just in time for the last tram. As their tram traveled up to the mountain top, Alice turned to Joey, her eyes flashing with excitement. "This is amazing! I never heard of it before."

"It's actually pretty new. I think it was finished in the mid-60s sometime and I hear it's the longest tramway in the country."

"Joey, look at the view! Even at night, it looks like we're seeing the whole city and the whole state from up here."

"Not sure it's the whole state of New Mexico, we're pretty good-sized. People who live on the east coast are only used to baby-sized states in comparison."

"I have to give you that. Everything out here is bigger and more spread out. There's a lot more desert too."

"I've never been east of Oklahoma, let alone the Mississippi River."

"Four years ago was my first visit to the West. It's a whole new world. Maybe you can come visit us in New York. If you haven't been, it will surely be a shock to your system. It's built up rather than out and chock full of diversity."

"That would be great, but not likely. I don't have the money to vacation and have to work to save for the fall; then I need to get back to school. Just starting my sophomore year, you know." He paused, and in a quiet voice said, "The diversity and crowding in Vietnam gave me enough system shock for a while."

"Mike told us a little about your high school years and your father. That must've been a tough time for you."

"It was okay. It all started when I was young so I never knew how my life could've been different."

"I know what you mean, I guess we all only have the lives we're born into when we're kids and that has to serve as what's normal."

"It's funny Alice, I've never heard you talk about your family, or the past at all. You are so present in the here and now. What's your family like?"

"Not much to tell. Maybe that's why I don't talk about it. I am very present-oriented. I drive Gail crazy because I can't plan the future well at all, even the near future like what I'm going to do tomorrow. I think I decided a few years ago that the past just makes me depressed and anxious and I can't do anything to change it, but you asked about my family, my childhood. Hmmm, I'm an only child of my parents although both of them have had other children in other families."

"So you have brothers and sisters?"

"Not really. None of them has ever lived in the same house as me, even my mother's kids. I don't know how else to describe it, my parents were both totally over having kids and a family life by the time I came along so I was mostly left alone. My mother has an alcohol problem and the only time I spent with her, from the time I was pretty young, was dedicated to her telling me about her teen years when she was the belle of the ball. I knew she was miserable if that was the highlight of her life, but I was the designated audience and that was how I got attention. In retrospect, I guess she was the one who was getting attention. The funny thing was that she decided by the time I was about 6 years old, that I was totally competent and independent. She used to tell people she never worried about me and believed I could be left on a street corner and would find a way to thrive. So I learned early on to never be a child with her."

Joey tried to imagine what that could be like. His mother was the complete opposite.

"What about your father? Did he think of you that way?"

"Hard to tell Joey, I don't believe he thinks of me one way or another. As I mentioned before, they were older and he had already been around the block with raising kids. When I was growing up I didn't think he liked any of us very much. He definitely had no use for female children, especially ones with brains. He used to tell people I was "precocious" and because of the way he said it, I grew up believing I was a bad person. In any case, he was seldom around because of his work. If he wasn't in his office in New York City, he was traveling for business. That's one of the other reasons my mother was drunk all the time. They both seemed happy when I went away to college and chose one on the other side of the country. None of us cared to see each other much, but I don't want you to think I'm bitter. My father has always been there with the money. I've never wanted for anything I've asked for."

Joey looked at Alice as she said these words without emotion. Then he reached over and put his arms around her.

Alice surprised herself by accepting his caring touch. She had already surprised herself by telling him about her family.

For some reason, she knew he wasn't feeling pity for her, which she would have hated. No, he was simply caring about her. There was no judgement.

Both Joey and Alice recognized this was an important moment and they also knew that neither of them was ready to put into words what they were feeling. She pulled back and said what she didn't need to say, but did out of respect, "It may be because of growing up without feeling trust, but I'm really driven to keep moving. I've been told I have itchy feet and that's probably as clear a description as I can come up with. I need to feel unencumbered and free to try new things, have new experiences. I like you so much, it almost makes me hate that this is the way I am."

"I like you a lot too, Alice, and that's not something I've said to anyone in a long time, but I understand and appreciate your being honest with me. We aren't in different places that way. I've been fighting depression for a long time which makes me incapable of giving or accepting. This past week, since I met you, I've experienced a few flashes of relief but I'm no-where near over it. It may just be who I am."

This time Alice put her arms around Joey and held him for a long time. For those moments, they experienced a meeting of hearts, souls, and minds and knew they were strengthened by their connection.

Chapter 21

June 19-24, 1973
Albuquerque NM, New York City

Alice and Gail spent the following day playing tourist in Taos and other places Mike felt they needed to see. They even went back to the Sandia Peak Tramway which Alice found equally charming in daylight. Mike and Gail noticed a new sense of comfort and warmth between Joey and Alice that had obviously flared on their first visit to the tram and began to wonder what went down between them the previous evening.

Early the following morning, the two women climbed aboard the bus that would take them all the way to Harrisburg, Pennsylvania. While it wasn't the Ritz, the seats were comfortable and reclined enough to allow them to sleep. In the spirit of adventure, they quickly got into playing social directors, sang songs with children and chatted with fellow travelers who joined them where they had carved out a small world at the back of the bus.

As planned, Gail and Alice considered the bus ride itself to be an adventure. The forty-four hour non-stop trip allowed them to view a chunk of Middle America, traversing through eight different states with a variety of landscapes ranging from the ubiquitous grassy plains and wheat fields littered with natural gas and oil wells of the Texas Panhandle and Oklahoma, through the forested flat Ozark Plateau highlands of Southern Missouri.

As they had expected, the highlight was seeing the Mighty Mississippi River which they celebrated with song. Alice took out her guitar and taught a group of traveling children the famous song from the Broadway show, Showboat, *Ole Man River.* By the time they reached St. Louis and crossed the Mississippi River, they were pretty tired of scenery but agreed the River and the Gateway Arch were the highlights of their trip. Gail continued to be awed by the country's size and geographical diversity, but had to admit she was relieved to get off the bus and into a motel in Harrisburg Pennsylvania where they both took showers and washed their hair. Alice was also happy to catch up with the Watergate Hearings on the television in their room. The next morning they headed for the Amtrak train station and the last leg of their journey. Within a few hours, they arrived at Penn Station in Manhattan. Stepping outside of the station, Gail and Alice began their New York City adventure.

The hustle and bustle of the city was both overwhelming and stimulating so they walked to the closest restaurant and sat down for lunch to plan their next move. They had decided to find a place to live as soon as possible, but, meanwhile, find a hostel where they could share space with other people. Someone they met on the bus told them New York City had a lot of hostels and the best way to find one would be to go to a central location on the Upper West Side. They splurged on a taxi whose driver told them the Upper West Side was a nice neighborhood.

Dropped off in front of a long building, they went inside and found a place to sleep and a bathroom to share. By the next day they were determined to move on. The kind lady at the front desk told them summer was a particularly good time of the year to find temporary housing. She suggested they visit local college campuses where students posted housing information on bulletin boards. Picking up both street and public transportation maps, they set out on foot. While they found the many strangers they met along the way to be friendly, and sometimes helpful, the next several hours turned out to be frustrating.

Then they hit pay dirt. After failing to come up with anything on the large, well-known university campuses, they literally ran across a small, liberal arts college that seemed to pop out of nowhere. Called "Ensaladilla," a Spanish word they later learned simply meant "salad," it was apparently spread out with classes held in various locations throughout the City. Their first encounter was something that looked like a storefront with a colorfully painted entrance. Not sure whether it was a real college or a daycare center, they went in partly because they were curious, and because they needed a break from their morning frustration. They were also drawn to the name.

Walking down the corridor, they sighted a bulletin board covered with announcements but nothing advertising places to live. Discouraged, they decided to stop for the day and continue their search at another time. After all, they had a place to sleep that night and had only been looking for a few hours. But just as they began walking away, a young woman with long strawberry blond hair tied up in a braid approached the bulletin board and put up an announcement for an apartment sub-let. Alice asked if it was her sub-let and told her they were looking for something right away.

The woman, whose name was Charlotte Norton, smiled, and said, "Do you have a minute? It sounds like we may have a fit."

Alice and Gail followed her outside to a small courtyard furnished with wooden benches and a few tables and chairs surrounded by a well-established flower garden.

Looking around, Gail said, "Amazing! I never expected to see something like this in New York City."

Charlotte laughed, "There are a ton of such treasures around here; you're new to New York?"

Alice answered, "I'm Alice Lyons and this is Gail Song; we are new as of yesterday although I spent some time here when I was a kid."

"It's nice to meet you both. Are you also from around these parts, Gail?"

"Nope, this is my first visit to the Big Apple. I'm from the Caribbean."

Charlotte smiled. "I thought I heard a slight island accent. You'll be comfortable here, this is a city where many cultures meet."

Charlotte told them she had just graduated from Ensaladilla, a small liberal arts college where students and faculty created individualized academic programs according to their common interests. Charlotte wanted to study ethnomusicology so her curriculum tapped into a wide variety of fields in addition to the arts.

Alice was impressed. "It sounds like an amazing college experience! So, the big question, will you be able to get the job or profession you want with this in your toolkit?"

"I sure hope so. Ensaladilla requires all students to learn about networking. I'm hoping to put that into practice over the next few months, which brings us to why I'm looking for someone to sublet my apartment. For personal reasons, I need to leave for my travels sooner than I had originally planned, but I'm not quite ready to give up the place forever. What about you? Why are you interested in a sublet? Actually, before I go on, I'm not talking about a rigid, traditional sub-let agreement and probably should start by asking you how flexible you are about our arrangement."

Charlotte was pleased with Alice's response.

"We're pretty open-ended at the moment. We just graduated from Coral University in California and are looking to spend at least the summer in New York. Do you have any idea when you'll be back?"

Charlotte twirled her braid nervously. This was the first time Alice and Gail saw that she was a bit anxious.

"I honestly don't know, but I want to keep my options open. I guess it's important to me that the people who live in my place this summer are flexible. I wouldn't throw someone out on their ear without a conversation, but I also need to have that conversation." She looked at Alice and Gail, and saw they were listening carefully. "I have friends I could sublet to but I'm in a hurry to leave. Putting up this notice was a last ditch effort to find someone right away."

"We spent last night at a hostel and are definitely ready to move in right away. We're traveling very light. Can we take a look at the apartment before signing on? I'm assuming it's furnished."

"Of course, and that's part of the deal. I need someone to watch over my stuff. I need to travel light too." She laughed. "Are you free now? It's not far from here and we can walk."

The apartment was a small space in the basement of a medium-sized five story building. The building looked old, but seemed to be in good repair. The apartment included an open living room-kitchenette area and two small bedrooms. There was a below grade window in the kitchenette facing an alley that was furnished by trash bins. It looked like there was another window in one of the bedrooms, but that was blocked by an overflowing bookshelf. Gail and Alice found it charming. In addition to its inner charms, the apartment was located only a couple of blocks away from Central Park.

"Great location, do you spend a lot of time in the park?" Gail asked.

"Yes and no. You have to be careful about the time of day. There is crime in this area, but if you're watchful, and I never go there by myself, it's great. It's like an oasis in the middle of a bustling city."

"What about the building? What are your neighbors like?"

Charlotte started to fidget again, then spoke slowly. "The neighbors are fine. There's a mixture of college students and single older people. I'm happy to contribute to the rent and other expenses, but it is super important that the landlord gets the money on time. I have a coupon book with invoices for each month. I always try to send it to them a week ahead of the end of the month."

"What happens if you're late? Do they evict you?"

"Of course not, it's just a good idea to avoid contact with their office, and as long as they get their money, they won't bother you."

"Is there a problem with you subletting?"

"I don't think so. There's nothing one way or the other about subletting in my rental agreement but I'd prefer that we all avoid them. Are you interested?"

Gail and Alice looked at each other and smiled simultaneously. They felt fortunate to come up with such a good deal, an affordable deal that accommodated their need for flexibility.

"Where do we sign?"

"If it's okay with you, I'm going to tell anyone who asks that you're old friends staying with me for a few months, and that's how I'll treat this. This is such a relief. Today is Sunday? I can be out of here by tonight."

To their surprise, Charlotte handed them a set of keys, showed them where the mailboxes were located on the first floor of the building, and went to a desk in one of the small bedrooms where she retrieved a checkbook and the rental agency coupons. "Do you mind if I give you a check upfront for a couple of month's share of the expenses? I promise I'll stay in touch as soon as I have contact information myself, but meanwhile, you probably won't hear from me."

As they left the apartment, Alice and Gail talked about how lucky they were. They had a place to stay in a nice neighborhood and a check for over a thousand dollars in their pockets which would really help them as they settled into their summer adventure. Then they began to talk about the part that made them slightly uncomfortable.

"This is almost too good to be true." Gail said. "Charlotte is clearly hot to leave town and I think she's nervous about something relating to this building. It doesn't seem to be about the park, even though she said it isn't always safe. It was more about the landlord or the rental agency. What do you think?"

"I agree, and hope it doesn't come back to bite us in the ass, but I'm going to ride the good luck wave. Since we have an address now, I'm going to open a bank account with the check she gave us. I hate the idea of losing that!"

Gail laughed as she watched her loosey-goosey friend get down to business. She had seen this side of Alice once or twice before and wondered who she was deep down. It was clear she had a baseline of competency and self-confidence which gave her the inner strength to expand, try things out, and be creative. Gail hoped some of that self-confidence would rub off on her, but meanwhile she would be content to bask, and hopefully learn.

Chapter 22

June 24, 1973
New York City

Alice put the kitten down on the floor and turned to Gail.

"What shall we call this little guy?"

"Since you found him wandering around the trash cans, why don't we call him *Trashy*."

"I guess that's a possibility—at least we can start with that—but he'll probably have a number of names as we get to know him. Let's see if he likes this one."

"Hey *Trashy*, come to Mama."

Absorbed in playing soccer with a wad of paper he'd found on the floor, the kitten ignored her.

Alice and Gail laughed, then Alice said, "Perhaps when we associate the name *Trashy* with food in his mind, he'll come around to responding to it, but meanwhile, I'd like to explore one or two other names."

"Like what?"

"Oh I don't know, maybe Mephistopheles."

"Ah, a T.S. Elliot cat."

"Or a Faustian devil cat."

"What ever happened to cat names like Fluffy? Why do they always have to have meaningful names these days?"

Alice smiled, "Okay, his name will be Fluffy. I actually like that."

Gail was increasingly content with her decision to spend the summer with Alice. Everything about it so far had been magical beyond her wildest dreams: their time in the Southwest, getting to know Mike and being in his family's luxurious home and even their cross-country bus trip. For the most part, she had put aside her feelings of guilt for lying to her parents, but she did worry that she would never be ready to go back to Jamaica. She didn't want to disappoint her parents, but was afraid that, given the chance, she would find a way to stay in the United States because deep down, that was what she wanted to do. *Coming to New York could be my way of buying time to come up with a solution to this complicated problem. How can I remain in the U.S. without a student VISA or Green Card? How can I get a job that would help me to obtain a Green Card and begin the process of becoming an American citizen? Ultimately, how can I become a professional dancer? I know, I know, I have no real training; it's just the thing that makes me happiest. I know it's a pipedream, but New York is the cultural center of the world and I can't lose hope!*

Alice looked at Gail who seemed to be completely lost in thought. "I'm going to run down to the little store on the corner and pick up some cat food. I can also pick up a box of spaghetti and a jar of sauce for dinner tonight. Can you think of anything else?"

"Oh, sorry, I was lost in thought. Can you add a carton of orange juice and a couple of bagels? Oh, and a package of cream cheese? I need something in my stomach in the morning."

Alice laughed. "Have you ever had a bagel with cream cheese or is this just what you think one must eat in New York?"

"I've had frozen."

"Then you are definitely in for a treat. New York bagels (and bialys, which are similar) are unlike anything you can find around the country. A lot of bakers around here make them fresh every morning and because they're in competition, they all taste a little different." Alice grabbed her wallet and opened the door. "I'll be right back. Do you want to take a walk downtown after breakfast?"

"Absolutely, I'm ready to rock and roll."

After breakfast, Gail and Alice began their walk along Central Park facing south. It was Monday morning and the sidewalks were pleasantly filled with fast-moving, fast-talking people. They had decided not to stop along the way, but to return for deeper experiences at another time. Today was devoted to getting a feel for the west side of the City as they passed well-known landmarks including The Museum of Natural History, Columbus Circle, Lincoln Center, Times Square and the Theatre District, and Penn Station. By the time they reached Washington Square Park in Greenwich Village, their feet had had it.

While their walk had taken them through a variety of neighborhoods, some sketchier than others, Washington Square Park felt safe and comfortable. It was full of young people, many of whom were probably students from the nearby campuses of NYU and the New School for Social Research.

Exhausted, but feeling invigorated by the surrounding activity, Gail and Alice sat in the park drinking cans of Coca Cola as they took it all in.

They saw people playing guitars and singing folk songs, creating anti-Vietnam War and Richard Nixon signs, selling tie-dyed tee shirts, and loudly sharing their political opinions. These were familiar activities, similar to what they had left behind in Southern California. But in the end, their eyes settled on something they were not familiar with as they watched a group of people conducting what they called a "happening," a theatrical performance of the mundane, "everyday." Alice was fascinated. They were actors but were claiming to "just being" as they performed. She had so many questions—did people play themselves or characters created by writers? Was there any prescribed dialog at all? Was it entirely ad-libbed? Did someone decide what the setting, situation, would be ahead of time? It seemed like a drama school exercise, but they were presenting it as a finished product, or were they? How much audience input would be allowed and would that change the story as it went along?

The actors had created a set in the park. They had brought with them a few chairs, and of all things, an ironing board. Throughout the time Alice and Gail watched, a woman stood ironing, or pretending to iron, since there was no electricity, in the middle of their set. Five or six other people came in around her, sat on chairs, had conversations, and walked in and out. She never spoke and never stopped ironing. She reminded Alice of Boxer, the cart horse in George Orwell's political satire *Animal Farm*, who represented laborers whose life and hard work never changed no matter who was in charge. There must have been a reason, a statement being made about the fact that she just ironed and didn't speak. All the action happened around her.

No-one interrupted the action, or inaction, as it seemed to Gail and Alice, and although they decided to explore "happenings" further, agreed it was time to return to the apartment. This time, they would take a subway train, a brand new experience for Gail, who had fallen in love with everything New York so far. Some of the sketchier neighborhoods, like Times Square with its wall to wall porn shops, felt overwhelming, but experiencing the streets with Alice, who seemed secure and comfortable, helped her feel safe. However, walking into the subway station was disturbing. It was dark, smelled of urine and populated by beggars, druggies, and drunks. If she had been alone, Gail would probably have turned around and found a cab, no matter how much it cost.

After climbing down what seemed like a hundred filthy steps, they arrived at their destination. Gail was extremely grateful Alice knew which train to take. At various levels they needed to choose between Uptown and Downtown; Alphabetic (A,E and C) and Numerical (1, 2 and 3), all of which apparently went both ways, but veered off along the way; and Local and Express lines. They also encountered signs proclaiming things like "the Local train will be traveling along the Express track between X and Y and then move back on to the Local track. Alice seemed to take it all in stride. Gail was happy she wasn't there by herself.

When they finally reached the correct level, Gail saw there were four tracks, two each for trains going Uptown and Downtown, respectively, and when the trains weren't blocking their view, they could see the platform on the other side of the tracks. There were a few benches along the wall where the lucky passengers who got there first could sit while they waited, but most people stood along the side of the track with hopes of finding a seat on the train itself. The trains and people were moving so quickly, Gail was barely registering what was going on. However, across the tracks, she could hear haunting exotic music. Someone was playing a huge kettle, producing sounds that echoed magnificently throughout the chamber created by its location in a subway tunnel.

The combination of the music with the cacophony of trains coming and going, along with the hum of many simultaneous conversations made it impossible for Gail and Alice to hear one another, so they stood with one-hundred fellow travelers as they waited for their train, listening to the music, and staring across the tracks.

They noticed the tall man on the other side of the tracks at the same time. He was jumping up and down and gesturing dramatically with both arms and seemed to be trying to get their attention. Although competing with all the other sounds, they heard the man yell out "Alice, don't get on a train, I'm coming over!"

Chapter 23

June 25, 1973
New York City

Gail watched curiously as Alice and the tall African-American man threw their arms around each other and hugged without words for what seemed a long time. She had always thought of the leggy Alice, at 5'9" as a tall woman, but this guy had to be well over six feet and Alice looked tiny next to him. As they hugged, Alice's feet were off the ground by at least six inches. Gail herself was only 5'7". Odd that relative height was the main thing on her mind as she witnessed this scene.

When they pulled apart, Alice looked at Gail and said, "Gail, meet Rocco."

"Oh my God, this is the famous Rocco of high school Chemistry!" Gail exclaimed, smiling. She reached a hand out to shake his. "I've heard so much about you, Rocco, I'm surprised I didn't recognize you from across the tracks."

Rocco smiled back at Gail and said, "Now I'm at a disadvantage here. Who might you be?"

"This is Gail, my college roommate. We graduated last month and have traveled across the country to the Big Apple in search of fame and fortune," Alice said beaming. "What about you, Rocco? How long have you been in New York? What are you up to these days?"

"Many long stories. Want to go back upstairs and find a coffee shop?"

Alice looked at Gail, who nodded. Turning back to Rocco, she said, "Of course, we're free at the moment. We literally just arrived, found an apartment on the Upper West Side and were walking the streets to familiarize ourselves with our new home."

Once settled in the shop, they bought coffee and began catching up.

Blowing on her coffee, Alice looked at Rocco. "How long have you been here? Did you finish school? If I recall, you were going to Gilmore College in Connecticut."

"Yes and yes, I got my B.A. in Poly Sci about a month ago and came to the City because a friend of mine offered me an opportunity to play in a band."

Still beaming, Alice turned to Gail, "I don't know if I mentioned to you that Rocco is a musical genius. He composes and plays every instrument known to mankind."

Rocco laughed, "That's an exaggeration, but music is basically my reason for living."

Gail smiled. "Yes Alice, I think you mentioned Rocco's musical gifts a few thousand times over the years! That's really exciting, Rocco. What kind of band is it?"

"I have to step back and tell you I'm not like a regular member of the band. My friend's father plays tenor sax in a small jazz combo and I get asked to fill in when someone has something else to do. I'm mostly valuable because I can play a variety of instruments, but these folks have been playing together for a long time as a second gig. They all have day jobs where they make their livings. To them, the band is a fun thing to do on their nights off."

"Do you make enough to live here?"

"Well, so far, but that's only because I've been staying for free at Phil's house—that's my friend. I met him at Gilmore. They live on Long Island, but I really want to move into Manhattan and need to get my own day job to afford to do that."

"We found an amazingly inexpensive place on the Upper West Side."

Rocco looked skeptical.

"And we have no money or prospects at the moment."

Rocco looked even more skeptical.

"It's a tiny basement apartment we're actually subletting, but the woman we're subletting from is traveling and may end up doing that for a long time. We literally just moved in, but I'm willing to bet there are other apartments in the building that might be cheap and available. We haven't really met anyone who lives there yet, but from what I've seen, it looks like most are college students. Do you want to go back with us and take a look?"

"Sure, it's worth a shot. Do you think there would be a problem with your bringing a black guy around?

"I don't think so. The place seems pretty mellow, but we haven't been there long enough to inventory who lives there."

Gail piped in, "I always notice. That's probably because of where I come from in the Caribbean."

Rocco looked at her with a puzzled expression. "Where are you from in the Caribbean? I figured you to be from Southeast Asia or the Philippines."

"I was born in Suriname, in South America, where we lived until I was eleven. Then we moved to Kingston, Jamaica. That's where my family lives now. Along with my weird accent, I get a lot of extra looks so I'm super aware of what I'm stepping into. With the Vietnam War going on, I sometimes run into hostility from Americans I don't know."

Rocco nodded. "It's never ambivalent where I'm concerned. Large black men are always noticed and people react. I try to ignore it, but it never fails to get to me when I'm walking down the sidewalk and women coming the other way take two steps to the side and clutch their bags."

"That really sucks, Rocco. You'd think New York City is diverse enough to be used to our differences. Anyway, the vibe at our apartment building has been pretty good, so far. Might be that half the people there seem to be students." Gail laughed nervously. "Please come back with us. Give it a try."

"Yes, seriously Rocco, if there isn't anything available at the moment, you can crash on our couch." Alice added. "It will probably take a few days to catch up anyway, so we may as well all be in the same place!"

Rocco laughed and was secretly relieved. He hadn't been sure where or how he would be living, but knew he had to get out of Phil's family house. He was uncomfortable there for a lot of reasons, beginning with their underlying attitude towards him and the way he was treated. There was something odd he couldn't put his finger on, something he partly attributed to the lifestyle of wealthy white people. The way they treated him was intolerable, a combination of being the family "pet", an educated, musically talented, black person to be trotted out to family friends and neighbors to show how liberal and open-minded they were. The minute he walked into a room, family conversations stopped, everyone greeted him with automatic smiles and banality ruled. He honestly would have loved a little conflict, even if it was about racism, but ultimately didn't care what these people had to say anymore.

As Rocco had told Alice and Gail, Phil's father played tenor sax in a jazz combo that performed in small venues in and around Manhattan, but his real job was in the financial world where he had obviously been successful. Their house was a huge gated property with its own swimming pool, tennis courts, and even a putting green. To Phil's credit, this came as a shock to Rocco. He had always found Phil to be a regular guy, but he was pretty quiet and no-one talked much about their families on the college campus anyway. Rocco, himself, had made it a point to never tell anyone that his father was a college professor.

Rocco thought Phil would understand why he needed to move out of their house, but his official statement would be that it was time for him to find a nine-to-five job and begin his life as an adult in Manhattan. He wanted to be careful not to offend Phil's father and screw up the band gig. While he didn't expect to become a permanent member, he knew it was a great opportunity to hone his musical chops and for exposure and networking. Although he had little hope of making it big in the music world, making music was his first love.

Rocco reached over and hugged Alice. He felt lucky to have run into her in the City and wondered why they hadn't stayed in touch during their college years. As he held her, he found himself saying aloud what he'd been thinking. "You know, we probably lost touch because we were both so hot to leave high school and our childhood lives behind."

Alice nodded, "Yep, I chose to go to a college on the other side of the country and you probably didn't know it, but my parents left Connecticut the summer after high school graduation, so I basically never went home again. This is the closest I've been to New England since I started college."

Looking at her, Rocco thought, *she seems the same, but different. I guess that's true of me too. I can only make that judgement through my current lens. How's she different? Well that's just a feeling. She looks the same, same long curly auburn hair, same casual clothes. Alice was never what you would call "stylish" but she did have a look that was distinctly "Alice;" no noticeable make-up, pink lips and long eyelashes that emphasized dark brown eyes that always seemed to be exploring. Yet, there was an even more comfortable air about her. After all, she was a college graduate now, four years older, no longer a teenager.*

Rocco hoped she still had the qualities that had attracted him when they were in high school. The Alice he remembered was very friendly and came across as self-confident and non-judgmental, so she attracted a wide variety of friends. It didn't matter to her what they looked like or what they liked to do. In fact, she was drawn to people who were different from her and tended to give everyone the benefit of doubt, sometimes tolerating behaviors other kids rejected as out of hand. This worked unless, and until, they violated her trust. When that happened with some people, she pushed them away, and that was that. Always on the move, Alice was never boring. Rocco was happy the fates had brought them together at this crucial time in their lives when he needed all the help he could get to figure out how to go about beginning the next chapter.

"Okay, I'm in," Rocco said as he stood up and stretched his long legs. "Let's go to your new digs and see if we can come up with a cheap place for me to live."

Watching him pull his legs out from under the table, Gail whispered to Alice, "He's going to have to fold himself in half to sleep on our sofa."

Chapter 24

It was approaching five o'clock when they arrived at the apartment and Gail was exhausted from the long walk, bumpy train ride, and underground air, or lack thereof. Figuring Alice and Rocco wouldn't object to private time together, she announced that she was going to take a short nap.

Alice turned to Rocco and said, "Would you like to join us for spaghetti tonight? I need to run to the corner store for wine and bread."

Rocco stood up. "Sounds perfect, I'll walk with you."

Just then, a furry orange streak ran out from under the sofa into the kitchen. Rocco jumped as Alice laughed. "Oh yes, this is our kitten Fluffy."

"Thanks for warning me, I thought it was a rat! How long have you been here again? I thought you said this was your first night!"

"It is. He just showed up this morning outside the door rooting around the trash bins, and we almost named him Trashy. I suspect he's pretty feral but young enough to adapt. At least I hope so. Isn't he cute?"

"If you say so," Rocco said, looking into the kitchen where the kitten had already disappeared, "all I've seen so far was an orange streak that scared the shit out of me!"

As Alice laughed and grabbed her wallet, Rocco opened the door and said, "Put that away, I'll pay for the wine and cheese."

Alice put her wallet back into a bag that was hanging on the doorknob and said, "Great, what's today, Monday? I'll start looking for work tomorrow, but at the moment, all contributions are welcome."

There was a wonderful feeling of spring evening in the air. The weather was perfect, temperature in the upper sixties with a slight, gentle breeze. Alice was feeling like she had come home. Having Rocco with her was the bonus that made it complete. He was the perfect person with whom to explore the City and make decisions about her new life. It felt totally natural to take his arm as they walked down the block. While a few people stared, she felt this was a neighborhood where diversity would be accepted.

The local deli turned out to have a nice variety of cheeses as well as Mateus in both rosé and white versions. They bought one of each, and a six pack of Black Label beer along with a loaf of French bread and a package of brie.

After they returned to the apartment and put down their purchases, Alice handed Rocco a small dish and a bag of cat kibble. "Here's your chance to bond with Fluffy." Sure enough, as Rocco shook the food out of the bag into the dish on the floor, the kitten came running into the room and began to devour the food, his shyness, at least temporarily, no longer an issue. Turning to Alice, Rocco asked, "Are you sure you're going to keep calling him Fluffy?"

Alice smiled and ignored his question as she popped the wine bottle cork. "Can I pour you a glass of wine?"

"Don't mind if you do."

Alice started to laugh. "Remember that time we broke into the lifeguard shack at the beach and drank a whole bottle of Mateus, just the two of us?"

"Oh yes, I could barely make it home. Thank God my parents had already gone to bed when I got there. They never knew I drank at all. But, breaking in must've happened with someone else. I had borrowed a key from my friend Ray who was a lifeguard."

"Really? I thought we were there in the middle of winter."

"We were there in the middle of winter. The lifeguards all kept their keys after the summer. It was one of the few private spaces in town so it was rare for it to be available. There were parties there a lot of weekends, but if I recall correctly, we were there in the middle of the week. You and I had been at some musical rehearsal and our parents didn't know how long it would be, so I took a chance and asked Ray for the key."

Alice shook her head. "I did attend a few parties there, but honestly, you remember more about it than I do. I think I've shut out a lot of memories from that time in my life. I wasn't happy at home and I was totally focused on getting away and not looking back."

Rocco nodded, "You know, I've never forgotten one thing you said to me that night. You told me you believed you could get through a wall if that was what you wanted to do. I've thought about that a million times since then."

"That's something my father once said to me and I decided it would be my philosophy of life. It was one of the few conversations I ever had with him about anything that mattered and I do believe he had that level of confidence, for himself, not me."

"Maybe he was trying to tell you something about how important self-confidence is for making life decisions."

"Could be, I tend to agree with that. But what about you, Rocco, do you believe you can go through that wall over there?"

Rocco looked at the wall. "I don't know. I have my moments, but then reality sets in. There are a lot of barriers that are thrown up by other people, beginning with parents and their expectations. Then there's the rest of the world and attitudes towards black males. It's just not that simple. This is getting heavy; can we talk about something else?"

"Sure, what?"

Rocco smiled, "I'm really glad we ran into each other. This summer is a big transition time. I can't think of anyone I'd rather be with while I shed college Rocco and get ready for the big bad world."

"What does that mean for you, Rocco?"

"That's the ten million dollar question, isn't it? My parents have such big hopes for me to make them proud, to achieve big in the big world that matters to them and I hate disappointing them. They're good people who care about me and they've always been there for me. College was an oasis where I got to be with more people my age who looked and thought like me. No offense, Alice, but it was great not being the only smart black kid in the class."

"I totally get that, Rocco, but what's stopping you from doing what you want now? I can't believe you didn't come out of college with straight As!"

"Well yeah, I've never had trouble with school that way. I just think my parents want me to go into business or get a profession, like being a doctor or lawyer. I don't think they like the idea of me being a starving musician."

"I always had the impression they were proud of you, Rocco. In any case, it's not surprising that people of their generation who grew up during the Depression want their children to make a comfortable living."

"Of course, but I needed a break from their expectations and college allowed me to try things they would never approve of."

"Like what, drugs?"

Rocco looked at Alice intently. He couldn't imagine her being judgmental. "I tried acid, and the occasional peyote button. I was in search of higher truth."

"Ah, a disciple of *The Teachings of Don Juan*. Everyone I knew in California read Carlos Casteñada. It was basically a rite of passage to spend a weekend in the desert hallucinating. I'm a little surprised peyote was part of things on the East Coast."

"Honestly Alice, everything was available and I tried a lot of drugs, but hallucinogens were my favorites. I've kept that from my parents, but I couldn't hide my Harley."

"You have a motorcycle! How did you pay for it? Do you have it here in the City?"

"It's currently in Phil's driveway. I'm not sure I want to bring it to Manhattan. Actually, I need to think about that. Phil's a good guy, so I'm pretty sure he'll take good care of it until I figure out my next steps. I think you'll like Phil. That reminds me, can I use this phone to give him a call?"

Alice poured wine into her glass.

"Of course, Charlotte, the woman we're subletting from, said she would let us keep the phone in her name. Please invite Phil to come by. I'm looking forward to meeting him. He'll be my first New York friend. So this is chapter one, we breach the first wall of 'adult' life. I know, I know, I'm totally into seeing this as an adventure I can write about when I'm old and have time to write my memoir. I have so many questions, both about all you've been up to and what you're thinking about doing now. Go ahead and make the call. We have lots of time to talk."

Rocco picked up the phone and announced, "Good start, there's a dial tone." Then, turning to face the window, he spoke quietly into the phone and hung up. "He's not home but I left the number so don't be surprised if and when the phone rings."

Refilling Rocco's glass, Alice said, "Tell me about the bike. I don't recall you being a biker type when we were in high school!"

"It's not a big story. I had a friend with a bike who let me try it out and I loved the feel so I found a way to get one of my own."

"How'd you do that?"

"Doubled up on the music gigs and saved a few bucks."

"That's it?"

"Okay, so last year I started doing a little racing. It kinda diverted my attention away from academic pursuits. And to answer your second question, I had always planned to go for a doctorate in Philosophy or Political Science, but now I'm not so sure. It might just be that I need some time off to play and the bike is my favorite new toy."

"Yet, you end up in New York City where you don't want to bring the Harley."

"Yep, what can I say, it just fell into my lap. Phil was dreading going home to the pressures of being the perfect son who will make his parents' dreams come true, so he asked me to come along, maybe to put off the inevitable. I couldn't say no. He offered me a chance to experience life and perform music in the Big Apple, an offer I couldn't refuse, but being at his house got old fast. Anyway, I really don't know what I want to do now. My immediate goal is to get out of Phil's family's house without pissing Phil off or losing my place in the Trotter Combo and finding a way to live in Manhattan, which I can hopefully do here. In the long run, I want to live my life on my own terms without disappointing my father."

"I think we're on the same page, Rocco, at least the part about living life on my own terms. My father has no expectations of me. That part has to be tough for you."

"It's a huge pressure. He had to overcome so much to get where he is today and I know it matters that I succeed on his terms. I'm his only son. I don't want to disappoint him, but I almost don't know what would be enough to live up to those expectations."

Chapter 25

June 25, 1973
New York City

"So, Alice Lyons, what are YOU doing here? What are YOUR plans?"

"Probably same as you, I'm not exactly sure what I want to be when I grow up, but I've always wanted to live in New York City. There's so much going on here, so much to fuel the imagination. It has to be the best place to have adventures to write about in my old age."

"This is the second time you've mentioned writing, Alice. Is that your passion?"

"I guess so, writing and experiencing new places, people, and things. I'm not joking when I say I need to have some of those experiences before I start writing. My imagination needs fuel. Remember when we were in high school how we used to talk about wanting to go to places that were really extreme just to get ourselves out of living in a routine? If I recall, your dream was to go way south to Tierra del Fuego or was it the South Pole?"

"Yep, and I still do. It's actually at the southern tip of South America, part of Argentina and Chile. My current fantasy is to ride my bike down there, see the Straits of Magellan and the original homeland of the Yaghan Indians, and maybe hang out with a penguin or two."

"That's so cool, Rocco. Why not? What's stopping you?"

"Actually, there's nothing stopping me, and when I'm ready, I'm just going to pick up and go. What about you? Are you still planning to go to the North Pole? What was the name of those islands, Svalbard?"

"Yes, I intend to go there and a lot of other places. I've always wanted to see the North Pole. Maybe even catch Santa's workshop."

Gail walked into the living room yawning and looked at the wine bottle. "I see the celebration has begun. Did you two get a chance to catch up?"

Alice went to the kitchen and came back with a glass for Gail.

"I think so. We were just reminiscing about our fantasy travel destinations when we were in high school."

Gail yawned again and rubbed her eyes. "Oh cool, where were they?"

"At the two ends of the earth; Rocco wanted to experience Tierra del Fuego, at the bottom tip of South America and I wanted to try the Svalbard Islands, up near the North Pole."

Gail smiled, "Brrr, they both sound awfully cold and remote."

Rocco looked at Gail and asked, "What about you, Gail? Where do you want to go you've never been before?"

"Honestly, I just want to stay in the United States. I've loved the three places I've been so far, Southern California, the Southwest, and now, New York City. Every place I've visited has been so different and the country is huge. You have to remember, I grew up in really small countries. I think I could spend the rest of my life here and never get bored. This is the best."

"I hadn't thought of it that way," Alice said quietly, "I guess people want to experience places that are different from what they already know. I would love to go to Jamaica and Suriname! So how was your nap?"

"It was great. I woke up thinking about the happening in the park. Wouldn't it be fun to do something like that ourselves?"

Alice jumped up, "Oh my God Gail, that's a great idea."

Turning to Rocco who had a puzzled expression on his face, she said, "We watched a happening in Washington Square Park this afternoon."

"Aren't those passé? I haven't heard about them for at least five or six years."

"I think they may have morphed into performance art. I honestly don't know what people are calling this sort of audience participation experiential art of everyday life these days. I know when I saw *Hair* in Los Angeles in 1968, the performers went back and forth between the stage and the seats. One of the songs, the one that sounded like Margaret Mead, was performed by an actress sitting in a third row seat. At one point, one of the actors gave me a flower. It was really fun, but that was different from what we saw in Washington Square Park today. That revolved around a woman ironing, or pretending to iron. She didn't speak, but other people came in and out of the scene talking about various things.

Subjects changed based on things people brought up, which weren't necessarily connected. It felt like real life. We couldn't distinguish between the actors and audience members because it was totally naturalistic. What a great idea Gail! This is something we could play around with, there's no-one telling us what or how to do it. I mean we're not in school anymore! Since we don't have to do anything in particular, or label what we're doing, we can make it up as we go along."

By this time, Rocco and the kitten had bonded. Perhaps attracted to the relaxed atmosphere, Fluffy had climbed into Rocco's lap and begun to purr loudly. Rocco stroked his head and scratched under his chin, but otherwise acted as if he didn't notice there was a cat on his lap. He was completely focused on the two women and their excitement about creating their own version of a happening. Their enthusiasm was infectious and he found himself wanting a say in what they came up with. He had already decided he would be part of whatever it turned out to be.

Rocco announced, "I'm in, maybe it's the wine but this sounds like fun. How do we start? What? When? Where?"

Alice thought for a minute, "Maybe tomorrow we can take a walk in the park and do some people watching. That might be a start."

"And then?"

"I don't want to predetermine how this goes. I just think it might give us some ideas about how to create our happening."

Gail smiled. "I love the idea of this totally belonging to us, with no-one telling us that we're doing it wrong, or even right. I love the idea of our happening evolving organically."

Alice added, "And if we come up with something the three of us want to do, we do it. I, for one, am willing to make a commitment to creative authenticity."

Rocco nodded, "I get it. This is a way for us to break away from other people's rules and create as artists. I like that, but we will need to agree on what and how it is, right?"

Alice looked at Rocco. "I guess that's true, we can't assume we're all on the same page all the time, but, shit, let's try. If it doesn't work, we stop doing it. So, you two relax and get to know each other while I start the spaghetti."

Alice headed into the kitchen and filled a large pot with water from the faucet; all the while, humming atonally what seemed to be her own tune.

Chapter 26

June 26, 1973
New York City

The following morning, Rocco surprised himself by waking up feeling refreshed. It had been a long fun night of catching up with Alice and getting to know Gail, who he found simpático, intriguing, and he had to admit to himself, very attractive. Although his body was achy from having to curl up on the couch, he was more all-around comfortable than he'd been since he arrived in New York the previous month. As he stood up and stretched, he thought to himself that he might take Gail's offer of the regular bed at least every once in a while until he found his own place. He couldn't help thinking he wouldn't mind sharing her bed, but stopped that thought in midstream. *No Idiot, that would be really really stupid! Of course Alice probably wouldn't mind. She's never been interested in me 'that way' but I don't want to do anything that would unbalance our relationship, and she might see it as getting between her and Gail. No, this won't do.*

The kitchen clock said it was 6:38 AM and Rocco didn't want to wake anyone up, so he decided to walk the few blocks to Central Park and go for a quick jog. It would also be an opportunity to see who might be out and about at this time of the morning, and how they would react to seeing a tall black man running along the park's paths. He figured that once he had the racial temperature of a neighborhood, he could find a way to negotiate it, or decide whether to stay or leave.

It was another nice day. The people he passed on the sidewalk appeared to be focused on getting from here to there. For the most part, they paid little attention to him, but if anyone looked at him, he made a point of smiling and greeting them. He believed that even a brief interaction with a stranger could send the message that he wasn't a threat. Once he got to the park, he didn't see a single soul. It was almost eerie. It felt like he could speak softly and his words would echo. He took advantage of his solitude to pay close attention to the woodsy surroundings, keeping his mind open to spots they might want to stage their first happening.

As he walked back to the apartment, Rocco tried to remember each promising spot so he would be able to describe them to Alice and Gail when he returned. Unfortunately, he failed miserably and decided the best way to move forward would be to follow the same trail when they were all together so everyone could take part in the decision-making.

Smiling broadly at Rocco as he entered the apartment, Alice asked, "How was your walk?"

"Good, it was both a walk and a short run and I scoped out part of the park. I think there's a lot of potential for happenings around here. Can I have some of that coffee?"

"Of course, just grab a cup. They're hanging on the wall over there."

Rocco did as he was told. Blowing on the steaming brew, he told Alice and Gail he really liked the neighborhood and was hot to start looking for his own place. "But first I need to take a quick shower if that's okay."

They decided to begin the apartment search by looking at the bulletin board they had seen next to the building's wall of mailboxes on the first floor. The board was covered with announcements and advertisements: people selling things, looking for lost pets (Alice and Gail were relieved to note that none fit Fluffy's description), various group meeting announcements, dance and exercise classes, language lessons, and three advertising apartments to sublet or share in the building. Two of the three were looking for roommates, and the third, like Alice and Gail's apartment, was a sublet.

"Sharing with someone would probably be cheaper, but of course it would be great to have my own place." Rocco mused. "I might as well check into all three."

When they returned to the apartment, Rocco remembered he hadn't heard back from Phil and made a mental note to try him again later. He then picked up the phone and called the number for the share, a request for a fourth roommate where he would have to share a bedroom. He figured that would be his last choice, but offered an opportunity to practice the "ask." A young female voice answered the phone and after a few questions, it became clear there were three women looking for a fourth. Okay, that wouldn't work.

The second call was more promising. When he first answered the phone, the man at the other end of the line sounded abrupt and suspicious, but when he heard it was an inquiry about the apartment, became very friendly. He said his name was Pete and was desperate for someone to take his current roommate's place. The roommate had suddenly decided to move out and he didn't have the funds to cover the whole thing. In exchange for fifty percent of the rent and other costs, Rocco would have his own bedroom and share the rest of the apartment, but Pete wanted Rocco to know he would need the first month's rent up front. While this didn't sound ideal, Rocco agreed to climb to the third floor of the building, take a look at the place and meet his potential apartment mate. The cost would probably be less than a whole sublet.

Hoping to see the sublet before making a decision, Rocco made the third call and was also fortunate enough to reach the tenant at home. He said his name was Kevin O'Reilly and was a professor at a local college. He was looking for someone to sublet the apartment for the next three months while he spent some sabbatical time in France. He wanted to leave his furniture and other belongings in good hands and, in exchange, was willing to share the costs of rent and utilities. Professor O'Reilly told him the apartment included two bedrooms, one of which was set up as his office. He would be okay with the sub-letter using the office, but preferred that none of his books or other belongings in that room be moved around. He was willing to move his clothes and other things out of the bedroom and closet, and would prefer to leave all kitchen items in place for use.

Rocco liked the sound of the sublet, although he still didn't know what the cost of the two choices would be and tended to believe the share would be less expensive, so he decided to visit both.

Climbing the stairs to the third floor, Rocco thought about how difficult it must be to carry furniture to the top floors of the building. *Maybe there's a freight elevator somewhere?* He knocked on the door of apartment 316 and was met by a young-looking, long-haired kid smoking a cigarette.

"Hi, I'm Rocco. Are you Pete?"

While he opened the door with a smile that seemed intended to express a certain level of coolness, Pete's facial expression immediately changed. His eyes dashed around as if he was trying to come up with something to say quickly. Rocco was almost amused. This boy was not happy to see a black guy at his door.

"Yep, are you Rocco? Hey man, I'm sorry you had to come all the way up here. It turns out my roommate already found someone to replace him. I would've called you back but didn't have your number."

Rocco smiled as he thought about the fact that they had spoken on the phone about twenty minutes previously. "No problem, glad you found the roommate you wanted."

As he walked down the stairs, Rocco wondered if Alice was right about the building being open and friendly to diversity. *The professor might even be worse. He's obviously an older guy. Oh well, he's expecting me.*

Rocco knocked on the door at apartment 209. This time he was greeted by a short man with a trimmed beard. He figured Professor O'Reilly was in his late 30s or early 40s.

"Hi, I'm Rocco, are you Professor O'Reilly?"

Professor O'Reilly looked at Rocco curiously and held out his hand. As Rocco shook it, the professor laughed and said, "Your name...I think I expected you to be Italian! Call me Kevin, I feel like I'm too young to be referred to as 'professor, even though that is my job title."

Rocco smiled back at him. "Ah yes, a lot of people think that. It's a nickname I got in elementary school that seems to have stuck. My full name is John Rockman." Then he stepped back and asked bluntly, "Do you have a problem with me being black?"

"No, No, of course not, come in and let me show you around the place." But he continued to look at Rocco curiously, as if he wasn't sure.

The living room was large and sunny with three windows facing the street. One wall was filled with two large bookcases and Kevin had decorated some of the other walls with colorful paintings, but the best part was a small upright piano. Rocco could barely take his eyes off of it. This place was perfect. *I wonder if he would be okay with me playing the piano.*

The living room opened up to a kitchen including a round breakfast nook. Kevin led him into a hallway that included the two bedrooms and a bathroom with a shower stall. While most of the apartment, with its high ceilings and huge old-fashioned windows reflected the age of the building, Rocco put it at the 1920s, the bathroom was totally modern. The longer he was in the place, the more he wanted it.

When they returned to the living room, Kevin invited Rocco to sit down and "talk turkey." Rocco braced himself for rejection, and the possibility that the cost would be way out of his range. Oddly, he hadn't even figured out what that "range" might be since he still had no job. He decided to see what the man had to say and was surprised when, instead of getting down to it, Kevin began by asking him questions about his life.

"I grew up in Fairfield County, Connecticut and graduated last month from Gilmore College."

"Oh yes, Gilmore's a great school. What was your major?"

"Political Science"

"Interesting, what do you plan to do with it now?"

"Not sure. I was planning to go for my doctorate, and may end up doing that at some point. At the moment, I need a break from school so I've come to the City for an urban experience. I've never lived in a city; both my home and school were in the burbs."

Kevin continued to look at him with great interest and Rocco began to wonder if this was simply the way he related to everyone. If so, his students were lucky.

"How long have you been here, Rocco? Where have you been staying?"

"I came last month because a college buddy of mine invited me to stay with his family on Long Island. His dad plays with a jazz combo and they were looking for someone to sub when they needed. I play several instruments, not great at any of them, but I know how, so I've been filling in every few weeks while regular band members are off doing other things."

Kevin laughed out loud. "I knew I'd seen you someplace! You play with the Trotter Combo. I've seen you play drums and gotta tell you, you are so much better than their regular guy. I saw you a couple of weeks ago at the Coven Cavern. Your solo riffs blew me away! It is indeed a pleasure to meet you, Rocco. I would be thrilled to have you sublet my apartment while I'm gone. Are you interested?"

"Thank you, I'm glad you like my playing. Yes, I'm very interested, but not sure I can afford to pay for such a great space. At the moment, the only money I have coming in is from the jazz gigs, and they are random. I mean sometimes twice a week and sometimes every other week so far. My plan is to find a day job as soon as possible, doing whatever for a regular paycheck."

"I'll tell you what, Rocco. I'll pay for the rent and utilities until you have enough to pay for half. Obviously you need to buy your food and stuff like that, but don't worry about the rest. The only thing I ask is that you take good care of my space and my stuff." Kevin smiled and looked at the piano. "And please play the piano so we can keep it in tune."

"This is amazing, Kevin. I can't believe I lucked into such a great place. I promise I will take good care of your things and keep your piano tuned to perfection."

"Oh Rocco, one more thing, will you be available to move in this week?"

"No problem, I'm basically homeless at the moment, staying with friends who live in the basement here. Well, here and at my friend's on Long Island. That's where my stuff is but I want to make my life in Manhattan."

"Oh, who are your friends in the building?"

"I doubt you would know them, they just moved in yesterday, subletting from a lady named Charlotte is all I know."

"Charlotte Norton? She's a student at the college where I teach. I didn't know she was moving out. Nice girl, although from what I hear, I'm not surprised she's taking some time away."

The conversation was going in a direction Rocco wasn't interested in pursuing. It sounded like gossip and as far as he was concerned, gossip about people he didn't know was even more boring than gossip about his friends. This was his summer to start fresh. He changed the subject.

"When do you want me to come by for the key and other instructions? I can wait to bring my stuff over after you're gone."

"What's today, Tuesday? My plane leaves late Thursday so how about coming by for the key tomorrow evening."

Chapter 27

June 26, 1973
New York City

Rocco returned to the basement apartment in a great mood. Alice and Gail were still drinking coffee, having a lazy morning. With a big smile, he told them he had already found an apartment. "Believe it or not, I just scored an amazing sublet on the third floor!" He proceeded to describe his experiences with Pete and Kevin O'Reilly ending with, "and it has a piano he wants me to play, to keep in tune."

Alice smiled, "I'm beginning to think this is a magic building."

Just as those words were coming out of her mouth, they heard noise at the apartment door. Someone was opening their front door with a key. Alice and Gail looked at each other with alarm, but Rocco spoke first, "What the fuck?"

A young man barged into the apartment. Staring at Rocco he demanded, "Where's Charlotte? What have you done to her?"

Rocco couldn't stop looking at him. He had a young face with fat baby cheeks, but very odd hair. While thick around his ears, it was quite thin on the top and dyed a bright pinkish-orange, almost the color of a clown wig.

While Rocco was musing over how to describe the man's hairstyle in his head, Alice smiled at this strange-looking young man and asked, "Are you a friend of Charlotte's? She's subletting her apartment to us for the next few months. I think she may be traveling around Europe. Maybe she didn't get a chance to say goodbye."

The young man said nothing and continued to stare at Rocco. A moment later, Pete also showed up at the door and addressed the stranger, "Hey Teddy, you really got here quickly. Thanks for caring about our security."

The young man named Teddy puffed out his chest and, sniffing loudly, said, "You did the right thing, calling me right away, Pete. They're telling me Charlotte is sub-letting the apartment to them. This can't be happening without my approval." Teddy continued to glare at Rocco, then looking at Gail, sneered, "You need to leave. We have standards here."

Alice looked at him with steely eyes. "I don't know who you are, but you need to give me that key to our apartment right now or I will call the police."

Teddy looked nervous and started shuffling his feet, then puffed his chest out again. "This building belongs to me. I have the right to have keys to all the apartments."

Alice smiled, "I believe there are laws that protect tenants' privacy. If you like, I'll call a policeman to explain them to you, but why don't we sit down and have a conversation so we can introduce ourselves to you and you can see that we aren't criminals."

Teddy looked uncertain and Pete was about to say something when there was a knock at the door. As Alice walked over to see who it was, she mumbled, "I hope we haven't annoyed our new neighbors with the noise." She opened the door to another young man, this one about her height wearing granny glasses, who said, "Hi, you must be Alice, I'm Phil."

Rocco jumped up and greeted his friend, happy to see a friendly face. He was starting to worry there was going to be trouble.

Phil walked in smiling, ready to meet Rocco's friends; when his eyes fell on Teddy.

"I sure as hell didn't expect to see you here. What're you doing here Teddy?"

Alice was starting to feel like she was in an *Agatha Christie* or *Columbo* story in which all the characters gather in a room to accuse each other of a crime. This was getting interesting. She decided to take over once again.

"I'm so glad to meet you, Phil."

Looking around the crowded little room, she continued. "I'm sorry we don't have places for everyone to sit, but we were just about to have a conversation with...this gentleman,"

Pointing to Teddy she said calmly, "I apologize, I don't recall your name." Then she pointed at Pete, "And your friend, missed that one too. Can I offer anyone something to drink? We have a little orange juice but not enough for everyone and of course water. I could also brew up some tea."

Rocco and Gail watched Alice with admiration. Everyone was quiet for a moment, then Phil responded, "I'd love a glass of water. So what's going on here?"

Rocco stepped in, "Well, Phil, it appears this gentleman wants my friends to leave the apartment they are subletting.

Oh, where are my manners, you've already met Alice, and this is Gail. They just got here from California."

Rocco looked at Teddy, "Small world, isn't it? Phil and I went to college together, how do you know each other?"

Everyone watched as Teddy's bluster seemed to melt. Looking with pleading eyes at Phil, he tried to recover his dignity.

"I was looking for Charlotte. She didn't tell me she was leaving."

Teddy sank into a chair looking devastated. Clear that nothing would come of his efforts, Pete walked out the door. No-one, including Teddy seemed to notice.

Alice went to the kitchen and poured Teddy a glass of water. As she handed him the glass with a kind expression on her face, she said sympathetically, "I'm sure she intended to tell you. Maybe she was under pressure to catch a plane. She'll probably let you know when she lands."

As Teddy continued to sulk, Alice turned her attention to Phil, "Rocco tells us you're interested in theater. Is that where you're headed professionally?"

Phil blushed. "I was a theater minor in college but doubt I'll ever make the big time. That's my dream; but there's nothing tougher to get into in New York."

"I think we all have artistic dreams, Phil. As you know, Rocco is an extremely talented musician, and Gail is a really amazing jazz dancer."

"What about you, Alice?"

"I'm probably a dilettante. I play around with music and writing, but really have no particular talents."

Gail spoke for the first time, "She's being too modest. Alice is the most creative person I've ever known. She's a great story teller, both in writing and music; and she sings and plays the guitar beautifully."

Rocco took over, "I have to agree with everything Gail just said. Alice and I went to high school together and she was always the imagination leader. Hey Phil, would you like to join us for a walk in the park? We have plans to do something theatrical."

Phil smiled, "Sounds like fun, now?"

Rocco nodded and started for the door. Alice grabbed her guitar and turned to Teddy, who was still looking miserable, and politely asked him if he wanted to join them. Gaining a little face, Teddy said, "Sure, why not? I don't have anything better to do at the moment."

Rocco, Gail and Phil walked ahead. Alice and Teddy followed. As they walked, he asked her why she was with Rocco and Gail. "Are you a hippie? One of those people who think it's cool to be inclusive?"

Alice was fascinated with this guy who seemed like an old man in a young person's body. It was like he totally missed the sixties. She found herself wanting to interview him, to find out who he was. Knowing the best way to get people to talk freely was to act as if what they were saying was normal, she answered his questions using an objective tone.

"Rocco and I grew up in the same town in Connecticut. His father is a college professor. Gail was my college roommate at Coral U in California. We all just graduated and came to New York from different directions. Gail and I accidentally ran into Rocco a couple of days ago. He's sleeping on the couch until he finds a place to live."

All of this was true except the part implying that Rocco hadn't found a place to live yet. Alice saw no reason to get Teddy agitated again. "How do you know Phil?"

"Oh, I've known him my whole life. We live in the same town and our parents are friends—you know, same country club and that sort of stuff."

Alice thought to herself, *sad to say, I do know that sort of stuff.* "Did you meet Charlotte in college?"

"Nah, I went to college for a while, but they were a bunch of losers. I can make more money in real estate. Business is definitely where it's at and I've learned more about business from my father than anyone at a college. I met Charlotte here when she rented the apartment. We have a good thing going."

"Then I'm sure you'll be hearing from her soon." Alice was doubtful, but wasn't about to have that conversation with Teddy. "I only met her last week. She seems like a really nice person."

Teddy looked at Alice as if he was squinting and sniffed loudly. "I guess if she wants you there, it'll be okay, but we have high standards for our tenants and prefer people who are like us. You know, Christians with similar backgrounds. Gail will probably end up being uncomfortable with people in the building; just giving you a heads-up."

Alice looked at him, amazed at what she was hearing. *Is he really this big an asshole?*

"I appreciate your concern for Gail's well-being, Teddy, I'll be sure to let her know you care."

Teddy looked at Alice to see if she was mocking him and only saw a straight face. That helped him to let his guard down. Without speaking, he began to think, *Maybe this Alice person understands what I'm saying. In any case, it's obvious she has the hots for me. I could go for it, but I don't know, I wonder; when was the last time she took a shower? But she's not that hot, pretty flat chested. The other one, the chink, has a much better body. She even has big boobs, which is weird for her kind. I suppose I could nail her without looking at that ugly face.*

Alice decided it was time to step away from this conversation. Although she found Teddy to be a real jerk, she was always fascinated with the idea of digging deeper. In this case, it was going to have to happen in small bites. She hated the way he looked at her and the way he talked about people. On the other hand, Phil seemed nice. Maybe she could learn more about Teddy from him before she shut him out completely. Smiling at Teddy, she said, "Looks like we're lagging behind the others, I'm going to catch up."

Rocco, who had been talking to Phil about their pseudo-happening idea, was also keeping an eye out for some of the locations he had run across earlier in the day. Not having much luck, he stepped off the path to a small woodsy area, and found himself facing a familiar tree with hanging branches. He turned around, saw Alice approaching and called out to her. "Hey Alice, this is the willow tree I was telling you about. The one whose roots laughed out loud at my ignorance of the way things really are in this place."

He pulled out a recorder and began playing a medieval-sounding tune. Gail, who had worn a colorful long skirt she had purchased in New Mexico, began to dance, climbing and dancing around a nearby rock pile. Meanwhile, to Teddy's astonishment, Alice ran up to the tree and spoke to it in rhymes. The rhymes evolved into a rhythmic chant-like sound, repeating the words with a funny accent, *I am the prophetess. I am the Sybil.* Rocco, Gail and a laughing Phil joined the chorus and trotted around the tree blending music and the chant. It sounded like *Ba-Dum, Ba-Dum* to Teddy. Phil then got on his hands and knees and began speaking in a squeaky mouse-dialect, asking the creatures of the underground to help him find his lost friend, "Green Mouse." Teddy was disgusted, but he didn't leave. Instead, he stepped back and pretended to be a casual onlooker.

Other people had different reactions, varying from curiosity to fascination. Some, including a couple of families with young children, stopped to watch, and within a short time a small crowd had gathered, many of whom began to clap their hands and move their feet along with the music. Among the participating audience were two African-American teenage girls who joined Gail as she danced from rock to rock. While they began hesitantly, their initial shyness dissolved as they quickly came to understand they could be creative. Gail was in awe of her young dancing cohorts who were so lithe, they seemed to float through the air without taking a breath.

Breaking from the tree, Alice picked up her guitar and, along with Rocco, began singing and playing a familiar medieval tune: *Down yonder green valley where streamlets meander, where twilight is fading, I pensively rove.*

At that point, one of the floating dancers joined in singing with Alice in perfect harmony. *Or at the bright noontide in solitude wander.... amid the dark shade of the lonely Ashgrove...Tis there where the blackbird is cheerfully singing, each warbler enchants with its notes from a tree; How then little think I of sorrow or sadness, the Ashgrove, the Ashgrove, spells beauty for me.*

By the time they finish the song, ten or twelve people had gathered around, listening in complete silence. It was clearly a magical moment.

Alice smiled at the young woman and reached out her arm. It felt completely natural for the two who had harmonized so perfectly to walk hand in hand down the path together.

Chapter 28

June 26, 1973
New York City

No-one said a word as the group stopped what they had been doing and left the scene of their performance. Their "happening" had flowed into the moment and the parents and children, and passers-by seemed delighted. In fact, some of the children continued to dance around the tree, calling out "where are you, Green Mouse, come on out to play." They didn't seem to notice the musicians and dancers had left.

When they were well past the tree, everyone in the group began to laugh and talk at once.

"This was perfect, Rocco!"

"Did you notice how seamless it was?"

"The children didn't notice when we left...isn't that the perfect outcome for a happening?"

Gail smiled at the teenage dancers who had walked with them. "Thank you so much for joining us. You girls are amazing dancers! My name is Gail, and you are?"

The girls blushed as the taller one answered, "I'm Melissa, and this is my sister Daphne."

Alice joined in, "You are both super talented dancers." Then turning to the smaller girl, said "And your harmonies are perfection, Daphne, I hope you'll come back to sing with me again."

The young teenager beamed at being singled out, "I will and you don't need to tell me, I heard you say your name. Your name is Sybil and you are the prophetess."

"Yes, I love that name."

Melissa and Daphne ran off in the direction they had come from as other people asked questions.

"Did you do this skit for a performance art class? Were the kids in on it? Are they professional actors?"

"No, we didn't know the kids but love that they got into our performance. It's just something we've been doing and everyone is welcome to join us. There's no script so basically we're expressing our creativity by doing what we feel like at the moment."

"There are no rules?"

"The only rule is for people to do something that flows and doesn't totally clash with what other people are doing."

"Can I assume you'll be back sometime?"

Rocco answered, "We haven't talked about it, but I'm figuring we'll be back this way, maybe around the same time on Sunday." He looked at his friends and they all nodded. This would be a great way to spend Sunday afternoons.

Rocco, Alice, Gail, Phil and Teddy headed back to the apartment. As they walked along, their conversation revolved around whether they had accomplished their goal; whether it had been a successful happening.

Gail was puzzled, "Doesn't even asking that question violate the spontaneity of the happening? I thought this was to allow anyone who wants to take part to be creative in their own way."

Alice nodded. "I agree with you Gail. Although this is our version of a happening, I think the spontaneity aspect is really important. We also have to make sure we're able to control what we start. I mean, it would be terrible if it led to someone being harmed. Then she added, "I hope Daphne and Melissa come again. They were wonderful."

Gail agreed, "I have to admit, their effortless dancing put me to shame."

Alice took her arm, "C'mon Gail, you are a super talented dancer, you don't need to compare yourself with anyone!"

Rocco turned to Phil, who had a quiet smile on his face, "Hey man, your green mouse shtick was awesome. Did you just make it up?"

"It's hard to say. I've been playing around with the idea of getting into children's television. Green Mouse is one of the characters I've been thinking about, but this was the first time I've had a chance to animate him. It was great to have a place to do that, and a welcoming audience."

"You sure wowed the kids!"

Alice said, "It added a really cool dimension, Phil. I hope you'll come back and join us next time."

"Sure, it was fun. When's the next happening?"

"I think Rocco told everyone, Sunday at one pm—Be There or Be Square."

Everyone laughed except Teddy who simply didn't get the joke. He had found himself in a familiar situation where he was the only one who just didn't get it. In his mind, this was a bunch of hippie-dippy bullshit. He neither liked nor trusted these people and didn't want to be thought a part of their group, but decided that he had to keep an eye on them to protect his father's interests at the apartment. Besides, his father would probably like him hanging around with Phil. There might be other benefits too. This might be a way to pick up chicks. It was well-known that women in theater were easy pickings.

When they returned to the apartment, Teddy left the group and went upstairs to see Pete. He told everyone he had to get back to work. There was a collective sigh of relief when Teddy left. Rocco asked Phil, "Who is this dude? There's something wrong with him, and I'm not just talking about the obvious racism."

Gail agreed. "I'm no psychologist, but he made me feel really uncomfortable—the way he looked at me and violated my space was really creepy."

Phil sighed. "He's always been like that. Our parents are friends and I've been around him since we were kids. No-one likes him and he doesn't get why. I guess he's a poster boy for a person with no social skills. I don't even think his parents like him. He was always mean to his brothers and sisters. I've tried to feel sorry for him because he's such a loser; failed at everything, lousy in school, lousy in sports, no friends to speak of, but he can't seem to notice that what he does to people isn't acceptable."

"Why does his father let him be the face of his business?"

"Good question, Rocco. His father's creepy too. It's almost like he uses Teddy to be an enforcer of unpopular practices. I don't know if his father cares what people think, but we all know Teddy doesn't care about anyone but himself. You know, Teddy's the sort who gets a charge out of throwing a single mom with small children out of her home."

Alice was listening to this with great interest. "I wonder if he's a sociopath."

Rocco smiled. "That's a ten dollar word, right out of Psych 101!"

Alice looked serious. "You know how I hate labels, but if he's so screwed up, we should be careful how we treat him, don't you think? I mean he has power over us while we live here. Do you think we should find another place?"

Thinking about the piano, Rocco wasn't about to give up his great new space before he even moved in. "I think we're putting the cart before the horse. We're here temporarily no matter what. I mean, both of the folks we're subletting from will be back in a few months and Teddy might not even be interested in us after today. He seemed to think our happening was stupid. Let's just let it ride and see what happens."

Gail agreed with Rocco. "Let's just let it ride. Rocco and I are probably more used to dealing with negativity from strangers than you are, Alice. I can ignore him."

Alice nodded, but Rocco and Gail worried about her basic inability to write anyone off without doing all she could to help them "see the light" through kindness. Her next words reinforced their concern. "I just hate being mean to people without giving them a chance and you know our living situation will be much easier here if he's okay with us being around. Besides, maybe giving him a way to express his own creativity will make him happier. Everyone has an inner artist—it just has to be tapped. I'm sure creative authenticity evolves from doing creative things."

Rocco looked at Gail. He could tell they shared the fear that "rehabilitating" Teddy by appealing to his "inner artist" was destined to be one of the invincible Alice's summer projects.

Chapter 29

June 27-September 9, 1973
New York City

Thoughts of Teddy were relegated to a back burner as Rocco, Alice and Gail devoted themselves to finding work. By the end of the week, Rocco had scored a job as a Manhattan bicycle messenger/courier and Alice was working part time as a waitress in a coffee shop in the West Village. For the time being, Rocco's motorcycle remained at Phil's family home where he thought it would be safe, but riding the bicycle around Manhattan gave him some of the feeling of freedom associated with riding at high speed in the open air.

Although primarily working for tips, Alice loved her job because she was allowed to bring her guitar along and perform on occasion. This, along with getting to know people in the local folk music scene and hearing their stories, was her idea of heaven.

While it took her a bit longer than her friends to find the perfect situation, Gail ended up working as a receptionist at a dance studio near their apartment where she was able to get a discount on dance classes and to interact with people who shared her love of movement.

On Friday, Rocco moved into Kevin O'Reilly's apartment. Kevin had apparently had it out with Teddy and his family's holding company. Much to Teddy and Pete's chagrin, he succeeded in demonstrating a hole in their rental agreement that allowed him to sublet to whoever he chose. Kevin also sweetened the pot by paying the next two months' rent upfront so Teddy's father, figuring it to be a temporary arrangement, decided to leave the sublet alone. Nevertheless, Teddy was assigned the task of keeping an eye on things so the Farrow's property wouldn't get the reputation of being a harbor for non-white people, an outcome they were convinced would lead to a significant decline in its value.

While they were all too busy much of the time to pay attention, Teddy didn't go away. Gail and Rocco ignored him when he came around acting as if he was part of the group. While neither spoke directly with Alice about it, they privately blamed her for being too friendly and allowing Teddy to join their Sunday afternoon happenings in the park. For reasons they would never understand, Alice seemed to continue to have faith that Teddy's inner artist would eventually emerge and make him a better person.

In some ways, Rocco and Gail's mutual dislike of Teddy contributed to their own bonding, which had begun early on with conversations about how they had dealt with racism. The two shared a fondness for Alice but occasionally vented frustration because she kept a lot of her thoughts and feelings private. It was subtle, but she seemed to be holding something back and, over the summer, began to spend a lot of her free time with the West Village crowd she met through work. This was not an entirely unwelcome outcome from Gail's point of view as she was beginning to have feelings for Rocco separate from their mutual friendship with Alice. She found herself treasuring the time alone with him more and more as the summer progressed.

However, every Sunday afternoon at one o'clock, the three, usually accompanied by Phil and Teddy, went into Central Park and launched a happening. Each happening evolved uniquely, as originally intended, but they always started at the magic weeping willow tree where Alice and Rocco invoked it to allow them to go through what they called its "wall of creativity."

Gail knew what they were doing, but was incapable of that sort of magical thinking. To her, the magic was the enjoyment she experienced dancing in the park. That was when she felt most free; but even then, she was weighed down by the realization that it was temporary. Her family obligations would be taking over in a short time. For her, the "wall" was impenetrable. Being a professional dancer and living a comfortable life in the United States were simply unattainable dreams.

The teenagers who had participated in the first happening, Daphne and Melissa, also often showed up. Coincidentally, shortly after their first encounter, Gail recognized them as students in a summer program at the dance studio where she was working, and encouraged them to share new steps and moves they were learning. The girls were thrilled to be recognized and welcomed by a founding creator of the "happenings in the park", as they were beginning to be called.

Melissa and Daphne didn't reveal many details about their lives, but Gail knew they were sisters who lived in Washington

Heights on the upper west side of Manhattan. While their parents allowed them to travel back and forth to their dance lessons on public transportation as long as they were together, the girls often found ways to stretch their time in the City. They had discovered the happenings by accident and got in the habit of finding ways to sneak out for the adventure. Knowing their parents would be unlikely to approve of their dancing around the woods with older hippie-types, they usually left as soon as the happening was over so they wouldn't be late getting home. However, Alice and Gail noticed when, for the first time in early September, they didn't show up at all.

A couple of weeks previously, Melissa had told Alice that she and Daphne were uncomfortable because Teddy had been hovering around them during the happenings and threatening to follow them home. Alice told Teddy he would no longer be included unless he promised to leave the young teenagers alone. Needless to say, Teddy did not take being excluded well and, while he didn't participate in the happening the following week, unbeknownst to Alice, he did go into the park and followed the girls home. Beginning the next day, he stalked Melissa wherever she went. She was terrified but afraid to say anything to her parents and didn't want to scare Daphne, so she kept it to herself. Then one day, her worst fears were realized, when he pushed her up against a building, put his hands under her clothes and molested her, all the while threatening to tell her parents what she had been doing and that she asked for it.

Not wanting to frighten Daphne, Melissa kept what had happened to herself, but from that day forward, found excuses to avoid participating in future happenings. Despite Daphne's pleas, she began making plans to hang out with school friends on Sunday afternoons .

After the girls failed to show up, Alice asked Gail if she had seen them at the studio. Gail responded that the summer dance classes were over, but she had run into Daphne with her mom a few days earlier. They were signing up for a round of after-school lessons.

"Did you ask Daphne if she would be coming around again soon? I really miss their energy."

"Her mother was with her, so I didn't ask; but I did tell her that I would be leaving for Jamaica soon and she took me aside and whispered that she would come next Sunday for a farewell dance in the park."

"Huh?"

"This has been a dream summer, but I have to go home to Jamaica. I've made plane reservations for next week."

"Oh no, Gail, I had almost forgotten! I'm so sorry! We'll have to do something special before you leave. I'll talk to Rocco. When are you leaving?"

"A week from Monday; I can do one more happening. Then it's off to the real world."

"Okay, Sunday after the happening, the three of us will do something special. It'll be a surprise. Shit Gail, I'm going to miss you, but I know you're going to kick ass in Jamaica and save your parents' business and help your little sisters grow up and all the other things that are in front of you."

"I would love to have your optimism. This is one of those times I wish you really were a prophetess predicting my future—a real Sybil."

Alice smiled, "I must admit I'm a believer in making your own luck. I know this is coming out of the blue, but have you been in touch with Mike Lucas? He seemed to have a major crush on you when we were in Albuquerque and I thought there were some mutual vibes."

"We've written back and forth a few times, but he's been super busy with work. He said he wanted to visit us here, but hasn't had the free time to get away. You're right, he's very sweet, and attractive, but that was like a three-day crush, and we're destined to live many miles apart."

Determined to give Gail an enjoyable send-off, Alice and Rocco put their heads together and made plans to spend their last afternoon and evening together. They decided to start by taking her to one of her favorite places in the City, the Museum of Natural History, followed by treating her to a dinner of Indonesian rice at Chumleys, a well-known restaurant in the West Village. After dinner, they had tickets for an African dance performance.

Daphne showed up at the Sunday afternoon happening by herself and began by dancing spontaneously around and around the magic tree. While Rocco pulled out one of his funky instruments, what he called his "xylo-frog", Phil began one of his mouse whisperer chants. As usual, they were quickly joined by children squeaking as mice as they danced along with Daphne and Gail.

Then, as if planned ahead, Daphne and Alice sang a song from the Broadway musical *Carnival.* The song was *Mira,* a haunting tune about belonging and homesickness. The opera singer Anna Maria Alberghetti had made it famous and was especially known for hitting an incredibly high note with total purity.

Everyone became quiet just after Alice began:
"I come from the town of Mira,
Beyond the bridges of St. Clair"

And weren't at all surprised when little Daphne joined in, in perfect harmony.
"I know you've never heard of Mira
It's very small, but still it's there"

They had all heard Daphne sing before, but this time was even more amazing in the way she picked up the harmonies so effortlessly. Like her dance moves, her voice was flawless, and while Alice dropped back when it was time to hit the famous high note, "I'm very far from Mira now, but there's no turning back," Daphne blew right through it. For the first time, the happening ended with everyone but the two singers stopping what they were doing to focus on listening. This was unprecedented. When they finished the song, the other participants and observers began to applaud and gather around Daphne and Alice. Tears welling in her eyes, Gail was aware this special performance was for her and didn't care whether it had been planned ahead or not.

Daphne enjoyed the attention, but after a while began to fidget. Escaping to the park that Sunday afternoon by herself was a bold move, but when she realized she had been away for over an hour, worried that she would be late getting home. Looking at Alice, she said, "I have to go, Sybil. I'm late." She gave Gail a warm hug and said, "I will never forget you," and started running through the park.

Alice watched as Daphne ran off, and immediately noticed she was heading in the wrong direction. She called out, "Daphne, I think you're going the wrong way." But Daphne didn't respond.

Noticing her concern, Rocco said, "Hey, she's a New Yorker, she knows what she's doing. Anyway, it's time to get moving if we're going to make it to the Museum of Natural

History this afternoon." Smiling at Gail, he said, "This is part one of our farewell to Gail celebration."

The three friends started walking towards their apartment, talking about the exhibits they wanted to visit. Nonetheless, Rocco and Gail were not surprised when Alice turned around and started walking quickly in the other direction, announcing she would catch up with them later.

"I'll catch up, I promise. I just want to make sure Daphne's okay. Give me an hour at most. I'll find you at the museum."

Meanwhile, unbeknownst to anyone, Teddy had also decided to follow Daphne. As he followed her through the park, he thought about what he would do when he caught her. He wondered if she was a virgin and decided it was unlikely since she was black and everyone knew all black girls were easy. It actually made him a little sick to his stomach thinking about it.

Driven by worrying about how her father would react to her being gone for so long, Daphne was focused on finding the quickest route through the park. Then she heard someone running behind her and panicked. She saw a large rock and decided to climb to get away from whatever was chasing her. The rock had crevices she was able to step into and pull herself up as she climbed. When she was about three-quarters of the way up the rock, she heard her name and looked down to see Teddy starting to climb up behind her saying things that scared her even more. There was something really slimy about the way he talked, saying things like, "C'mon honey. I can give you the thrill of your life. Your sister loved it."

Sensing danger, Daphne tried to climb higher and faster. Then her right foot got caught in a crevice, and she screamed with pain as her leg was twisted. This led her to fall, hitting her head as she landed on the ground.

Teddy decided there was no way he was going to be caught in this place with that girl and ran off.

Daphne was in shock at first and may have passed out for a moment, but when she came to, she realized she was not only in severe pain, but couldn't move her legs at all. She started screaming for help.

Within minutes, Alice heard the screams. When she saw Daphne was injured, she did what she could to make her comfortable and ran out to find help.

Chapter 30

Rocco and Gail walked back to the apartment without speaking. Neither Gail nor Rocco wanted to wait for Alice, so they left a note and walked down to 81ˢᵗ Street and the Museum of Natural History where they spent the next two hours. When they returned to the apartment, there was no sign that Alice had been there. Flopping on the couch with Fluffy, Rocco turned to Gail and said, "Alice must be someplace with Daphne. I'm getting hungry. Do you want to go out and find a sandwich? Or do you have anything here to snack on?" It was only five o'clock and the dance performance wasn't until nine. There was plenty of time.

Gail went into the kitchen and came out holding a half bottle of wine and an almost empty bag of pretzels and laughed, "I don't think there's enough of either of these to hold us over. I guess we can go out, but it's Sunday and we probably can't find anyplace cheap."

Rocco stood up. "Let's go up to my place. Kevin left all sorts of food I haven't really gotten into—a lot of fancy things in the freezer, Why don't we bring the wine and pretzels along in case we can't find anything we like."

Gail laughed and followed him out the door to the second floor of the building. Feeling relaxed, Rocco and Gail continued joking and laughing as they speculated about what they might find in Kevin's freezer. They were feeling so much better that it didn't even bother them when they ran into Teddy who was chatting with Pete at the stairwell. They simply nodded and continued on their way, but both sighed in relief when they were able to close and lock the door of Kevin's apartment.

Gail, who hadn't stopped giggling, made a joke about Teddy always being where he wasn't wanted, then paused and said, "Did you notice how harried he looked just now? He didn't have his usual charming snarly expression."

Rocco replied that he hadn't looked at his face. "I must admit, the only part of that asshole I ever look at is his back, and sometimes his ass itself. Then I find myself gagging, so I have to hum songs in my head."

"Like what?"

Rocco started singing, "I've got you under my skin. I've got you deep in the worst part of me. And deep in that part I need to start fart—ting.."

That got Gail giggling again, and opening up the half-empty bottle of wine, she took a long sip and passed the bottle to Rocco who gulped some down himself and went to the kitchen to grab a couple of glasses he then filled with the rest of the wine from the bottle. As they sat and drank, they munched on the pretzels and made fun of Teddy.

"I really think he sees himself as God's gift to women. Did you see the way he was ogling Daphne today?"

"Oh indeed; and his smarmy shtick where he gets super close to people's faces and makes that creepy laugh. And the constant snorting; he claims he has allergies but it sure sounds to me like he snorts coke or some other drug he puts up his nose. Then after he's done nothing creative, nothing to contribute, he talks about how great he was. Wasn't it today when he was giving himself credit for being our 'stage manager' when people were talking about how cool the Alice Daphne harmonies were?"

"I can't believe this is the first time we've done this, Rocco; really letting our feelings out. I know you and I have agreed about this jerk since we met him."

"I agree, Gail, this is long overdue."

As soon as these words came out of Rocco's mouth, both he and Gail recognized that they were describing much more than being able to talk about their mutual disdain for Teddy. They also had the attraction they felt towards each other in common. As they continued to drink, finished the bottle from downstairs and opened a new one, their mutual attraction became easier and easier to acknowledge. Everything melted away but being together.

It was getting dark when Alice finally returned to the apartment. Still in an emotional state, she was anxious to share her news about Daphne with Rocco and Gail. She had been completely caught up in being with Daphne as she was taken to the hospital, and sitting with her parents and sister while they learned about the surgery she would need to undergo to save her legs. At some point, Alice realized she hadn't called home to tell anyone what was going on, but figured they would understand when they finally heard what happened. The apartment was dark and she was greeted by Fluffy who bumped her leg and led her to the kitchen. For some reason, he seemed very needy. There was definitely something going on in the universe that day! It was unusual for Gail not to leave a note.

Walking into the hall, she decided to see if Rocco was home. Maybe he would know where Gail was. As she climbed the stairs to the first floor, she saw Teddy and Pete coming into the building.

Daphne had been confused when Alice first saw her. In addition to her leg injuries, she had hit her head on a rock when she fell. She was later given pain medications that made her sleepy, so there wasn't a lot of conversation about what had happened. But the one word Alice heard was "Teddy." She wasn't sure about any details, but had the feeling that Teddy had something to do with Daphne's fall. Being Alice, she would not jump to conclusions until she knew more, but couldn't help asking Teddy, if he had seen Daphne after the happening.

Teddy's face turned a bright red, but he denied he had seen her. "Of course not, why would I bother with someone like her?"

Alice glared at him, then headed towards the stairs. Teddy called after her as he and Pete laughed, "Are you looking for your friend Gail? I think you'll find her in Rocco's apartment. They've been there all afternoon." Teddy and Pete giggled again and walked down the hall in the other direction.

Alice, once again thought to herself that she may have been too nice to this guy. *He really is an asshole... takes all kinds, but I think he may end up being the exception to the rule of my theory that everyone is capable of creative authenticity. This has been such a terrible day, I can't wait to be with my friends.* She began to take two steps at a time.

When she reached Rocco's apartment, she banged on the door and called out, but no-one answered. There was a shuffling sound, then Rocco opened the door wearing a short robe. The robe was black and white with stripes like a zebra. Her first reaction was that there was no way Rocco had ever bought such a robe; it was too short and dorky. It probably belonged to Kevin O'Reilly. But that was just the beginning. Rocco rubbed his eyes and said he was taking a nap and could they get together later. Alice started telling him about Daphne, but it was evident he wasn't listening and wanted her to leave. She began to walk away, then turned back to ask if he had seen Gail, but Rocco had already closed and locked the door.

As she walked down the stairs, Alice thought about what Teddy had said, that both Rocco and Gail were in his apartment. This explained Rocco's strange behavior. He never slept during the day, never. Gail was there and they were screwing. Alice tried to absorb this and couldn't. Then she remembered Teddy's sniveling voice and his and Pete's giggles when he said *she's been there all afternoon.*

Leaving the building, Alice began walking and instead of heading for the Park, walked in the other direction where she stopped at Ensaladilla. The hidden garden would provide her with a private place where, surrounded by flowers, she could take a breath and sort through her thoughts and feelings. Upon entering the small courtyard, she was relieved to see she would be alone with her thoughts. It would be impossible to even smile at another person. There was too much to process.

Rocco walked back to the bedroom feeling uncomfortable about his encounter with Alice. Gail looked up as he walked in the door. "I think I just blew it, Gail. That was Alice. I lied and told her I was napping."

Gail smiled, "Well, I guess napping was part of it."

Rocco remained serious. "No, she knew something was up. She had something to tell me and I cut her off. We don't do that to each other."

Rocco started putting on his clothes while Gail looked at him. All of a sudden this felt completely wrong. As her feeling of closeness with Rocco was being shattered, Gail attempted to hold on to her pride by making them partners. "What do you want to say to her, Rocco? I think we need to be on the same page."

Gail's hopes were dashed when Rocco looked at her. It was obvious their moment of intimacy was over. This confirmed her deep down belief that his feelings and connection with her had always been about Alice, who he obviously loved deeply. She was just a way for him to be close to Alice. While not surprised, Gail was hurt. She had just made love with Rocco. Even though it was fueled by alcohol, she had meant it. Now she had to pretend it hadn't happened because Rocco cared more about Alice's feelings than hers. *Well, Rocco cares more about*

Alice than me. I'm not sure I care more about her than Rocco. But right now, I have to rise to the occasion and help him bring things back to 'normal', whatever that means.

Rocco sat down hard on the bed and covered his face with his hands. When he looked up, there was pain in his eyes. "I don't know Gail. I'm so sorry; I didn't mean to have this happen."

Gail flinched, "Hey Rocco, it takes two to tango. I may regret it in the morning, but honestly, I've enjoyed being with you today. Don't you dare think you made me do something I didn't want to do. This was very mutual."

Rocco smiled wanly. "Thanks for saying that. You know, maybe Alice doesn't know what was going on. Maybe we can just say you were out and came looking for me to see if we wanted to pick up a pizza or something. I'll bet she's down in your apartment hanging out with Fluffy."

Gail wasn't so sure. She had just learned that Rocco was in love with Alice. She couldn't think about anything else, so when they opened the door to her apartment, she was relieved to find that it's only occupant was Fluffy. She needed time to herself to lick her wounds. She turned to Rocco, "I think I'm done for the night. I'm exhausted and I have to get up early tomorrow for my flight."

"But we made plans to take you to an African dance performance in the Village tonight."

Gail looked at Rocco and thought about how clueless men could be. Without another word, she kissed him on the cheek, closed the door and walked back to her bedroom. She was dreading facing Alice. So this was the way her magical summer would end.

Rocco knew he had screwed up. He walked back up to his apartment and put on his headphones to listen to Billie Holliday. His head would be clearer in the morning and he always found riding his bike up and down the avenues cathartic.

Chapter 31

September 9, 1973
New York City

Alice sat in the courtyard, but nothing came into her mind with words. She experienced a few colors, mostly purples and charcoal grays, but they didn't do anything for her. Then she heard a soft voice, "Are you okay? I hate disturbing you, but I'm beginning to worry. I've been back and forth watching you for at least an hour and you haven't moved a muscle and I have to tell you, you're emanating a really sad vibe."

Alice looked up and was surprised to see Charlotte, the Charlotte they had sublet the apartment from. For some reason, her presence had the effect of thinning the mess that had been Alice's mind for the past hour and she was able to speak. "Charlotte! What are you doing here? Are you back from your travels? Why didn't you let me know?"

Relieved she had broken through the clouds encircling Alice, Charlotte smiled. "I'll tell you about me later. First, talk to me about what's going on with you. I was really concerned."

For some reason, Charlotte's kind words helped Alice to open up. Opening up was not easy for Alice, especially when she was feeling emotional. She had spent her life pushing emotion back and not sharing her feelings until she had words that separated the feelings from expressing how she felt. It was as if the words protected her from the feelings. She was most comfortable with that level of control, but the events of this day were overwhelming. They were painful for Alice and she was blaming herself for what happened to Daphne.

The words poured out and Charlotte listened carefully. Then she asked, "Is Daphne going to be alright?

"I don't know. It sounds like there was a lot of damage to her legs, hips, ankles and feet. And there may be some internal damage. She's only fifteen. She wants to be a professional dancer. She may never walk again!"

Alice broke into tears that felt like an explosion. Charlotte reached out and held her while her body vibrated. She knew it was going to take time for Alice to calm down enough to answer questions, questions like, why she was blaming herself.

"Daphne is very lucky you cared enough to follow to make sure she was okay. Were you alone? Did you have to leave her by herself when you went to get help?"

Alice wiped her eyes and looked at the ground. "Yes, that was horrible. She was so scared."

"It's too bad your friends didn't go with you. What did they say when you told them what happened?"

Alice looked up and blinked hard. She wasn't ready to talk about Rocco and Gail. She still hadn't processed the thought that they were 'coupling.'

"They don't know. I couldn't find them when I got home. It had been several hours. I didn't want to leave her. She was in such pain and so scared, she begged me not to leave her there alone. I explained that I had to find help. I couldn't lift her; I'm not that strong. I didn't want to move her because I was afraid she would become more injured."

"I'm sure she understood."

"And she was afraid someone else would come to hurt her more."

"I thought she had fallen accidentally. Did someone push her? Was she a victim of a crime?"

"I'm not sure, and I didn't want to falsely-accuse anyone. She wasn't totally articulate, but I do think someone had been there, someone who had been at the happening." Alice stopped for a moment and continued. "Oh shit, why am I protecting him? She said Teddy had been there. She didn't say exactly what happened, but she was definitely afraid he would come back to harm her."

"Teddy? You mean Teddy Farrow? He was part of your group?!"

"You know Teddy? Of course you do, I had forgotten, he's the guy who collects our rent. Yes, it was my fault that he started hanging around with us. No-one likes him and I just felt sorry for the guy, even though I completely understand why people find him so offensive. I let him come along. He never contributed anything to the happenings, I tend to doubt he has a single creative bone in his body, but he always wanted to come along. I just hate being unkind to anyone. For some reason, I always expect people's inner artist to emerge eventually."

Charlotte looked closely at Alice and sighed, "There's something I need to tell you. You asked me when I got back from my travels. The truth is, I didn't go anywhere. I just had to get out of my apartment so I moved in with a friend until the lease was up. I've been basically hiding from Teddy Farrow. I'm so sorry, Alice, I just couldn't cope with him anymore."

"What did he do to you?"

"I'm not sure I want to go into details, but he scared me and I needed for him to believe I was gone; but I still had time on my lease. That's why I sublet it to you. I figured I could stay out of his reach for a few months and then really move on."

"I'm so sorry you have to go through this, but now you're scaring me. Do you think he would do you, or me, physical harm?"

"I don't know about other people. I've always assumed that since his father has assigned him to be the face of his business here, he can't have hurt other people. But now that you're saying he played a role in Daphne's injuries, I wonder. It sounds like he knows that you know."

"Please Charlotte, tell me what he's done to you!"

Charlotte sighed with resignation. She had put Teddy behind her and didn't want to relive what she had experienced, but at some level, knew it wasn't over. Maybe sharing with Alice would be a good thing. "I guess the best way to describe it is that he became obsessed with me and when I didn't reciprocate, he started to stalk, and it didn't stop there. He told everyone we were in a relationship. That was bad enough, but then he started acting as if we were in a relationship."

"How weird! It's bad enough to have someone not believe you when you tell them you aren't interested, but to have them lie about it AND stay around and stalk you. Do you think he's mentally ill, that he's delusional?"

"I have to tell you Alice, I've stopped trying to analyze Teddy. I NEVER encouraged him. I found him creepy from the get go. I did everything I could to treat our relationship for what it was, purely business. He was the building manager; but I can tell you for sure that he isn't normal. He has no capacity for empathy. I guess the psychological term is narcissism. All I know for sure is that I needed to stay away from him."

Alice began to cry again. Everything was hitting her at once. She didn't want to tell Charlotte, or even think about Gail and Rocco. She just wanted to get away. Looking up at Charlotte again, she wiped her eyes and asked, "Would it be possible for me to sleep on your couch tonight? I don't want to go back there."

"Sure, I share an apartment with three other women. There's always room for one more.

Relieved she could avoid going back for the moment, Alice put Gail and Rocco out of her mind and began thinking about how she could help Daphne and her family. She decided to think about it overnight, but began leaning towards going to her father. Now she just had to find him. Oddly, that felt easier than digging into her feelings about Rocco and Gail.

Chapter 32

September 10, 1973
New York City

When Alice got up the following morning, her head was clear. She had two things on her agenda: moving out of the apartment and finding her father to ask for his help. If she had time, she would go to the hospital to visit Daphne. Knowing Gail would probably be on her way back to Jamaica, she went first to the apartment, packed her few belongings in her bag and backpack and grabbed her guitar. All the while, Fluffy coiled himself in and out of her legs purring loudly. Alice looked at him and said, "Oh Fluffy, what am I going to do with you?"

At first she thought about letting him out where she had found him in the alley. He obviously had street skills, but the more she thought about it, the more unwilling she was to let him go. Grabbing a few cans of food, she put them together with Fluffy into her backpack, all the while hoping Charlotte and her roommates were okay with cats. At this point, she had no plan B.

Alice had left Charlotte's place before anyone else was up and about, but when she returned with Fluffy, Charlotte and her roommate Nola were up drinking coffee. Charlotte had told Nola that Alice's stay was temporary, a fact Alice repeated. "Thank you both for helping me out. I hope my kitten can stay here with me too. I don't want to leave him behind, but I promise I'll be finding my own place very soon."

Nola reached out to hold Fluffy. "He's adorable. I just lost my kitty, Banana. Banana was almost 20 years old; I really miss her. It will be nice to have a baby in the house. Alice smiled at Nola gratefully and asked. "Do you have a litter box? I brought a few cans of food and his dish but forgot all about the litter box. My arms were kind of full."

Nola continued to hold and pet Fluffy who purred contentedly. Alice was once again amazed at how adaptable he was. Most cats she'd known in the past would run and hide until they knew where they were.

Nola responded, "Nothing to worry about; we are very well equipped cat-wise. I think Fluffy and I will get along fine and I can see that you need to be out and about."

"I do need to head out. I can't visit the hospital until two but I have a few other things to do first anyway. Thanks again, I'll try to be in touch but not sure how late I will be."

Alice was thinking, and even making decisions, as she walked to the subway station. Finding her father might not be the easiest task. He traveled a lot and she literally had been out of touch with him and her mother since the beginning of the year. She supposed he might have known she was in Albuquerque when he looked at her American Express bill, but that bus and train fare was the only way she had used it. So she decided to stop off in the Village and give his office a call from the coffee house. She needed to tell her employer she wouldn't be working later that day as well.

As she dialed the office number, Alice was struck by how familiar it still felt, but was shocked to hear the office was no longer located at 17 Battery Place across from Bowling Green at the bottom of Manhattan. Lyons Shipping had moved its headquarters several blocks north to the recently completed World Trade Center complex. Alice had, of course, been aware of the huge twin towers, which now dominated the New York City skyline but it felt strange to think of her father's office being anywhere besides 17 Battery Place. He'd worked at the same address her whole life.

This was the first time she had traveled below Greenwich Village since coming to New York. Lower Manhattan was her father's territory, something she had never shared with Rocco and Gail. She had avoided it, not wanting to run into her father or any of his business acquaintances. Yet Alice had no doubt her father would be happy to help once he heard what had happened to Daphne. It was hard to explain to other people how it was with her and her parents. They took family seriously from a financial support perspective, but no-one really enjoyed one another's company so there was never any need to pretend to know or care. Alice's parents, who had named her after the curious, adventurous Alice of *Alice in Wonderland*, prided themselves in raising a completely socially and emotionally independent daughter.

Walking into the building, Alice couldn't help but be impressed. Brand new, the World Trade Center was the tallest building in the world. It definitely made her dizzy to look up! But, sadness equally matched her sense of awe. The old office building, 17 Battery Place with its marble walls and brass bannisters, was so much more elegant in an old-fashioned way and simply felt more substantial.

Not unexpectedly, the visit with her father was brief. When she told the receptionist who she was, she was ushered right in. When her father heard she was there, he stepped out of a meeting and greeted her warmly. "What a pleasant surprise, Alice. How nice to see you. Is there something I can help you with?" Looking back at the people sitting in his office, he added, "I only have a minute."

Alice kissed him on the cheek and said, "Actually, I only need a minute. I have a friend who's going to need major surgery. Her family doesn't have the resources and I don't think they have much in the way of insurance."

Her father smiled and without blinking, said, "Of course, we'll cover it. Just let me know how much and when you'll need the money and I'll write you a check. Do you have my private number?"

"Thanks Dad, yes, I think I have your number unless it's changed. I'll get back to you as soon as I know. It might be a lot. She has a lot of broken bones."

"No problem, anything for a friend of yours." His next smile was indulgent, like that of a tolerant parent whose three year-old mispronounced a word in a cute way. Then he looked at his watch. "Now I really have to get back to my meeting. Oh, and drop in to room 9812 and say hello to Lucy. Remember my assistant? Just let her know what you need and she'll take care of things."

"Wow Lucy, she's been with you forever! I hope she remembers me."

Her father laughed distractedly and turned back towards his office. It was evident he was finished with Alice. "Just tell her I sent you down the hall. No-one gets this far without permission. My meeting awaits."

"Okay, Room 9812, just down the hall. Thanks again, Daphne's family will be relieved; and Dad, say hi to Mom for me."

Relieved that she had reached her father and found him willing to help, Alice headed to the reception area of her father's office. She looked at her watch and was happy to note it was just twelve noon and she had time to grab a bite to eat before heading up to the hospital. She was remembering a moment in her childhood when one of her father's employees took her out to lunch, promising "the umbrella club" which to her delight was a hot dog truck. The hot dog, smothered with sauerkraut, mustard and onions, was the best she had ever tasted and it cost twenty cents. Maybe she could find an umbrella club today and eat a hot dog on a park bench. Walking past the reception desk, she gave the distracted receptionist a wave. The receptionist looked up and called out to her, "Alice? I have a note for you."

Alice read the note from her father as she ate her hot dog. It was brief:

"Your mother is in Galway. Do you have any interest in joining her there?"

As soon as he returned from work, Rocco knocked on the basement apartment door. There was no answer. Of course Gail was gone. Her flight had been earlier that day. He knew he would spend the rest of his life regretting not making things right with her. He cared a lot about her but was well aware that he remained as confused about where his life was going now as in the beginning of the summer. As much as he cared, he knew he didn't currently have anything to offer her, a woman who was basically very needy. Then he thought about Alice and hoped he hadn't screwed up their friendship. Maybe he could stop in at the coffee shop on his way to tonight's gig, but that was probably not a good time and place for them to talk. He would wait until the time was right. Nothing was the way it was supposed to have turned out.

That night, Rocco went to his gig where he played drums, the perfect outlet for his confused feelings. While he was playing, he inhabited a singular dimension that enveloped him with the rhythms. So caught up, he didn't notice Alice standing in the back of the room as he played, nor did he see her leave.

By the end of the performance Rocco had made a decision about his next steps. He would hop on his motorcycle and take off to parts unknown. He needed to be alone. On his bike, he could feel the world fly by without having to participate. He had always planned to take a road trip to Tierra del Fuego, why not now instead of later? Before he walked out, he thanked Phil's dad for the opportunity to play with his band and told him he was moving on. He would be coming out to Long Island to pick up the bike by the end of the week. After that, the future would take care of itself.

PART 3

April 26 - June 30, 2002

Chapter 33

April 26, 2002
Montreal Canada, Jersey City NJ

Melissa was in shock, "I need to wrap my head around this, Sybil. You're telling me you accidently met Rocco and Gail, the people who started the happenings in the park all those years ago, and Rocco is an attorney!

"An amazing coincidence Mom, Rocco was the man who stayed with me after I was injured in the carjacking. He and Gail were meeting at the Newark train station after not seeing each other for twenty-nine years. They had my glasses case which helped everyone figure out my identity when I was so out of it. It took a while, but last week, Rick and I invited them over for a thank-you drink. That was when I recognized them as being in that old photo."

Melissa smiled, "Rocco was so hot! I had a huge crush on him. I think all the women in the group had a big crush on him. He was an artist, a musician, super good-looking, and when we were performing, he always had a twinkle in his eye, like he knew a secret. Man oh man, could that guy play and even invent instruments! Sometimes he brought a flute or drums, or even a banjo, but my favorite was what we called his xylo-frog."

"Huh?"

"It was a sort of drum shaped like a frog with ridges along its back. He made the most amazing sounds with it using a pointed stick." Melissa paused, "He's a lawyer? I have to say, I never imagined that life for him. I guess I just always figured he would make his living as a musician, or at least an artist of some sort."

"Do you remember Gail?"

"Of course I remember Gail. She was a jazz dancer who worked at the studio where Daphne and I took lessons. She was gorgeous, and a really talented dancer. Daphne and I learned a lot of technique from her."

"From what they told me, Rocco and Gail created the happenings group along with Alice. I think they had just finished college and came to Manhattan for a summer adventure before heading out into the world. They describe Alice as the creative leader of the group. I believe they both knew her before they met each other."

Melissa was silent for a moment. Alice had been kind, and protective of both Melissa and Daphne throughout the summer. In retrospect, Melissa was very grateful, for although they liked thinking of themselves as grown-up enough to create art with a group of older people, the sisters were basically naïve teenagers. Of course she could never forget Alice, but during the years they were in touch after that summer, Alice never mentioned Gail and Rocco. Melissa never knew what went down between the three friends, but thought it was somehow tied up with Daphne's accident. There was always some mystery around what had taken place in the park, but neither Daphne nor Alice ever spoke of it when probed. Their story was consistent throughout Daphne's life. The basic outline was that Daphne had sneaked out to participate in the happening because it was her last chance to see Gail. Fearing she would be late getting home, she decided to find a shortcut through the park and ended up getting lost. Daphne had never been alone in the park before and didn't know her way around. Feeling increasingly lost, she had been frightened by unrecognized sounds and climbed the rocks where her foot got caught in a crevice. She twisted her leg and fell. Meanwhile, fearing Daphne might get lost, Alice went in search of her and found her lying on the ground, incapable of walking. The rest was history.

After the accident, Melissa and her parents thanked God on a daily basis for Alice's caring presence, which continued until the day Daphne died. She was indeed Daphne's guardian angel. She paid for a lot of her medical expenses over the years, and stayed connected with the family. Melissa sometimes wondered if Alice felt responsible for Daphne's accident, but she knew the truth, that it was her own fault for not being there that day. It was her responsibility to take care of her little sister, and she had failed miserably.

The family was more than grateful for Alice's help, and when it was time for Melissa to name her own little girl, she named her Sybil, the name Alice used in the park that summer. Alice told them she had taken Sybil as her "stage name" in the park based on a book by Par Lagervist called *The Sybil* about a mythological Greek woman with the ability to see the large picture about the present, and predict the future. Whether she actually had special powers or not, Melissa admired and respected the strength and kindness she saw in Alice/Sybil. She liked the idea of giving her daughter any boost possible as she traveled through her own life. She wanted her Sybil to always feel powerful.

"This is amazing! I don't suppose they told you where Alice is these days? I lost touch with her after she brought over the kachina doll and *Alice in Wonderland* book for you. That was, what, seventeen-eighteen years ago?"

"No, I don't believe they're still in touch. They both spoke of her kindly, but it sounds like those relationships ended a long time ago. I think they would have mentioned it if she was still part of their lives, but Rocco and Gail hadn't been in touch over the years either. This was actually the first time in twenty-nine years. I guess what they say about those hippie-dippy days is true; people drifted in and out of each other's lives and made no commitments."

"Well, that sure wasn't the case with Alice and Daphne. I was always amazed at how committed she was to helping Daphne get better and have the best life she could have. I don't know what we would have done without her. Alice paid for everything and did the research to get her the best care. Although she dressed the part, there was nothing hippie dippy about Alice!"

"I agree Mom, but she was also at the center of the happenings, which seem like a very hippie-ish activity, you know, loosey goosey, letting it be totally natural and go with the flow."

"It was, and that was part of why Daphne and I loved it so much. We could just dance any way we wanted and what we were doing was never judged by the other people there. They were respectful and even let us lead some of the moments. That meant so much to us."

"I totally get it. You were getting to hang out with, and have the approval of older kids. That would be heaven for fifteen- and seventeen-year olds."

"It was. Say hello to Rocco and Gail for me. Maybe we can get together next time your dad and I come for a visit."

"That would be awesome. I'm feeling better every day, but I'm still edgy around cars and crowds."

"Have you been able to do any work?"

"I haven't been to the office yet. My ribs still hurt quite a bit going up and down stairs and the only place I ever want to sit is this chair where I still sleep at night, but I have kept up, mostly by phone and email. I want to get back to work full time. I just need to feel more comfortable physically."

"I understand, Dear, I'm glad you're taking care of yourself and that you're obviously healing. It's good to take the time to do it right. Your body will tell you when you're ready."

Melissa sat back after they said goodbye and thought about what was really worrying her. She was confident that Sybil's physical injuries would heal, but not so sure about the trauma associated with the carjacking. Like her, Sybil tended to bury her emotions in places they couldn't be reached to air. Melissa believed this traumatic experience needed airing, but she felt powerless to change what happened. She would always struggle with her inability to protect Sybil along with her failure to save Daphne. On the other hand, Melissa was happy to hear her daughter speaking with so much animation. Sybil had been uncharacteristically quiet in the wake of the carjacking. It was great to hear her enthusiasm, but at the same time, Melissa felt the familiar clutch in her chest associated with reminders of that summer. As usual, thoughts of the summer of 1973 brought back visceral memories of her own trauma, the trauma of being molested by that horrible man and not being able to tell anyone about it. It was a secret she had kept to herself throughout her life. She had originally kept it quiet for fear of losing her parents' trust and the privileges and freedoms she had only recently earned. Then she failed to protect Daphne from harm and just could not go back there. It had all been her fault. As was her habit, she pushed negativity aside and focused on the positive for her daughter.

Sybil laid her head back and thought about the conversation with her mother. Her mom was, and always had been, the Rock of Gibraltar in her life. Yet somehow Sybil found herself incapable of being completely honest about how she was feeling. It wasn't because she was afraid her mother would think she wasn't trying hard enough to heal quickly. That was probably true of Rick, but in both cases, she knew they only wanted the best for her. It was more that, while she believed she was doing the right things to advance her physical healing, she felt totally helpless in her efforts to control the emotional side. She had never known how much being a helpless victim could trigger depression, but even with the meds, she woke up in the middle of each night because of her physical discomfort and stayed awake as her mind tortured her with what seemed to be unrelated failures and cruelties she had experienced (and doled out) throughout her life. It almost seemed as if a veil that had been created to deal with past hurts had simply been lifted. When she woke up, she was always still exhausted, and while the depression no longer dominated, it was often replaced by a crippling feeling of anxiety.

A part of her believed if she could remember the moment she was pushed out of the car, a moment she knew must have been terrifying, she would be able to exorcise the noxious humors that were buried deep inside. Carmela had explained to her that when a person experiences trauma, they often react with 'fight, flight, or freezing'. It was clear to everyone that Sybil was a "freezer" who had put the memory of the traumatic moment away into some inaccessible cell of her body. While it protected her from falling apart, Sybil sometimes felt it was festering. She wasn't walking around feeling unsafe, per se, but despite the anti-depressants, which had succeeded in taking the edge off, it was clearly debilitating.

Dwelling on her emotional discomfort made Sybil feel sorry for herself, and if there was one feeling she hated more than anything, in herself or anyone else, it was self-pity. Sitting up straight with determination, she decided to do something. Then it hit her, the one specific experience she had in the wake of the carjacking that made a huge difference was the initial visit with Pam, her magician massage therapist. Still not sure how much she wanted to be touched, Sybil picked up the phone and told Pam where she was in her healing process. While she had yet to start, she had spoken with a physical therapist who told her that massage could be a beneficial addition to her treatment. Pam was a miracle worker who combined her deep knowledge of human anatomy and alternative medicine with an intuitive understanding of the spiritual part.

Pam agreed to come over the following week. While on the phone she asked Sybil some interesting questions, beginning with "have you ever had a spa treatment?" Sybil had been rather taken aback by that question, *was Pam thinking about giving her a pedicure?* So she asked, "You mean like facials and mani-pedis? Not really."

Pam laughed, "No, I'm thinking about something deeper. I promise you can tell me to stop anytime if it feels weird to you, or causes pain."

Chapter 34

April 26-27, 2002
Jersey City NJ, Newark NJ

Rick went outside to make sure the front door to the building was locked after Rocco and Gail left. He was pleased with how things had gone with them, engaging Sybil's interest in ways he hadn't seen since before the carjacking. Although Rocco hadn't helped her remember what she experienced at the train station, he and Gail had awakened fond memories of Sybil's Aunt Daphne and her namesake, Sybil AKA Alice. The mysteries surrounding those times seemed to stimulate his typically curious wife.

On his way up to the apartment, Rick ran into their neighbors, Carlos and Pablo, who called down from the top of the stairs. They asked if he could come up to their place for a few minutes. When he hesitated, Carlos said, "Just for a couple of minutes, we have some information for you."

This wasn't the first time the three men had spoken privately about the carjacking. While Rick avoided sharing details with Sybil, he had been quite active in his efforts to stay up to date with the police investigation into what had happened at the scene. He was particularly intent on learning who committed the crime, and what they had done with the car. Rick had not had much luck getting answers and was told that until they found the car, the police would be unable to take the investigation further. They said they were operating on the assumption that it had been a random car theft conducted as part of a gang initiation, not an uncommon crime in the area. The only difference this time was there was a person (Sybil) in the car when the thief approached it and the carjacker took the initiative to push her out of the car before taking off with it. The thinking was that perhaps the carjacker figured it would be best not to complicate the car theft with the more serious crime of kidnapping.

Rick had shared his frustration with Pablo and Carlos, who became further involved because they had a friend who worked for the Newark police department who was sometimes willing to provide them with insider information. It was their friend

Hannah who had told them the police theory about the gang initiation. She also explained that they had little expectation of ever recovering the car or information about the carjacker. The police believed these folks knew how to cover their tracks and the car had probably already been stripped of any identifiable parts.

When Carlos and Pablo shared this information with Rick, he began to understand why the police detective he spoke with kept encouraging him to just go ahead and make an insurance claim to get the money to replace the car. Although he was reluctant, Rick filed the claim and was almost immediately rewarded with a check to buy a new car, but he continued to bug the police about finding the old one. The new car was fine, and was probably in better condition than their old one, but it wasn't the car he was worried about. The thief had also taken off with Sybil's wallet, cell phone, and, most importantly, a backpack full of work-related notes and documents that could be problematic if they got into the wrong hands.

Closing the door behind him, Carlos said, "They found the car. It was abandoned and left in a mall parking lot in another county."

Rick's first reaction was annoyance that he had to hear this from a secondary source, but he decided to get over that immediately and began asking questions. "Do you know where it is? Can I see it? Did Hannah say if they found Sybil's stuff in the car?"

Carlos sighed, "From what I gather, the car was totally empty. I'm not sure they'll allow you to see it. You are no longer its owner and it's seen as crime evidence. I think Hannah said they towed it to a police garage somewhere."

"But, did they find any fingerprints that would identify the carjacker?"

"I don't know."

Rick scratched his chin. "Maybe I'll just go by the station tomorrow and casually ask if they've made any progress. They're sort of used to me by now. I promise I won't blow Hannah's cover."

"No, you can't do that, Rick, but going by and asking in general makes sense."

"Thanks guys. I'll let you know what they tell me tomorrow."

Rick returned to his apartment where he was greeted by a happy Sybil who told him about her conversation with her mother about meeting Rocco and Gail.

"I'll bet she was surprised. What did she say?"

"She was very surprised but she had fond memories of Gail, and a big crush on Rocco."

Rick laughed as he went into the kitchenette to clean up. He was happily surprised when Sybil got up from her chair and came up behind him to touch his arm tentatively. This was the first time she had initiated a touch since the carjacking almost three months ago.

Sybil continued talking, "Guess what Rick? I called Pam and she's coming over next week to give me a special massage."

"That's great news!"

"Well, I completely trust her to be careful around the parts that were injured. My physical therapist says I can begin to add massage to my treatment without harm and to be perfectly honest, I think of Pam as having magical knowledge. Remember how she knew exactly what I needed when she came over when I first got home? I honestly believe my face would be scarred if she hadn't used the lavender essential oil on the wounds."

The following day, Rick went to the police station and innocently asked if there was any new information about the carjacking. The police officer, Detective Costa, told him the car had been found stripped of everything, and was currently under the control of the municipality where it had been abandoned. They had identified it as Rick and Sybil's car because of its Vehicle Identification Number, but were in the midst of discussion about whose responsibility it was. As part of a criminal case that hadn't been officially closed, no further action could be taken until that decision was made. When Rick asked whether he could take a look at the car, he was told he couldn't. He was no longer its owner and, if he hadn't heard this before, it was evidence of a crime that had crossed city/ municipal limits.

In an attempt to ease Rick's frustration, the police detective explained how they were viewing what had occurred.

"From what we can gather, your wife was simply in the wrong place at the wrong time. It sounds like the carjacker was a drugged-up teenager, probably a prospective member of one of our local gangs, who was stealing a car to fulfill a gang initiation rite. Since your wife can't remember anything about him or her, we have nothing to go on, but it fits the profile of how gang initiations happen around here. After they succeeded in getting away with the car, they probably took it for a joy ride and dropped it off in the mall parking lot."

Rick was frustrated with what he was hearing. It confirmed his fear that the police had written this investigation off without going any further, but while he had the officer's attention, he decided to try something else.

"I gather the two jurisdictions are debating over whose case this is, but since the car is available for official inspection, I'm wondering if anyone checked it for fingerprints or DNA evidence."

Detective Costa scratched his head and responded sincerely,

"I honestly don't know, but I'll check into that for you. It might require getting your and your wife's prints. Were you the only people who drove the car?"

"Yes, and we will be happy to give you our prints, and even hair samples, if it helps to identify the carjacker."

The police detective smiled at Rick and said,

"That's a great idea Mr. Morgenstern. Let me look into it and get back to you."

"I'll come by again tomorrow." Lying a little, Rick added, "I drive by here on the way back and forth to work every day."

While they both knew nothing would change in such a short period of time, Detective Costa got the message. Rick was not about to let go.

Chapter 35

May 3, 2002
Jersey City NJ

Sybil was feeling upbeat when Pam came for the spa treatment. She was excited about the prospect of getting help to break through what she had begun thinking of as a trauma wall. The events of the past week, especially meeting Rocco and Gail, had motivated her to try to conquer her fears so she could move forward with her life.

Pam came equipped with her folded massage bed, as usual. In addition, she had to make a second trip up and down the stairs to bring in other things she was planning to use as part of the healing massage. To Sybil's surprise, these included avocados and other fruits, various herbs and spices, flat and round rocks, a large pot, a small flute and various sized Tibetan singing bowls and mallets.

Unlike other massage therapists Sybil had known, Pam didn't usually employ musical tapes, so she was fascinated anticipating how this would work. Sybil watched as Pam filled the pot with water and put it on the stove to heat and set about creating a paste from the avocado, a mango and various herbs and spices.

As she worked, Pam apologized to Sybil for the delay. "This process usually takes a long time. I hope you have a few hours. It's important for everything to be really fresh."

Sybil laughed, "I have no other plans. Is there anything I can do to help?"

"Nope, I have everything I need to start."

What followed was indescribable to Sybil, in the literal sense of the word. She had always enjoyed massage and considered it a major contribution to a healthy body. She had often wished the medical insurance business would understand how beneficial massage could be as part of any preventive medicine routine. She completely trusted Pam to know how to protect her injuries, so it didn't take long before she was able to relax and allow Pam to perform her magic.

When asked later what she experienced, Sybil could only say she felt as if she drifted in and out and around and through a variety of states of consciousness. Some of the time she felt the soothing massage touch, and was aware of how Pam was addressing many of her senses as she applied the paste she had concocted, more than one heated stone, and warm wet and dry cloths. At times Pam placed metal bowls on parts of her body and made music with them. She also made music with the flute-like instrument. These were the parts Sybil was aware of, but much of the time, she drifted, saw scenes and colors, and even had a dream or two.

After a couple of hours, Sybil began experiencing a focused head pain. It was just above her forehead on the right side. The back massage was feeling so good, she didn't want Pam to stop, but the head pain seemed to be intensifying to the point where Sybil could no longer ignore it. She decided to ask Pam to stop what she was doing.

Although no words passed between them, Pam seemed to sense a change in Sybil's demeanor and stepped away to change her methodology. Sybil remained silent, lying on her stomach, and fell asleep, or at least went into a dream-like state.

I'm standing in a courtyard talking to a friend. Aunt Daphne and Alice Lyons are walking towards me engaged in conversation I can't hear. I call out to them to ask where they've been; they respond, 'we've been to the funeral.' My first reaction is to feel guilty that I wasn't there, but I didn't know about it. They tell me not to worry, using the words "it wasn't yours." As I'm puzzling over the meaning of that statement, someone in the courtyard picks up a large mallet and hits a giant gong that's hanging behind me. I turn around to see who it is and see a teen-age boy with an eight-pointed star tattooed on the back of his hand. He's wearing a red baseball cap. I ask him what he's doing there. He walks towards me without speaking, then mumbles, 'Teddy sent me' as he walks by. It all happens so fast, I barely register what I saw and heard.

Just as the gong was struck in the dream, Pam was striking a metal bowl she had placed on Sybil's back. The sudden sounds woke Sybil out of her dream. At the same moment, she felt a rush of air fly out of her right ear and her head pain was completely gone. She didn't have to say anything to Pam. It was clear the spa treatment had its impact.

As Pam began to pack up her stuff, Sybil said, "Can you stick around for a little? I'm not quite ready to be alone. That was amazing. I feel like a two hundred pound weight was lifted from my bones."

"Of course I can stay for a few minutes. I didn't want to presume. Some people need time to themselves after a spa treatment. Let me clean this stuff up. While I'm up and about, can I make you some tea?"

"That would be perfect. I would love a cup of Sleepytime, and help yourself to any of the other choices in the basket on the counter."

"Thanks Sybil, I'll have some of that spearmint tea."

Continuing to make polite conversation because her brain was totally fried, Sybil went on to tell Pam that she didn't use sweetener in her tea, but sometimes to give herself a treat, would add a little half & half or milk.

Pam brought the two cups of tea, sat on the sofa across from Sybil and asked how she was doing.

"To be perfectly honest, I think it'll be a while before I'll be able to process what I just experienced, but there's no doubt that it worked to lighten my psychic load. I don't know what happens next, but this feels wonderful. Did I tell you about my dream and how the gong released the horrible pain in my head?"

"I never know the details of what's happening, but I could feel you were releasing a heavy burden."

Sybil proceeded to describe the part of her dream in which Daphne and Alice Lyons told her it was okay that she missed the funeral saying it wasn't hers. "When they said that, I had been feeling guilty that I didn't know about the funeral and was sure I should've been there. At first it didn't occur to me they could be saying it wasn't my funeral with the implication that I didn't die. That blows my mind, to think there are parts of my body that believe I died from my injuries, or was supposed to die. Do you think my mind and body have been in conflict over all of this? Do you think that could be the reason I froze and haven't let go?"

"That makes sense to me, but I suspect only time will tell. Do me a favor and drink a lot of water today. I think you released some toxins you may want to flush out of your system. I hate to massage and run, but it's pushing five and I have a dinner date at six. I'll need to make two or three trips down to my car, so I'd better get started. I'd love to give you a hug, but don't want to hurt your ribs. I'm glad you had a good experience."

"Thanks Pam. At the moment, I'm feeling oddly energized, but I'm also exhausted. Is that possible?"

"That's a pretty common reaction, but don't forget to drink a lot of water."

As Pam was carrying her last load downstairs, she ran into Rick, who was unlocking the front door.

"Hey Pam, how'd it go?"

"I think it was good. Sybil seems to have let go of some of the poisonous junk that was clogging up her system."

"That's awesome! I was just thinking you could call your service 'roto rooter for the soul.' Here, let me help you with that stuff."

Pam laughed, "Roto Rooter for the Soul; I love that! I wonder if they have a patent."

Rick turned serious. "I've got to tell you, I've been learning much too much about how slowly the wheels of the legal system turn these days. Just trying to get information about our stolen car has been super frustrating. I understand the police have a lot on their plates all the time and have to prioritize, but I'm not giving up, and I must admit, the police are getting tired of seeing my face."

"I'm glad you're persisting, Rick. Even if you annoy the hell out of them, they won't be able to ignore the case. As they say, the squeaky wheel…"

Waving goodbye to Pam, Rick walked back upstairs and stopped at Pablo and Carlos' apartment. Pablo had called to say he had more news from Hannah. It had been a week since their last conversation, when he learned about the car being found. Rick had gone to the police department at least once a day since then and heard the same story. The two jurisdictions were still deciding who owned this case and no-one had done a thorough inspection of the car since they found it stripped of everything that had belonged to Sybil.

Pablo had good news. "Hannah says they finally decided. Since the car was stolen in Newark, they won the lottery. The car is now in their official custody."

Relieved, Rick said, "That's great news. My persistence might have an effect on what happens next."

"Well, apparently it has already had an effect, Rick. They took a closer look and found something that might help to identify the carjacker."

"What did they find?"

"I don't know exactly what to call it, but it is a really small packet of some kind of powder, obviously a drug of some sort. It was tiny and stuck in the crevice beneath the driver's seat."

Rick sighed, "So I guess that would confirm the police theory that the carjacker was a gang member? I hope that doesn't keep them from digging deeper just because it confirms their theory that it was a random gang initiation."

"Maybe, but Hannah said the police are intrigued. It's not a commonly known drug like heroin or cocaine. It hasn't been tested yet, but they suspect it's a new designer drug. And, this could be big, it's a glassine bag stamped with an eight-pointed star."

"What does that mean, Pablo?"

"She said it could be one of two things: the star either identifies the drug itself or who it belongs to, who has ownership rights to this particular drug."

"Holy Crap! I never expected the theft of our car to lead to a drug bust. This could give the police more motivation to find out who did it. I think it's the best news I've heard in a long time." Rick laughed, "Now I have to continue pretending not to know anything. It'll be really interesting to see when they succumb to my bugging."

Carlos walked into the room. "Hi Rick, I guess you heard the news about the car. Isn't it great?"

"It is great news, I don't know how to thank you two, and Hannah, for your help."

Carlos looked at Pablo, then turned back to Rick. "So, I ran into Stacy the other day. She still believes this wasn't a random act, that it was somehow connected with Sybil's anti-discrimination work. I think she'd like to meet with us to talk about her theories."

Rick scratched his head, "I've been curious about her theory since she first brought it up to Sybil, but Sybil's been adamant about not dealing with the idea that someone was out to murder her, so I've let it go. I have to admit, I've never understood why the carjacker bothered to take her backpack. I get them taking her cell phone, and wallet with the driver's license and credit cards. But why would they bother with a backpack full of papers?"

"I've been curious about that too. Maybe we can meet Stacy for coffee or a beer, whatever works for everyone. I'd like to hear exactly why she thinks Sybil could have been the target."

"Can you arrange it, Carlos? I'm pretty open work-wise at the moment, so whatever works for the rest of you. Let's keep

Sybil out of it for the moment. I'm not sure she's emotionally ready to get into something like this. Actually, I need to get back to her now. She just had what was advertised as a pretty intense massage."

Pablo laughed, "That sounds awesome, but I'm surprised she would let anyone touch her with intensity. Now, I, on the other hand, could really use one of those."

"I'm sure Pam would be happy to accommodate you, Pablo, but I think this was specifically designed for Sybil's current needs. I ran into Pam on my way up, and she seems to think it was a success. I guess I'll be hearing Sybil's opinion shortly."

Chapter 36

May 3- May 4, 2002
Jersey City NJ

Rick walked into the apartment and found Sybil sipping a cup of tea with Billy settled comfortably on her lap. Walking towards her, he said, "I ran into Pam outside. She said it went well."

"It was amazing. I'm feeling more relaxed, mellower, and at the same time, more energized than I have since this all started."

"Tell me about it."

Sybil described what she could of the techniques Pam used, but was mostly only able to tell Rick how she experienced it. "I drifted in and out. I had no sense of time or space, but what was extraordinary was that it didn't hurt, even my ribs."

"You must have been super relaxed."

"I was, and as I said, I drifted in and out of a dream-like place. Maybe I even slept some of the time, but in the end, I had a pretty dramatic moment that changed how I had been feeling. It was like a huge release, and I even experienced it as a rush of air that flew out of my ear. It started with a headache that, in retrospect, I realize was exactly at the site of my concussion. It was becoming unbearable and I was planning to ask Pam to stop. Then I seemed to have gone into a shallow sleep state and had a dream."

Rick was amazed. He had never believed the way Sybil did about alternative approaches to health care, but kept his skepticism to himself. "What happened in the dream?"

Sybil told him about the courtyard and the conversation with Daphne and Alice.

Then she added, "I came out of the dream and woke up to the sound of a gong. Well, it was a gong in the dream, but, as it turns out, Pam was making sounds with a mallet on a singing bowl she had laid on my back. I think the real and dream sounds came together. Miraculously, that was the moment the pain left my head and flew out of my ear. Rick, that was real, and with it, my whole body relaxed for the first time."

"This is making me really happy, Sybil! It's almost like you can begin to heal the psychic wounds along with your body now."

"That's what I'm hoping, Rick. I want to tell you something else about my dream. I didn't mention this to Pam because I'm still trying to figure out what it means."

"I'm all ears."

"In the dream, the person who hit the giant gong with the huge mallet was a teenage boy. He was wearing a red baseball cap and had a distinctive tattoo shaped like an eight-pointed star on his hand. In the dream, I turned around to ask him what he was doing and he ignored me. He started walking towards, then past me, and mumbled something I barely heard."

"What did he say?"

"Teddy sent me."

"Holy shit!"

A few minutes passed before Rick could speak again, then he looked straight at Sybil and said, "I have something to tell you. I haven't told you any of this before because I was just going on instinct and honestly didn't know if my efforts would come to anything. Putting what you just told me with what I've learned makes me believe we may be able to figure out who did this to you."

"What?!"

Rick caught Sybil up on his efforts to stay informed by the police and the role played by Carlos and Pablo's friend Hannah. He told her the car had been found at a mall parking lot in another township and there had been the conflict over who was responsible. But he had just heard from Pablo about their finding the unidentified powdered drug in a glassine envelope stamped with an eight-point star in the car.

"Did they recover any of my stuff?"

"No, the car had apparently been cleaned out, but the tiny envelope was found stuck in a crevice under the driver's seat."

"Does this verify the police theory that this was a gang initiation carjacking? Wait a minute, that eight-pointed star . . . that tattoo on the teenager's hand! I wonder if the spa treatment unlocked a real memory and I saw what this kid looked like AND actually heard him say it was Teddy's doing."

"Do you think you would recognize the kid's face?"

"I don't know, it happened really fast in the dream. You know, Rick, I think it would be hard to convince the police that what I experienced in a dream could be considered evidence."

"Carlos, Pablo and I are meeting with Stacy tomorrow to talk about what we've learned. I know you were reluctant to go down that road with her when she suggested there was a connection between the carjacking and your work, but I believe it's worth exploring. "

Sybil smiled at Rick, "You betcha! I want to be at that meeting."

Rick picked up the phone. "Carlos? It's a whole new ballgame. Can you and Pablo invite Stacy to come over to our place tomorrow at seven? Yes, Sybil will be here. Yes, we have some interesting news to share."

The following evening, Stacy arrived with Pablo and Carlos at seven on the dot. Rick began by catching everyone up to date with their efforts to find out what had happened, ending with the revelations from Sybil's dream. While Carlos and Pablo knew most of it, Stacy was essentially hearing Rick's story for the first time.

Pablo was stunned by the coincidence of the eight-pointed star. "This has to mean something! You must have actually seen that!"

Stacy asked, "Did you say none of the work materials you had with you were recovered in the car?"

"They apparently took everything. The documents were in my backpack, and I also had a cellphone and handbag that basically just had my wallet with a little bit of cash, my driver's license and credit cards. None of that stuff has shown up."

"Can I repeat my original questions now?

"Yes, Stacy, I think I can handle them better now."

"Let me start back at the meeting. How many people were there? Who were they?"

"I think there were around five people in the meeting. I was the only one from Sussex, but Angela had some people with her."

"Angela's the person who was heading the project out of Newark?"

"Angela Park, I think she was in charge. At least she did most of the talking. She had a couple of colleagues who were taking notes. I'm sorry, I don't recall any of their names. I think Angela and I did most of the talking."

"If I recall, the meeting was about the racial discrimination policies of the Farrow group, especially as they applied to Muslims, right?"

"Yes, we had heard they were doing similar things in and around Newark as in Jersey City and that the Jaffe Anti-Racist

Society was getting close to taking them to court. We reached out to see if we could work together to develop a stronger case by sharing data."

"How did you connect with them, Sybil? Had you met Angela Park previously?"

"I met her at a conference a while back, but only to say hello. This was the first face-to-face where we actually talked about things."

"You said she walked with you to your car."

"Yes. Wait a minute, are you thinking Angela had something to do with the carjacking?! That's really hard for me to believe. I mean, why would she do that? No, I don't buy it."

Stacy continued, "I understand how improbable it may seem, and I'm not accusing Angela of anything. Just trying to get a handle on what was happening that day. So, you got into your car and drove up Washington Street, heading back to Jersey City. Then, just before the Newark train station, you got a call on your cell, right?"

Sybil nodded.

"You pulled over near the entrance to the station parking lot to answer the call?"

"Yes, I don't talk on the cell when I'm driving."

"Did you see the number on the phone?"

"I may have glanced at it. I have a vague memory of not recognizing it but wasn't sure because it all happened very fast. My brain didn't have time to register that detail."

"And you have no memory of anything after that?"

"Just waking up and seeing Rocco."

Rick addressed Stacy, "What do you think? Are we onto something here?"

"I think we have a lot of what they call circumstantial evidence that points to the carjacking being a deliberate, pre-planned act rather than a random gang initiation. I also think we're hanging it together with loose threads that probably won't fly as is, but I absolutely believe we should, must, keep at it until we have enough to go to the authorities."

Looking at Sybil, Stacy continued, "The fact that you were endangered and injured is enough for me to keep at it, but this is also a threat to us as a business and our commitment to advocacy for helpless people. We can't let anyone intimidate us. We can't let it go."

Rick asked, "What do you see as our next steps, Stacy? I know I'll continue to bug the police regarding the car and hope they become willing to share what they're coming up with."

Carlos added, "I'm sure Hannah will keep us informed."

Rick continued, "I don't know when we go to the police with Sybil's dream. I have a feeling they would have trouble seeing that as legitimate evidence, but it so clearly is, especially in conjunction with the eight-pointed star on the glassine envelope being the same as the tattoo. We can't even tell them we know about the drugs they found in the car and they'll probably see that as evidence of gang activity anyway. What do you think, Sybil?"

"Did I hear that Hannah said the police thought it was a new designer drug? Wouldn't that be of interest? You know, I think we have a lot of important information to share with the police and am wondering if we should consider bringing an attorney into our group. Someone we trust, of course. They often think about things differently than the rest of us and have legitimate access to official information. I think we should reach out to Rocco."

Chapter 37

May 4-5, 2002
Newark NJ

Rocco was pleasantly surprised to hear from Sybil and Rick so soon after their visit. He liked them. Unlike other twenty-somethings he'd run across, they seemed to be focused on serious things. *When did I become the older generation? How quickly that happens.* However, this time, instead of offering another opportunity to reminisce about his misbegotten youth, they were asking for his professional help. The more they told him about what had been learned, albeit, some through rather strange communications, the more interested he became in helping them. Keeping his lawyer hat firmly planted on his head, he told them he would think about it because he was up to his ears with his usual workload and efforts to help Gail sort out her legal issues in New Mexico. In his heart he knew he would end up getting involved. This was close to home. If he could get anything on that slippery asshole Teddy Farrow, it was worth going into overtime. He got off the phone thinking, once again, how small this world is and how ironic that he was almost present at the scene of that crime.

Rocco wasn't exaggerating when he said he was up to his ears. Frustrated by the lack of response to his inquiries in Albuquerque, he had decided he would need to have a face-to-face with Mike's family lawyers. This should have been a straightforward process as the will was clearly written. On the other hand, with conflicting relationships, it was never simple. For a variety of reasons, he wasn't sure he should invite Gail to join him on his planned odyssey. To begin, her hostile relationship with the Mike's family would likely color any chance of amicable interaction. In addition, he had to admit there was a mutual attraction between them that could complicate their business arrangement.

Rocco was well aware that mixing business with pleasure was almost always a mistake. He also worried about the authenticity of what seemed to be Gail's attraction towards him. A lot of the time, he attributed her interest to having recently lost her husband, a state that often drove people to feel needy. He didn't want to feed his ego on this subject, but also knew he had mastered the art of closeness aversion. It was almost kneejerk for him to put up a protective wall at the first sign of emotional involvement. All of this complicated his planning, but he also knew he had to decide. The request he had just received from Rick and Sybil, along with the new information they shared about the carjacking, propelled him. He picked up the phone and called Gail.

"Hey Gail, I've decided to fly out to Albuquerque to have a face-to-face with the lawyers."

Gail was happy to hear Rocco's voice, as well as his news. Something had to give in this standoff. "I agree I need to move forward. I'm glad to hear you have the time now."

Rocco laughed, "I'm not sure I have the time, but it doesn't seem that long-distance communication is getting me anywhere. I'm also considering picking up another outside job to help Sybil and Rick find out what was behind the carjacking."

"Have they found the car?"

"The police found the car, but they still don't know who did it. That's what they're asking me to help with. Anyway, I want to focus on resolving your inheritance issues first. I'll tell you all about what's going on with them another time. Can we meet soon? I'd like to pick your brain one more time before I head west, just to see if there's anything we've missed."

"Sure, I'm free tomorrow. Do you want me to come to Newark?"

"That would be great, Gail. Can you come to my office late tomorrow afternoon, like around four or five? Maybe we can grab a bite to eat around here."

"That works for me. See you at your office."

Traveling by train during rush hour turned out to be crazy and Gail didn't arrive at Rocco's office until after six, so they went straight to a local Greek restaurant they could walk to. As they settled themselves in a comfortable booth, Rocco called out to the approaching waiter, "Two glasses of Chianti please."

Gail laughed, "You read my mind. My feet are killing me and I'm sure Chianti will be the best cure." Then turning serious, she said, "Having lived around the wide open spaces of the Southwest for so long, I'm never prepared for how exhausting being in crowds can be."

"Interesting, I guess I've never thought about it, navigating crowds is a daily reality around here. It's been pretty much the same throughout my life, except some of the time I was traveling around South America way back when."

"You've never told me much about those days, Rocco. Was that where you went after the summer of '73?"

Rocco got a faraway look in his eyes, as if he was visiting another place in another time. Then he sighed, "Yes, that was quite a year."

"Where did you go?"

"Can we do this another time? It's a long story and we need to focus on next steps. I'm thinking of calling the lawyers to set up a meeting sometime next week and need to make sure I'm as prepared as possible. So, if you don't mind, I want to ask you some questions. Forgive me if I've asked them before."

Gail was disappointed, but quickly realized this was the reason for their dinner. It was not a social occasion.

"Sure Rocco, ask away."

"When Mike was sick, did he talk with you about his will, his wishes, anything specific?"

"Yes, he told me exactly what I've told you. He said he was leaving everything to me and that was clearly spelled out in the will. He felt the only other claim, besides Brian of course, could come from his daughter Cindy. He seemed confident that the will, which he prepared with the help of his family lawyers, by the way, spelled out his wishes clearly. Even though he and Cindy hadn't had a relationship for years, he wasn't shutting her out to be mean. He knew she was well off in her own right through her mother's family and he was more concerned about me and Brian."

"Do you know if he spoke with anyone besides you about his wishes?"

"I don't know. No-one has come forward to tell me, if that's the case."

Gail took a sip of her wine, and gazed sadly at the table before finishing her thought. "He didn't have friends or supportive family in Albuquerque; at least when we were together. It was very sad. He seemed to stick with his job because it was what he was doing and that kept him in Albuquerque. I honestly think he believed they would all come around to accepting me and Brian." Her eyes filled with tears. "I also believe he hoped someday to be reunited with his daughter. I hate thinking it was my fault."

Rocco took Gail's hand, "Families can be such shit and unfortunately, really stupid things can make them feel justified in hurting one another. I'm glad you and Mike had a happy life despite that noise."

Rocco called the waiter over for a Chianti refill. As he was pouring the wine the waiter asked if they were ready to order. Gail and Rocco said yes at exactly the same time. It was a good moment to take a break and look at the menu.

"I think I'm going to go with the appetizer plate. I love baba ganoush and hummus. What about you, Rocco?"

"That sounds good to me too. And they have great homemade pita bread. Let's get an extra order."

Gail nodded as the waiter walked away. "You know, if Mike shared with anyone, it would have been Joey."

"Didn't you say you didn't have contact with him? Do you have any idea where he lives?"

"Not really. I never saw him in Albuquerque. He and Mike had obviously drifted apart by the time we got together. I think Joey disliked Mike's first wife and the lifestyle he had chosen. But Mike always spoke well of him and, more than once, told me he would trust him with his life. I'm sure that if he confided in anyone it would have been Joey."

Gail took another sip and said, "Well maybe I can find out where he lives. His mother Dora had a travel agency in Albuquerque. Maybe I can reach her."

Rocco smiled. "This feels like a longshot, but if she's still around, can't hurt to try. Even if she's retired, we can probably locate her through the people who still work there."

Having made some decisions about their next steps, Rocco and Gail settled into their dinner and talked comfortably about old times and how Gail had been spending her free time in the City. She told him she had been exploring the Upper East Side of Manhattan, visiting museums, and going to Broadway and off-Broadway shows. She had even taken a few dance classes for the first time in many years. Despite the uncertainty regarding what she had left behind in Albuquerque, Gail was enjoying herself. She had come to agree with what everyone said about how much fun New York could be for people with money.

They also went through a third glass of Chianti, which they finished in time for dessert and espresso. Both Gail and

Rocco recognized that their collective mellow feelings were at least in part, alcohol fueled. Without speaking about it, they separately remembered their last such encounter and were both determined not to end up in bed, but Gail finally felt comfortable asking Rocco if she could travel to Albuquerque with him.

"I need to see Brian and think I would have an easier time than you connecting with Joey's mother since we once knew each other. It was only once and a long time ago, but she might remember me as Alice's friend. She and Alice clearly connected. Did I tell you Alice gave Sybil a kachina doll when she was a child?"

"What's a kachina doll?"

"Kachina dolls are carved Hopi Indian figures that represent ancestral spirits. They're traditionally used as part of a ceremony for a girl's transition to womanhood, but I think the spirits they represent have even larger significance in Hopi culture. The dolls are popular among tourists and can be extremely expensive. Alice was fascinated with them and Joey's mother had some originals. She's part Hopi. I think they were handed down to her by her grandmother."

"And she gave one to Alice, who gave it to the young Sybil? That's pretty amazing. It makes me wonder about how close these relationships must have been. If she got one from Joey's mother, I mean."

Gail scratched her head. "I know Joey's mom didn't give Alice a kachina when we met her that summer. We were traveling together and I would have known. But I wouldn't be at all surprised to hear Alice stayed in touch with her, or at least with Joey. They really seemed to click but Joey was still in school in California. I believe he had a few years to go, having taken time after high school to serve in the Vietnam War. Getting back to my original question, I know I can help find Dora and I should probably stay away from the family's lawyers for the moment, but I would really like to go to Albuquerque with you. I haven't seen Brian since I came back east either, and would like to visit him. He's in school in Colorado, a hop skip and a jump, at least compared with here. I should probably go to my house too. It's been sitting empty for the past few months."

Rocco nodded, "Why not? Let's do it. I'll make travel arrangements as soon as I set up an appointment with the lawyers. Hopefully we can do this next week. Can you make it then?"

"Absolutely, just give me a day or two's notice." Gail stood up and said, "Now I have to get myself to the Newark Train Station and get back to my lovely little bed."

"I can give you a ride to the station, it's on my way home."

"Thanks, and thanks for the great dinner."

Chapter 38

May 8-9, 2002
Albuquerque NM

The planning and flight to Albuquerque went smoothly. Mike's family lawyers responded quickly to Rocco's request for a face-to-face meeting. Rocco began wondering if their previous avoidance was simply due to the fact that he was on the other side of the country. Face-to-face interactions always made things more real.

Anticipation of resolving this issue, along with their recently acquired personal comfort with each other enabled Rocco and Gail to relax and enjoy the flight while Gail told Rocco about her adventures in the Southwest with Alice all those years ago. Rocco had never been west of the Mississippi and Gail had plans to show him around once their business was accomplished.

As they flew into Albuquerque, Rocco was amazed at how a city of that size could be surrounded by so much sand.

"It's a different world out here, Rocco. I lived in Albuquerque for fifteen years and never got bored because I learned about new things all the time. The southwest has a really rich history and prehistory as well as a notable blending of cultures."

"Who's been here besides cowboys and Indians?"

"Ha Ha...to begin, a lot of different Native American cultures with different histories both here and other places they lived. There's also a large Mexican population. Are you aware that Albuquerque is the home of a really good state university and an awesome annual balloon festival? People come from miles around to experience that."

"I'm glad to have you to show me around, but, if it's okay with you, I think I'll take the first meeting with the lawyers by myself."

"Do you expect it to take more than one meeting?"

"Probably, this is a large estate and you may have to be part of the process. Meanwhile, you can be searching out Joey's mother."

Arriving in Albuquerque, Gail and Rocco went their separate ways. Gail went to her house on the edge of the city and Rocco checked into a centrally located hotel. They made plans to meet at the hotel for breakfast the following morning.

Gail had thought about inviting Rocco to stay at her house, but decided to avoid doing anything that could make either of them uncomfortable, even for a minute. Besides, no-one had lived there for a few months and she figured it would need some airing out. She was also unsure how she would react to being there without Mike.

As it turned out, she was okay at the house. Her time in New York had given her whole system time to heal and get back into some sort of balance. She was happy to be surrounded with her "things," the stuff that appealed to her sense of smell and general sensibilities: the comfortable chairs and sofa that had been imprinted by her family's unique bodies, the paintings on the walls that could absorb her forever, her gardens, her kitchen, and, most of all, her bed. After Mike died, she couldn't sleep there so she had moved into an extra bedroom with a single bed. That was probably one of the reasons she had wanted to escape when she did. There was no place in the house she had been comfortable sleeping. In the wake of Mike's death, she had Brian to care for and caring for him was the only thing that kept her sane. She left for New York shortly after taking him back to his boarding school. This was her first time in the house since then, and so far, it was okay.

Gail changed the sheets on her and Mike's bed and slept like a baby. As usual, the flight had exhausted her and she was feeling positive about resolving her legal issues. Although she was enjoying being in the home she and Mike had created together, Gail realized she would be okay with selling it and moving away from Albuquerque when it was time. She was ready to move on.

The following morning, Gail and Rocco had breakfast together and optimistically went their separate ways once again.

Driving her own car helped, and Gail found it easy to identify Dora's travel agency. She hadn't remembered the name of the agency, but a little bit of research enabled her to put the pieces together. Joey and Dora's last name was Knox, which was also the name of the travel agency, the Knox Travel Agency. She decided to walk in rather than call ahead. Her years of dealing with what seemed like deeply rooted mistrust between Mike's family and some people in the community led her to be cautious. Although she was pretty sure there was no particular animosity between Dora Knox and the Lucas family, she decided to take it slow and read Dora's reaction before asking to be put in touch with Joey.

When she walked into the office, it was like "deja vous all over again." Gail had only been there once in her life, twenty-nine years previously, but the feeling of the place was exactly the same. She immediately felt she would get the help she needed, whatever that might be, and began to wonder why she and Mike had never visited with Joey's mother when they lived in the same city. Mike always spoke fondly of Joey but as far as she knew, had not actually seen him during that period. As she reminisced about the magical few days she and Alice spent in Albuquerque in what seemed like a really innocent time, she wondered what she didn't know.

Approaching a middle-aged woman who was sitting behind a computer screen at a desk piled with papers, Gail asked, "Is Dora Knox available?"

The woman looked up and smiled at Gail, "I think she's out back. Who should I say is asking?"

"I'm not sure she would recognize my name, I'm Gail Lucas. I used to know her son Joey and am hoping to find him."

The woman reached out her hand. "Hello Gail, I'm Joey's sister Evie. Weren't you here with Alice back in the early Seventies?"

Gail smiled, "That was me."

Before she could ask the next question, Evie left the room, calling out, "Let me run out to grab my mother. I think she's doing something in the back garden."

Evie walked down a long hallway and opened a door to the outside. A few minutes later, the mother and daughter entered the room. Gail couldn't help noticing how much they resembled one another, both petite with thick dark brown hair.

Dora approached Gail with a polite smile and curiosity in her eyes.

Gail began, "I'm sure you don't remember me. We only met one time some twenty-nine years ago."

Dora responded politely, "I do remember you and later knew of your marriage to Mike Lucas. I'm so sorry to hear of his death. He was a good friend to my son Joey when they were young."

"Thank you. It has been a terrible shock. It was unexpected."

"How can I help you Gail?"

"I know this is going to sound strange after all these years, but I'm hoping to connect with Joey."

Dora began to withdraw. Joey was a private person who had made it clear to his mother that she was not to share his whereabouts with anyone. Sensing Dora's withdrawal, Gail decided to go all out and explain how it appeared that Mike's family was going to fight his will in which he left everything to her and their son Brian.

"You and Mike have a son? I'm sorry I haven't kept up with your family. How is he, Brian, doing? I remember how hard it was for Joey to lose his father at such a young age."

"Brian's in a very supportive boarding school in Colorado right now. I've been trying to protect him from the fight over his inheritance." Tears came into Gail's eyes, "I don't want him to know his grandparents have turned away from him. I always knew they found me unacceptable, but he's their blood!"

Reacting to Gail's distress, Dora offered her a cup of tea. As they walked back through the hallway, Gail noticed a glass-enclosed cabinet with knick-knacks including a miniature kachina doll. She stopped and asked about it.

"I remember my friend Alice was fascinated by kachina dolls when we were here. If I recall, you invited her to see some of your family's collection."

Dora smiled, "Yes, they are at my home. This is a more recent creation someone gave me. They are very popular with tourists."

When they sat down, Gail told Dora about her and Rocco's encounter with Sybil who was apparently named for her old friend and how Alice had given her a kachina doll when she was a child.

Dora was moved by the carjacking story and amazed at the coincidence of Gail and Rocco being at the scene. She was even more stunned by the fact that Alice had given the crime victim a kachina doll. She found herself opening a door she wasn't sure was hers to open but couldn't help herself.

"They must have been very close. A gift of a kachina doll is precious."

Gail went on to tell Dora about Daphne and how Alice had helped and cared for her and her family.

Dora looked at Gail curiously, "You must be proud of your friend Alice."

"I always was, I always admired her, but I only heard about this recently from young Sybil. As for Alice, I haven't had any contact with her since that summer. I can't explain it, but we just went our separate ways. Life took over."

Dora was taking all of this information in and made a decision. She would share it with Joey and let him decide whether to reconnect with Gail.

Finishing her cup of tea, Dora stood up. "I'm going to have to get back to my work. Thank you for sharing your stories with me, Gail. I'll inform Joey you would like to be in touch with him, but I can't tell you where he is or what he's doing as he has made me promise to respect his privacy. As soon as I have his response, I will share it with you. What's the best way to reach you?"

Gail wrote down her cellphone number and added that she would probably be around for a while, depending on how long the legal process required her to be in Albuquerque. Reaching out to shake Dora's hand, Gail thanked her and hoped for the best.

Chapter 39

May 9, 2002
Albuquerque NM

Gail and Rocco met at the hotel and shared their news. Rocco came away from his meeting with the lawyers with the feeling they were planning to pursue Mike's daughter's claim to his estate. "They believe the will, as written, doesn't preclude going forward with her claim. I'm not discouraged, but I will need to find a local law library and study the nuances of New Mexico's inheritance laws. I'm sure there has to be a way to honor Mike's intentions. I'm in no way ready to give up."

"Somehow, I'm not surprised, Rocco, but I have complete faith that you'll find a way. I'm also convinced Dora will reach out to Joey to tell him what's going on with Mike's estate. Of course we don't know if he can help my cause, but it may be something. Joey's mother is really nice, and I remember him being a good guy too."

Rocco smiled at Gail, "I think we both accomplished something today and have a plan for tomorrow. How do you want celebrate? Would you like to go out on the town after dinner? What do people do for fun around here?"

"I would love that. I've been thinking about how to celebrate tonight and I know the perfect place to go for dinner."

Rocco didn't know what he had expected, but was both surprised and amused as they pulled into the parking lot of a rustic looking cottage on the outskirts of the city with a large sign advertising **Sarah and David's Mac and Cheese Emporium.**

Smiling at the puzzled expression on Rocco's face, Gail said, "This is my favorite place to eat in Albuquerque and it's run by two of my favorite people in the world. You'll be amazed at the variety of delicious macaroni and cheese options they offer, and their coleslaw is to die for."

As they walked into the restaurant, Sarah and David greeted Gail warmly. She was obviously a regular customer. The ambience was homey and casual and Rocco was pleased to notice there was a small stage set up for musical performances. Gail told him David and Sarah were professional musicians as well as gourmet cooks.

Lynn Gregory

Their small restaurant doubled as a prestigious performance venue known for supporting up and coming musicians.

Although quite busy, Sarah and David made a point of visiting their table to welcome Rocco. When Gail told them about Rocco's musical talent, everyone urged him to get up on the stage to play the instrument of his choice. Relaxed and comfortable, he chose an acoustic guitar and brought the house down with a creative rendition of *Classical Gas*. David and one of their customers joined in with banjos. This launched a variety of spontaneous performances including instrumentals, singing and dancing as Rocco impressed everyone with his creative musical talent. It had been a while since Rocco had last performed in public and he really enjoyed himself, as did Gail, who also joined in with the dancing.

Although Sarah and David would have liked Rocco to spend the evening on their stage, Gail was determined to move on to show him an historic part of the city before the night was over.

As they were leaving, Sarah took Rocco aside and said, "I hope you'll visit us again before you go back east. I haven't seen Gail this happy for years. I can tell you agree with me that she's a very special person who's had it rough recently. She may not have told you, but she helped us fund this business and all she asked in exchange was a place to offer free dance lessons to children in the community. I don't know what I would have done without her in my life these past ten years, she deserves the best."

Rocco nodded and said, "I agree Sarah, and I also think she's lucky to have friends like you and David. Thank you, I had a great time this evening and promise to come back before I head back to New Jersey. By the way, your mac and cheese is the best I've ever tasted!"

Their next stop was a completely different part of the city that looked and felt like a stereotypical old western town. Rocco loved it, "This is awesome Gail. It reminds me of my favorite childhood cowboy shows on television. I almost expect to see someone emerge from a saloon drawing pistols with both hands. What's it called?"

Gail laughed, "Hard to forget, it's called Old Town Albuquerque."

"I really like it, do you mind walking around?"

"Not at all, I've always found the old west aspects of Albuquerque to be charming. And I love the variety of musical sounds. Have you heard of Al Hurricane?"

"Sure, isn't he the guy who brought ranchero, rock and country music together? I think they call him the Godfather of New Mexican Music. Is this where he performs?"

"Sometimes, he's definitely a legend in these parts."

It was a comfortable spring evening and Gail was happy to revisit the historic neighborhood with a new set of eyes. Rocco was fascinated by everything he saw and was particularly charmed by the central plaza that was surrounded by ten blocks of one- and two-story buildings where you could actually see the sky. Everything was open and they were able to stop and listen to live music coming from various themed bars and restaurants.

After walking for a while, they stopped at a bench to take a break and Rocco began to talk. Gail had never heard him open up this way. She had often marveled at how little he ever revealed about his life and his inner feelings. She had assumed that part of his reticence was the natural learned reaction to dealing with the racial politics people of color in this country had to negotiate.

"The Pueblo music takes me back to my travels around South America. It reminds me of some native tunes I heard in the Brazilian jungles, in the Amazon."

Gail wanted him to continue and thought carefully about her next comment. She was thrilled he had opened the door and didn't want him to close it as he had in the past.

"Did they have the same kinds of instruments, guitars, drums, flute? I can't imagine they were connected as tribes. Is that possible?"

"Yes, flute-like and drum-like; the sounds are the same and different. I've always been amazed when I hear people from different parts of the world play the same instruments. They produce sounds I've never heard before."

"Like what?"

"Well, I once met a guy in New York who had just come over from West Africa, I think Cameroon. He came in to hear our jazz combo and afterwards asked if he could play my guitar. He started playing it and everyone in the room stopped and looked to see what instrument was making that sound. It didn't sound like a guitar, it didn't sound like any instrument we had heard before, but it was my little Alvarez guitar. I have often wondered if the ways people use their vocal apparatus when they learn to speak affects the sounds they make with instruments. You know, like trills and clicks that are totally natural to Spanish and African languages and almost impossible for English-speaking adults to master."

"Did you get to play for them when you were in the jungle? What did they think of your music?"

"Of course, and I think they found it intriguing. They always seemed interested in everything about me."

"Like what?"

Rocco laughed out loud, "Well, for one thing, they thought I was a giant. I'm tall in my own culture, but next to them I was huge. I think the average guy was maybe five feet tall."

"And you're, what, six four?"

"Somewhere around that, I haven't been measured in a really long time."

Rocco looked at the ground with a thoughtful expression on his face. Then he turned to Gail and said, "I may have missed out on a lot when I was there. I was heavy into hallucinogens at the time. In fact, the reason I ended up visiting the Yanomamo people in the Amazon was because I had read about their plants. An anthropologist, Napoleon Chagnon, wrote a book about them, and there was also a film."

Gail wasn't completely surprised. A lot of people she knew back in the late 1960s and early 1970s experimented with all sorts of drugs and Rocco was also part of a music culture that was notorious for drug use. She always figured drug use was a consequence of the self-imposed pressures a lot of artists experienced. *Could this be why Rocco had been so reticent to speak freely about his time traveling around South America on his motorcycle? Was there more to his story than it being his last gasp of freedom before settling down to adulting?*

"I saw the Chagnon film when I was in college. I think it was required viewing for our generation, but not many of us got to live it! How long did you stay with the Yanomamo?"

"I don't know, not long. I had always wanted to make it to Tierra del Fuego, at the tip of the continent. I wanted to see what it was like where the Yaghan people lived. I had read they traditionally spent most of their time naked and covered their bodies with bear grease to dive in the water to catch fish with their hands."

Rocco paused to see how Gail was reacting; seeing she wasn't bored, he continued.

"They actually had lived that way, right on the Straits of Magellan where it's freezing cold, until they ran into Europeans who decided they needed to be civilized, which basically meant putting on clothes and becoming Christians. Darwin wrote about meeting them and I think his Beagle gang took some Yaghan people back to England to be exhibited as savages."

Gail sighed. "I can't understand the need to make everyone in the world exactly the same. It's never worked in any case."

Rocco agreed, "It was not benign. Even though the missionaries thought they were saving souls, and I assume they really believed that, a lot of Yaghan were killed off by European diseases like smallpox. They had no immunities. That's what happened in North America too."

"Did you get there, Rocco? Did you meet any Yaghan people?"

"I did get there, and was in awe. It's really cold down there. There are still some people who identify as Yaghan, but not many, and the language is on the verge of dying out. I think there are only one or two native speakers left. I didn't get to meet them. It's hard to tell who's who down there."

Rocco became very quiet, as if lost in deep thought. Then he began to talk again.

"That wasn't my only encounter with South American Indian cultures, or drugs when I was there."

Rocco went silent again and Gail began to wonder whether she should change the subject. Instead she sat quietly, waiting to see if he would continue, or change the subject himself. This topic belonged to him, and although she wanted to know, she also knew he needed to be in control. When she finally looked at him, what she mostly saw was shame, an expression she had never ever seen on his face before.

Gail took Rocco's hand gently. "Are you okay? I don't want you to feel uncomfortable. Whatever you want to share with me, or not share, is fine. I will never violate your privacy and I will never judge you."

Looking closely at her kind expression, Rocco knew Gail was speaking truth and that he could trust her. He had never spoken about his time in South America to anyone. Twenty-eight years had passed, perhaps it was the right time and place to let go of some of those demons.

Chapter 40

May 9, 2002
Albuquerque NM

"I'm okay Gail. It's just that I've never opened up about that part of my life before. It's probably time to do it." A look of pain crossed Rocco's face again, but he continued, "I guess I'm still ashamed, even after all these years. I know I was a kid, but I did things that showed how little judgement and self-control I had."

Gail thought about the afternoon that led to the sad end to their idyllic summer of '73 and the end of her friendship with Alice; the afternoon when she and Rocco ended up in bed. It brought back her own feelings of regret for her lack of judgement and self-control, but she had forgiven herself because she had to move on with her life.

"Rocco, I think we all did things…"

Rocco interrupted, "Let me finish before you accept my stupidity."

As he was speaking, Rocco was realizing he wanted Gail to hear the whole story before gaining her acceptance. He was surprised at how much it mattered to him.

"I'm going to start at the very beginning and the first thing I want you to hear out of my mouth is that I have never regretted our last afternoon together in New York." Seeing that Gail was about to say something, Rocco interrupted again, not giving her a chance to step in. "Let me try to explain to you what was going on with me and how it all came down."

Gail sat back and pulled her jacket closer.

Rocco asked if she was cold and whether she would like to go somewhere indoors before he continued. "This might take a little while."

"No, I'm fine. Please go on."

"I think we were all at a major moment in our lives that summer, finishing college, making decisions about where we wanted to end up, what we wanted to do, and, at least for me, who we wanted to be. I grew up in a privileged environment. My parents were successful professionals and I got to go to good schools and be with mainstream white people who generally seemed to accept me. Of course, that was always unclear to me, the 'who I was' part, because I wasn't those white people and I wasn't my parents as far as I could figure. Although I appreciated them, and was proud of their accomplishments, I didn't share a lot of their values. I didn't want to live like they did and the more I was out in the real world, at least some gently scrubbed version of the real world, I came to feel like I didn't belong anywhere."

"That summer was wonderful because of the music and the creativity you and Alice added to nurturing that part of me. I dreamt of being a professional musician, but deep down knew it wasn't going to happen even though that summer allowed me to pretend. I just don't have the right personality to spend my life as an artist, but that summer was a great fantasy. To live a life of happenings in which I could just bump into a tree and have a conversation about, I don't know, what it was like to be a tree, no, what it was like to be that particular weeping willow tree. That had never been allowed before, it wasn't real and it was never going to be allowed again. Whoever I became, that freedom wasn't part of it and I knew it. I know I'm dwelling on this too much, but in a way, this is my first attempt at trying to describe what I was about that summer."

"Running into Alice, and meeting you, was the icing on the cake. You were in the same head space as me, even though it was clearly coming from three different directions, but the similarity, the spirit of it, was the same. I felt like we really understood each other on that plane. Then it changed. I'll never totally get my head around it, but it was probably a juncture for all of us. You had to go back to Jamaica, Alice started pulling away and being more interested in being with other people, and I became even driftier than I had been at the beginning. I stopped being able to concentrate. All I wanted to do was get away, to fly with the wind and stop thinking."

Rocco looked at Gail. "Sleeping with you wasn't just a drunken act for me and it wasn't a way to get back at Alice for pushing us aside. It may have been a way to tie up a loose end, to have a special moment with someone I had come to care a lot about. I really want you to believe that."

Gail interrupted. "I guess I thought it was about Alice; especially when you pushed me away after she came to the door. I was very hurt, but in retrospect, it helped me to get off my ass and do what I needed to do. I may have tried to find a way to stay in New York if it hadn't happened that way."

Lynn Gregory

"I'm sorry I hurt you, Gail, but I can assure you our time together that day had nothing to do with Alice. I was really attracted to you and had held back all summer because I didn't want it to complicate my friendship with her. Yes, I loved her, but not as a partner. I loved her as a cherished friend. She had been the one person I knew in high school I trusted to be who she was with me. There was no pretense so I could relax and be me. At the time, I thought I had everything under control and that we were all playing by the same rules. It seemed so easy for the three of us to be together. My leaving abruptly was not at all thought out. When I think about it now, maybe it was one of the few goals I had set for myself, you know, going to Tierra del Fuego. From the minute I heard about it when I was in high school, I was fascinated by how people could live in extreme environments. I remember sharing that fascination with Alice but her fantasy was to go to the North Pole. Funny I hadn't thought about this before either, but we were headed for totally opposite poles that were equally cold."

"Did you travel mostly by motorcycle?"

"Yes, and I took my time. There were times I didn't have enough money to eat, but for the most part I met good and interesting people along the way. I worked at a lot of things, mostly physical labor, and even some music gigs. Being as big as I am has the advantage of making people think I'm strong. I have to say, by the time I got through Mexico, I was probably in the best shape of my life, and I learned how to communicate with people with different languages. I became pretty fluent in Spanish but also ran into a number of other tongues, especially in places like Chiapas where there are a lot of different indigenous tribes and villages. Most people were really nice.

"How long did it take you?"

"I must admit I lost track of time, but I tried to stay on top of weather changes. I think I spent about six months traveling in Mexico and Central America. I met people along the way who gave me tips on places to go, other people to meet, and what I needed to know culturally. Whenever I was in a city, I found libraries and universities. That kept me sane. I have to admit I sometimes reached out to my parents for money. As usual, they were wonderful. I have been lucky in so many ways."

"How did you connect with the Yanomamo? I think of them as being in a very remote part of the Amazon."

"Actually, everyone I spoke with in universities knew about the Yanomamo." Rocco laughed out loud. "The Yanomamo I met were used to 'tourists' and very generous with their drugs."

"You said you did a lot of hallucinogens. Did you try theirs? I remember the Chagnon film with men sitting around snorting with green mucous dripping out of their noses."

Rocco laughed again. It was definitely not a funny haha laugh. "I did, but that wasn't where it all started. I was doing all sorts of drugs from the time I left New York. It might have been funny if I was doing it for scientific reasons, but I wasn't. I was just doing it to get stoned, and to have alternative reality experiences. I got really hooked. When I'm being honest with myself, I know that most of my networking, traveling from contact to contact—I started referring to these people as my travel agents—I just went from one drug scene to the next."

As he told this story, Gail didn't change her expression at all. Rocco kept waiting to see a look of disgust on her face, but what he mostly saw was something like curiosity. Then she asked, "Did you get what you were looking for? Did you ever have that moment of enlightenment that's supposed to come with hallucinogens?"

"Good question, Gail. I suppose there were times when I felt that way. There were times when I left my body and experienced greater truths and the whole universe, but none of it stuck. I always came down feeling worse than when I started, but I also became addicted. Like most junkies, I stopped caring about anything but the drug and whatever it was that particular drug was offering."

Rocco paused fearing that by going further with his story, he would lose her sympathy, and worse yet, her respect and friendship. Yet, he knew if there was to be a future for them, he had to take the chance. For the first time since he returned from his travels all those years ago, he actually wanted to invite someone into his life. That someone was Gail so he had to take the chance.

"Gail, I want you to know I have never spoken about this to another person in all these years."

"I'm honored to be your first, but if you want to stop, I'll understand. I can see how painful it is for you to talk about that time in your life. The good news is that no matter how far into the hole you fell, you got out and have made such a success of your life since."

Rocco stopped her, "Let me finish. I hit the worst bottom you can imagine. One night, I left some people I was doing drugs with and they followed me, beat the shit out of me, stole my bike and all of my belongings, and left me in a ditch on the side of the road. I was left for dead."

Gail gasped, "Oh my God, how horrible!"

"That wasn't the end of it. It turned out some of the people in the gang were local officials and when it was learned I hadn't died in the ditch, they became afraid I would go to an American embassy somewhere and blow their cover. So they found me and had me thrown into prison on drug charges."

"Holy shit!"

"I was in prison for a long time. I was seriously afraid I would die there and simply disappear from the world."

"What happened? How did you get out?"

"I eventually found a way to get in touch with my parents. I convinced a guy I met in prison, actually one of the guards, by promising him a lot of money, to contact them and tell them where I was. When they heard what was going on, my parents engaged the help of the country's American Embassy and the rest is history. I came back to the United States determined to stay sober, many pounds lighter, and chastened. I had a lot of time to think when I was in that hell hole and vowed that if I ever got out, I would go to law school and dedicate my life to helping helpless people."

"Oh Rocco, I'm so glad you made it. Your parents... you're so lucky to have them on your side. Did you go back to Connecticut with them?"

"Yes, I spent my first year back sleeping in my childhood bed. That is, when I wasn't in the hospital or in rehab."

"Rehab? I figured you would have to go cold turkey in prison."

"It's not that simple, Gail. My body was completely broken. I don't think I had an unbroken bone. There were drugs in the prison and I took as many as I was could get for the pain. I promised everyone there whatever I needed to promise to get what I wanted. They saw me as a rich Americano who had the potential to live up to the promises. That's probably the main reason I'm alive today."

"Did you live up to those promises after you got out?"

"Believe it or not, I did the best I could to help those guys. You would not believe the poverty, the terrible living conditions. It takes very little money, at least very little from our privileged perspective, to provide people with a decent life there. I go back every year, and when I turn my head to avoid getting in the still corrupt local government's crosshairs, have been able to help some of these folks and their families."

"Wow, no wonder you were the guy who sat by Sybil after the carjacking."

Rocco looked at Gail. "You know, I never thought of that connection. It could be true."

"Tell me the rest. You spent a year recovering your health and then went to law school?"

"It was probably more than a year, closer to two years. Towards the end, I started exploring and decided to specialize in real estate law. While I was at law school, I did some volunteer work in an impoverished neighborhood, mostly minority families. That was when I started a credit union that would help poor people become property owners. I followed law school with an MBA program. That turned out to be really valuable. Neither of these programs had anyone teaching us how to help people get out of poverty directly, per se, but I learned everything I needed to know by paying attention to the fine print."

Gail smiled at Rocco and said words he was happy to hear, "Thank you for sharing your story with me."

"Oh Gail, I'm the one who's thankful for your acceptance. I know I'm being presumptuous, but am I wrong in believing there's something important going on between us?"

Gail burst into tears and put her arms around Rocco. Holding him tight, she said, "I sure hope so."

Chapter 41

May 10- May 12, 2002
Albuquerque NM

Dora called Gail the following morning with good news. "Joey will be coming to Albuquerque this weekend and would like to meet with you."

"Did he say whether he had evidence of Mike's intentions?"

"He didn't say exactly, but sounded delighted at the prospect of seeing you. I think I told you before, although they hadn't been in touch for a while, he and Mike were very close at one time. I'm sure he wants to give you his condolences in person."

Although that sounded sweet, Gail was hoping he had more than condolences to offer her. She held her breath and thanked Dora for playing go-between.

When he heard the news, Rocco had similar questions. "Did she say anything about whether he can help you?"

"Not exactly, but I got the impression he wouldn't be coming unless he had something to offer. I know you have a lot of work waiting for you in New Jersey but obviously it would be great if you could stick around to meet with Joey on Sunday."

"Of course; I'd really like to resolve this while I'm out here. I talk with my team every day and we're moving along nicely collecting data for the fraud case against Farrow and some of their collaborators. I can take a few more days here if it helps me to remove something from my job jar."

"I can't thank you enough! I'm glad you're working with people in Jersey who can keep the ball rolling there. You haven't talked much about the case you're so involved with. Is this about housing discrimination?"

"Yes, ultimately, but that's always a tough one to prove. At this point we're going after them on financial fraud. They've been slippery but I think we have enough to cause them to be uncomfortable continuing their practices."

"What practices?"

"You name it: a lot of financial fraud, bank fraud, insurance fraud, tax fraud. All of those are complicated and hard to pin down, especially when they typically outsource, but it looks like they may have crossed a line by undervaluing properties on some documents and overvaluing the same properties on others. I know it sounds like technical bullshit but it's easier to prove than slippery slopes like racial discrimination. I'm just hoping, if we can get them on this, it will open the can of worms to deeper investigations."

"What you're doing is so important, Rocco. I'm grateful for your help with my problem but completely understand if you need to get back to Newark sooner rather than later. I know I'm being optimistic, but if all goes well with my inheritance battles, I can return back east week after next."

Rocco was surprised. "Will you be coming back east soon? I figured you'd be staying in Albuquerque to plan your next steps."

Gail was silent. *Does he want me to be on the other side of the country?*

But before she could say anything, Rocco added. "It's not that I want you to stay out here."

More silence.

"Shit Gail, we need to have a conversation about what happened between us last night. We need to talk about who we are together."

Gail began to breathe again and thought to herself. *It seems like I've been holding my breath a lot lately.* Then she felt herself smile.

"I really want to do that too, Rocco, but first I need to go to Colorado to visit Brian. I would invite you along, but I'm not sure it's a good time. He's still struggling with losing his dad. I'm thinking I'll drive up there on Monday, after we meet with Joey."

Rocco was both disappointed and relieved they wouldn't be talking about things for a few days. It would be good to get the business part done. It would be good for Gail to have time with her son. It would be good for both of them to have time to see how they felt with the benefit of some distance. But he was convinced they were on the same page.

Gail woke up Sunday morning hoping for the best, and trying to prepare herself for the worst. Best-case scenario, Joey would have evidence that Mike wanted to leave everything to her and Brian, and Rocco would not regret or shrink back from the closeness they had experienced. Not sure she was yet ready to trust any feelings while still grieving for Mike, she was quite sure she didn't want to lose that closeness.

Rocco was in the same emotional place. He felt a hundred pounds lighter in the wake of the unburdening, as he had come to think of it. As they met in the hotel dining room for breakfast, he greeted her with a huge smile and a warm hug.

Gail took a sip of coffee. "I have to admit I'm nervous about seeing Joey. I have high hopes, but a nagging fear that he doesn't have what we need to resolve things. On the other hand, it seems unlikely he would come here just to say hello. I haven't seen him since we met all those years ago in '73.

Rocco nodded. "I guess we'll know soon enough. I spent some time looking into New Mexico law on the subject and am convinced the law is on our side, but the Lucas' lawyers may have the resources to fight you for a long time. Having clear proof of his intentions could put a damper on their arguments."

The conversation was all business as they drove to Dora's travel agency where they had arranged to meet with Joey. Dora greeted Gail and Rocco at the door warmly and didn't act surprised that Gail had brought her lawyer along. Gail wondered if Dora was ever surprised about anything.

As she led them through the corridor, Dora said, "Joey's in the backyard. He's really looking forward to seeing you, Gail, and he has a surprise for you."

That was an understatement. When they got to the backyard, they were greeted by a smiling Joey AND a smiling Alice. Everyone was stunned. While Gail hadn't expected to see Alice, Alice hadn't expected to see Rocco. Joey and Dora watched as the three old friends hugged one another. At some point they pulled up chairs and sat in a circle looking at each other. Joey broke the silence.

"I'm happy to finally meet you, Rocco. Alice has told about your high school days and your amazing musical talent. You've become the stuff of legend in our house."

Everyone laughed, then looking at Alice and Joey, Gail said "I'm assuming you two are a couple, and can't wait to hear how this came about, and when it came about."

Alice said, "Yes, Joey and I are a couple. As for how and when, that's a long story. I suspect we all have a lot of catching up to do. Tell me, did you two stay in touch after that summer? I tried but couldn't find either one of you."

Rocco answered, "No, we all seem to have gone our separate ways. Gail and I only recently reconnected."

Gail interrupted, "I have a ton of questions, but before we get into it, Joey, I'm wondering if you can help me convince Mike's family and their lawyers that Mike honestly wanted to leave everything to me and our son."

Joey pulled a piece of paper out of a bag and handed it to Gail. It was a letter from Mike dated, July 2001. Tears flowed from Gail's eyes as she read it. In it, Mike wrote about his illness, his heart disease. He wrote that he was feeling guilty because he had married Gail knowing it would take his life at an early age and keeping that information from her. He had been reluctant to have a child, but when he saw how much she wanted one, he deeply wanted to share that experience with her. He wrote that it was the best decision he'd ever made and despite the conflict with his family, had not regretted a day of his life with Gail. He felt she had sacrificed a lot to be with him, to stay with him while his family actively made her and Brian feel unwelcome. By the time he was writing this letter, his heart disease had advanced to a point where he was sure there was little hope of recovery. He wrote that he had gone back to his will with lawyers who told him it was written clearly, but he didn't completely trust anyone connected with his prominent family. Joey was the only person he knew he trusted completely. He had written the letter shortly before he died but managed to have it notarized. The last paragraph was written in very straightforward language:

"I, Michael P. Lucas, wish to leave all of my estate, without exception, to my wife Gail Song Lucas. She is to be my single heir and I want it to be clear that no other member of my family has a legitimate claim to any of it unless she decides to distribute parts of it once it is totally in her control. I have confidence she will make only good decisions."

Gail handed the document to Rocco. "Will this convince the lawyers to let go of the other claims on his estate?"

Rocco nodded, "I think this will do the job. Thank you Joey, you've made my work here a lot easier."

Gail added, "Yes, Joey, I can't thank you enough, but I can't help wondering, were you and Mike in touch all these years or did he send this to you out of the blue?"

"We were never estranged, if that's what you're asking. It was just that our lives took such different directions and we had less and less in common. For whatever reasons, Mike couldn't pull away from the power his family had, and it did provide him with a good living. We were traveling in different circles and when he married that woman, his ex-wife, I just couldn't be there. It was like a disastrous dynastic thing. After that, I moved away. I didn't even know about his divorce and your marriage for a really long time but it was already too late for us to go back to being buddies. So, when I got this letter, it had been several years. I hate to say it, but I only recently heard, from my mother, that Mike had passed away. For that, I'm really sorry. He was a good man. He really helped me when we were young and I was pretty screwed up. I'm glad he trusted me with this, and that I can repay him for his kindness and the positive impact he had on my life."

Alice nodded. "I didn't know you were with Mike in Albuquerque, Gail. Isn't it weird we both ended up coming back? We only spent a few days here with these guys on our way east that summer. Had you and Mike stayed in touch? I remember there were vibes between you when we were at his house."

"That's true. As you may remember, I was committed to going back to Jamaica to help my parents get their business off the ground and I was definitely not ready to settle down with anyone at that young age. Mike and I were in touch for a short while, but that fell off within a year or two. I stayed in Jamaica for fourteen years, the business went under, my father died and my mother remarried and moved to Switzerland. I went through a tough time, depressed and feeling like I had failed my parents and accomplished nothing for myself. When I hit bottom, I decided it was sink or swim time, so I found a therapist. I'll never forget my first conversation with her. She asked me to remember times when I had felt truly happy. That was easy, the summer of 1973, which began with our trip back east and the few days we spent in Albuquerque. So I picked up and went to Albuquerque."

Alice smiled, "You were always so cautious back then, Gail. This was pretty impulsive."

"You're right, Alice. I climbed over my wall and took a chance, reconnected with Mike and had fifteen happy years with him. My only regret is that I didn't know you were in New Mexico."

Rocco looked at Alice, "You always said you needed to wander and explore the fringes of the planet. I know people say such things, but in your case, I believed it. You always did what you said you were going to do."

"I thought you knew me better than anyone, Rocco. It's true, I did a lot of wandering, including making it to the North Pole as planned. Did you get to Tierra del Fuego?"

"I did."

Joey stepped in, "I'm getting hungry. Anyone interested in Mexican food? There's a great takeout place a few miles down the road. If you give me your orders, I'll be happy to be your waiter."

Rocco pulled out his wallet and gave Joey a couple of twenty dollar bills. "Will this cover it? I want to treat."

Handing the bills back to Rocco and grabbing a pad of paper and pencil, Joey said, "That's probably twice what it will all cost, but if you want to split the bill, I'll give you an accounting when I get back. Now, what are your preferences?"

Following Joey back into the building, Dora asked if anyone was interested in lemonade. The three old friends said yes and settled into their lawn chairs.

Chapter 42

May 12, 2002
Albuquerque NM

Watching Dora, Alice said, "I adore that woman. Not only is she the mother of the finest man I know, she has also become the mother I never had. Ever since I met her all those years ago, she's pulled me out of fires more than once. I should probably tell you both before going on, she's the grandmother of my two daughters—the best grandmother in the world."

This news took Gail and Rocco by surprise. For some reason they could imagine the Alice they knew doing all sorts of crazy things, but never as a mother. Gail recovered her voice first. "Congratulations. How old are your daughters? Are they here with you?"

"Amanda's thirteen and Ginger is six. They're both involved with kid things at home this weekend."

"How long will you be here, Alice? I hope we'll have some time together. I want to hear all about your life."

"And I can't wait to hear about yours, Gail, and yours, Rocco. I'm still in shock running into you two together at this time in my life."

Rocco laughed. "I'm in shock to run into you here too. So, what have you been doing with your life since the summer of '73, besides traveling to the ends of the world and becoming a wife and mother?"

"In a nutshell, for a long time, I was doing what I always wanted to do, traveling to strange places and collecting stories."

"What about the writing? Have you written the great American novel yet?"

Alice laughed, "Not yet, but I have written a number of ethnographically-inspired children's books. I guess some of them have an element of fiction to make them attractive to their target audience, but they've mostly been written with the goal of teaching kids about other ways of living and thinking."

Gail jumped in, "How did I never hear of you? I have a thirteen-year-old son who has always been an omnivorous reader. Those types of stories would have been right up his alley. Oh wait a minute, is it possible that you are Alice Boaz?

You wrote *The Svalbard Stories?*" Alice nodded as Gail continued talking, "We have everything you ever wrote! I can't wait to tell Brian I know you."

"How great that you have a son, Gail, and that he's enjoyed my books. I'll never get tired of hearing that kids AND their parents like my books."

Rocco said, "I haven't had the pleasure, not ever having kids, but will definitely look out for your books in the future. You always said you were going to be a writer and you obviously found a compatible niche. But I want to know what happened to you at the end of that summer. Did you leave New York right away? Oh, before you answer that question, I need to tell you that Gail and I only recently learned what happened to Daphne and how you helped her and her family out."

"You didn't know? For some reason I always assumed everyone knew. So I guess you know Daphne passed away at a young age, probably caused by internal injuries she sustained when she fell. It was horribly tragic, she was so young, such a lovely soul, with an incomparable singing voice." Alice was silent for a moment, then continued, "You only heard about it recently? How did you hear?"

Gail said, "Just to add to our slew of coincidences, Rocco and I met Daphne's niece Sybil earlier this year and learned about what you did for their family."

"Oh my God, Sybil must be in her twenties by now, how is she doing?"

"This too is a longish story, but we met a few months ago when she was the victim of a carjacking at the Newark train station. Rocco was at the scene and stayed by her until the ambulance showed up. Meeting her was a total coincidence."

Alice's face turned white, "How awful! Is she okay? When did this happen?"

"About three months ago, I believe it happened February first. She seems to be healing physically, but struggling with what sounds like PTSD. She has a great husband, Rick, who takes good care of her and is heading an effort to discover what actually happened. The police haven't been very aggressive in their investigation."

Gail gave Alice a minute to absorb what she had just heard. She wanted to know about Alice's relationship with the young Sybil, but first, about what had happened to Daphne that day.

"Alice, you just disappeared that day. What was going on?"

"You may remember, we were going to go the Museum of Natural History after the happening, but I started worrying that Daphne was going to lose her way. She had been frantically worried that her father would curtail her freedom if she got home late, so she decided to take a shortcut through parts of the park she didn't know. Anyway, I ended up finding her lying on the ground with several broken bones. So I went for help and contacted her parents. At the hospital, I learned her family had no medical insurance and decided I had to help them financially. I have to admit, I was in a state of panic, but I've always been good in emergencies." Alice looked up and laughed, "Unfortunately they're usually followed by major emotional crashes."

"We didn't know where you were!"

"I'm sorry about that. I was in a really emotional state and I ran into Charlotte, remember the woman we were subletting from? She invited me to crash with her and her current roommates for the time being. She had a story to tell that involved Rute, remember Teddy Farrow? It turned out she had never left the City and was simply hiding from him until her lease ran out. One of her roommates had recently lost a beloved cat and wanted Fluffy. You were heading back to Jamaica and I was happy to find him a loving home. And Gail, I'm really sorry I never got to say goodbye. Attending to Daphne took up all of my time for the next several days and then I didn't know how to find you."

Rocco asked, "How were you able to get money to help Daphne?"

"I went to my father and he paid for all of her medical expenses for several years."

Looking at their surprised expressions, Alice went on, "My father owned and ran a really big export-import shipping enterprise. I know I never told you. I didn't even tell him I was in New York that summer. His office was way up high in the World Trade Center. It's always been hard for me to explain how it was with me and my parents. We were never close, but they always helped me when I asked."

"Is your father okay? Was he there on 9-11?"

"No, he had retired and passed away by then. It's weird though, when I went to ask him for the money to help Daphne, he had only recently moved into the twin towers and I had to search for him."

"Did you try to find us?"

"I did and I didn't. During the weeks following her fall, I spent most of my time with Daphne and her family. I felt totally responsible and really guilty."

"How could you have blamed yourself, Alice? It was an accident."

"She was only fifteen years old. If you recall, that was the first time she joined the happening without her older sister Melissa. I should have found a way to get her home safely. But there was something else she told me that made it even worse. She told me Rute followed her and scared her with things he was saying. She climbed the rocks to get away from him and when she fell, caught her foot in a crevice which made the fall even more traumatic. I will always feel responsible for including him in our group. I knew everyone disliked him; hell, I disliked him. He was a piece of shit, but I was in a mindset that wouldn't allow me to reject anyone. For some screwed-up reason, I thought it made me a better artist."

Alice took a deep breath and continued, "Before you ask me the next question, Daphne and I talked about this a lot. Neither of us felt we had a chance of making him legally responsible for what happened to her. It would have been her word against his. Daphne had been terrified and traumatized and didn't want to relive the experience, ever. It may have been a poor decision, but I let it go. I basically didn't leave her side until she was in recovery, then I took up an offer from my mother to visit her in Galway, where she had parked herself for a few months. As I mentioned before, I grew up in an unusual family. From Galway, I made my first trip to the ends of the earth. Rocco, I actually went to the Skalbord Islands, basically the North Pole. That was where and when I began my life as a nomad. I was driven to experience new things, people, and places. Someone once said I had 'itchy feet', and I think that was a good description of me, even to this day. It just enters my head and I have to experience something new. But it doesn't have to be exotic, just new to me."

Rocco smiled, "It sounds like you haven't changed. I always had the impression you noticed things I took for granted and ignored, and you always wanted to keep the door open to new experiences. So, did all of this go into your writing? Have you written anything besides children's books?"

"Of course, but the children's books are the published ones. In fact it started with Melissa's daughter Sybil. I used to make up stories and poems for her that got me in a particular headspace, so when I was traveling around, I often thought about what she would want to know about the people and places."

Rocco looked at Gail, "Did Sybil mention the stories?"

Without waiting for an answer, he turned back to Alice, "She told us you were always close to Daphne and you were like a fairy godmother to her. She told Gail you gave her a copy of *Alice in Wonderland* and a kachina doll when Daphne died. It sounds like you made her feel very special."

Alice teared up, "Thank you for telling me that. She was a wonderful child. I was proud Melissa named her for me. I think she was only about seven years old when I last saw her."

"That was a long time ago--I'm guessing sixteen or seventeen years? What happened then? Why did you stop visiting the family after Daphne died?"

"Daphne died in May 1985 but my journey had started earlier. I was in and out of her life for several years during which time I also did a lot of traveling. Once, when I was in New York, I decided to explore going back to school, so I enrolled in a graduate level program at Ensaladilla—remember them? I knew they would value my travels and what I already brought to the table. As I expected, they encouraged me to study with faculty in a variety of schools in the region. Right around the time Daphne passed away, I was looking into Ph.D. programs. I ended up going to a university down the road from here in New Mexico. The next time I checked in, Melissa's family, including little Sybil, had moved away. It saddens me to think my little namesake felt abandoned. I had basically moved my base from East to West. Also, things had changed for me with my family by that time. My parents were no longer living together. I first learned about that when I visited my mother in Galway in 1974. Unbeknownst to me, she had been living in Ireland for the past two years while my father had stayed in New York. I saw my father every once in a while and he continued to pay for Daphne's medical needs all through her life. He died six years ago and my mom outlived him for only about six months. They left me very comfortable financially, but I guess I was always starved for family. So the short answer is that I wasn't living in New York."

"We all have stories to tell that will take some time, but I will give you a thumbnail about how I ended up back here and with Joey. Dora and I stayed in touch over the years and when I came to New Mexico for school, I reconnected with her and Joey. I mostly saw Dora because after Joey graduated from college he decided to forego engineering and became a school teacher in a remote village several hours from here. I only saw him once in a while. I was still doing a lot of wandering then and hadn't come up with where or whether I ever wanted to settle. Then in 1988 I got pregnant and the only person I wanted to be with was Dora, so I came to Albuquerque and had my first daughter Amanda. As with everything else, I hadn't completed the requirements for my doctorate, but was basically still on the books as a student because I had continued to pay tuition and now I had a child and felt I needed to make a home for her. That's when Joey came in. He had been transforming the education system in his community, creating a progressive school with curricula that brilliantly incorporated native knowledge and values with what was good about American education in general. He convinced me I could probably get a dissertation out of studying their work while I helped them to get grants. It was a win-win, so I did it. Amanda and I moved there and stayed, and yes, I did do the research and finished my doctorate."

Chapter 43

May 12, 2002
Albuquerque NM

Gail smiled, "Congratulations! I can't believe you and I were here at the same time and never crossed paths. Did you ever reach out to Mike?"

"No, I'm sorry to say. I was so caught up with my new baby, trying to finish school, my new life. I honestly never thought to reach out to the Lucas family. I never in a million years would have expected to find you here, Gail! Then Joey and I got together, and I moved to be with him. We've been together with our girls ever since."

Rocco and Gail stared at her, trying to align this contented woman with the restless Alice they knew back then.

Reading their minds, Alice laughed and said, "Oh okay, I sometimes get itchy feet and need to take a day trip somewhere I've never been before, but mostly I get my rocks off just living my life. There's never a dull moment with Joey and the kids, and I'm very active in the school and local arts community, and my music, research and writing."

Alice looked up as Joey and Dora came through the back door carrying bags of food. It was a great time to break, but after everyone ate their fill, she turned to Rocco, "Okay Rocco, your turn. How did you end up being a lawyer? How did you end up being Gail's lawyer?"

Rocco laughed, "Like yours, mine is a convoluted story that will take a while to tell; but your second question is easy to answer. Gail reached out to me a few months ago. We hadn't seen each other since New York in 1973."

"And you two were together at the Newark train station the day Sybil was carjacked?"

Gail smiled, "That was where we met for the first time. Oddly, her tragic event got us involved in a little adventure that reminded us of the way we all used to start our happenings in the park. It was way beyond amazing to discover Sybil's relationship with Daphne and Melissa and now that we may have resolved my inheritance problems with Joey's help, it looks like Rocco can move on to his real work."

Alice asked, "What's your real work Rocco?"

"I mostly specialize in financial and real estate law, but, in the wake of the 9/11 attacks on the World Trade Center, racial discrimination in those areas has taken center stage. There's a lot of discrimination against Muslims in northern New Jersey which isn't particularly surprising but is completely illegal. In fact, we're involved in a big case against Farrow Holdings."

"Is Teddy involved?"

"Oh yes indeed and I need to get back to that work soon. Thanks to Joey, I'll be able to finish up with the lawyers here in a day or two and head back to Newark."

Alice sighed, "I was hoping I could get both of you to come visit us, meet our girls, and just spend time really catching up. I hate to lose you so soon. What about you Gail, will you be sticking around for a while?"

Gail felt like she was being hit from all sides with everything that was happening. She wanted to stay in New Mexico to be with Alice and meet her kids, but couldn't let Rocco go without having the conversation they needed to have. She also knew she would need to be in Albuquerque to collect her assets and make decisions about the property. Everything was happening so fast, and although she believed she and Rocco would find a way to be together, this moment mattered a lot to her. She decided on the spot to return to the East Coast with Rocco.

Not knowing what Gail was thinking, but directly addressing Alice, Rocco said, "Unfortunately, a deeper visit is going to have to wait until this trial takes place. While we don't have a firm date, I think it'll be starting within the month and there's a ton of prep work left to do. The Farrows are very slippery. I've also promised Sybil and Rick I'll try to help them go after the carjacker."

"Do they know who did it? I thought the carjacker got away with the car."

"At this point I don't know much about it as we only had time to speak briefly. However, when Sybil and Rick asked for my help they said there's new evidence. Believe it or not, they think our old friend Teddy Farrow was involved. Talk about the bad penny!"

Alice jumped up, "What, how on earth?!"

"Sybil works for a nonprofit advocacy organization that focuses on racial and economic discrimination. She has apparently butted heads with Teddy in her professional capacity and he hasn't taken it well. I have yet to meet with them to get details, but it sounds like they have some evidence tying Teddy to her carjacking. Although it's totally separate from my firm's current court case, I find it interesting and, if I can help Sybil and Rick, I will."

Alice turned to Joey who had been quiet throughout this reunion conversation. He knew what was coming and smiled before she opened her mouth to say she really needed to go back east with her friends for a while. Joey said, "No problem, the girls and I will keep the home fires burning."

Armed with Mike's letter to Joey, Rocco was finished with the lawyers in a few days and returned to Newark. Gail and Alice decided to follow him later in the month. In addition to finishing with the legal paperwork, Gail needed to drive to Brian's school for a visit to make sure he was okay.

As expected, Gail's visit with Brian was emotional, but she was happily reinforced with the feeling his teachers and counselors were doing a great job. He was very active in sports and thriving academically. Just in the few days she was there, Gail got to see him play basketball, and play his guitar in a school concert. He was still young enough to be happy to have his mom there to watch him perform. She hadn't told him about the problems with Mike's inheritance and hoped never to have to bring it up as he tended to worry about her as much as she worried about him. She also didn't mention that she was seriously considering moving to the east coast, but when she left, her mind was at ease, Brian was okay. Now she just had to move the rest of the peanuts of her life along.

Gail and Alice met in Albuquerque on May 21st and traveled to New York together. They were both excitedly anticipating the surprise reunion between Alice and Sybil. Rocco had arranged a get-together with Sybil and Rick for the evening after they were scheduled to arrive in New Jersey.

Chapter 44

May 4-May 21, 2002
Jersey City NJ, Newark NJ

Although they had decided to hold off contacting the police with their evidence, Sybil, Rick, and the rest of the group continued to meet and share information. Needless to say, they were thrilled when Rocco called shortly after returning to Newark with the news that Gail's inheritance issues had been resolved. Rocco also reported that while Gail had to remain in Albuquerque to visit with her son and tie up some loose ends, she would be returning soon thereafter with a big surprise for Sybil.

One reason they were eager to consult with Rocco was to determine if they should engage the services of a criminal lawyer. They also wanted his advice to make sure they didn't make mistakes in their efforts to get the police to look further into its investigation of the carjacking. With the help of Pablo and Carlos' friend Hannah, and other acquaintances with knowledge of police procedure, Rick, Sybil and their group had learned the police were honing in on identifying local gangs known to be involved with specific drug trafficking. They hoped the symbol on the packet found in the car would help push forward that process. At the same time, they feared the source of Sybil's strange AHA moment, when she remembered the carjacker's tattoo and haunting words, would be met with skepticism.

Upon hearing their story, Rocco scratched his head and said, "I think we have enough to take to the police investigators, but I agree we can leave out that the memory came in a dream. I'll go to the police department tomorrow and see if we can get them interested in setting up an interview with you, Sybil. Are you okay with that?"

Sybil smiled broadly. Bringing in a lawyer and waiting for Rocco had been the right move.

In her interview, Sybil described the carjacker, his tattoo, and the words he said to her. Her demeanor convinced the police investigator she was telling the truth and that the trauma had resulted in her burying the specific memory in the deep recesses of her mind until she felt safe enough to handle it. The investigator was especially impressed that she described a hand tattoo that mirrored the symbol on the drug packet they found in the car. There was no way she would have known about that.

As Rocco predicted, Sybil was asked to look at photographs of gang members, followed by a line-up of individuals who fit the profile. As she went through this process, Sybil became increasingly confident in her ability to recognize the person who victimized her. He was a baby-faced teenage boy named Joreth.

While he walked in with a brave expression, Joreth confessed to the carjacking, but seemed to feel that since he didn't kidnap or kill the driver, he hadn't actually committed a crime.

The police investigator corrected him, "Joreth, carjacking is a crime. You stole a car."

"But I didn't keep it! I was hired to take it, so if someone stole it, it was the guy who hired me."

"Maybe you're right, Joreth. Who was that guy?"

"I don't know. I was in my buddy's car. He was driving. We were told to wait outside the parking lot for a signal from someone who would be walking to the lot with the driver of the car. We knew the car's make, color and model. Then we followed it up Washington Street and when it was a block or two from the train station, called the cell number."

"Did you know the person who was giving you the signal?"

"No, it was some woman. She was wearing a red coat, that's all I knew."

"I'm going to need your buddy's name."

"You'll never find him, he's left town."

"I'll still need his name. So what were your instructions?"

"All I know is we weren't supposed to do nothing unless the driver pulled over to answer the cell. But she did, so I was dropped off and my buddy drove off. I'm known to be pretty quick so they picked me to take the car. The deal is to be really fast so the driver is taken by surprise. And it worked. I wasn't going to hurt her, just get her out of the car and drive it away."

"What were your instructions after that?"

"Drive the car to another township—to the mall where we left it, meet my partner and leave."

"What about the stuff that was in the car?"

"What stuff? Oh that bag of papers, I didn't steal nothing. They told me to leave it there and I did."

"Are you telling us everything? You're in big trouble for stealing a car, drug possession, and maybe even attempted murder and you can't tell us who hired you to do this?"

"I told you, I never met anyone. I'd been taking some of the drugs so I was pumped up but we don't talk about where our directions come from."

"But who gave you the directions?"

"I don't know. It came to me as a text. It was anonymous."

While he continued to talk with a young man's bravado, Joreth nervously picked at a hangnail as he added, "Oh wait, I was told to tell the driver that Teddy sent me. I almost forgot. But I didn't know who Teddy was. I was just doing what they said to do. They paid me a lot of money."

"One more thing, how did you know who would be giving you the signal in the parking lot?"

"I already told you, I got a text message saying two women would be walking out to the blue CRV sometime between ten and ten thirty. One would be wearing a red jacket and she would brush her hair off her forehead just after she said goodbye to the driver when she got into the car."

"So it was that woman, the one in the red jacket, who gave you the go-ahead to steal this car, to do this carjacking?"

"I guess. Never met her, but that was how we knew who to follow."

"Do you still have the cell phone where you got the signal? We can get that record so you might as well tell us the truth."

"Are you kidding? We don't keep cell phones!"

"So you threw it away?"

"Of course, I'm not stupid."

"Destroying evidence is a crime."

"It's not evidence, it's my phone!"

Chapter 45

May 21, 2002
Jersey City NJ

Alice threw her arms around Sybil and said, "Oh my God, Sybil, it's really you! I've often dreamed of meeting you again."

"Me too! I can't wait to tell my mom I've been reunited with the amazing woman she named me for, the woman who saved my Aunt Daphne's life. You will always be a hero to me and my family."

"I'm not sure I deserve that, and I feel terrible about losing touch with you and your family after she died. I was so sad to lose her, and for a while, I retreated from everything and everyone, but that wasn't why I lost touch. I was at a crossroads in my life and had decided to move out to New Mexico to complete my education. I think I may have told your mother, or maybe it was your grandmother, but never got to say goodbye to you, and I'm very sorry for that."

Sybil responded, "I did miss you. It was especially hard because I had lost my Aunt Daphne, but we didn't stay in New York either. I think it was less than a year later when we moved to Canada. My mother and father still live there, in Montreal."

Alice sighed, "Life just takes over sometimes, but it sure is wonderful seeing you now, all grown up and living in such a great place. What an amazing coincidence that you met Rocco and Gail, but, what a terrible way to meet them! The carjacking had to be really traumatic. How are you doing now?"

"Yes. I have had all the symptoms of post-traumatic stress and I suspect it's going to take a long time to get over it. I'm not a person who deals well with loss of control."

Alice laughed, "Oh my yes, we are cut from the same cloth."

A faraway look came into Sybil's eyes and with a smile, she began to recite a poem, "*Poetry makes me feel better; it opens my heart and my soul; It gives me an anchor of structure when my life unravels its scroll.*"

Alice was stunned, "You remember that?"

"Of course, I remember the whole poem you taught me. "*When everything seems to be broken; and arrhythmia is all around;*

Poetic themes are the da-das that focus my brain with their sound. There isn't a pill in the cosmos; food, drink or something to smoke; that can help me put all those ducks in a row when the row is the thing that is broke."

"You were only seven or eight years old. How on earth could you remember it?"

Sybil smiled again, "I remember other poems you made up for me too. One of my other favorites was *There's Something About a Sidewalk*. Both of these have always been like songs in my head that have gotten me through some tough times in my life. I've often pulled them out for perspective, but this time, I think the universe decided I need the big guns—I needed you in the flesh and here you are!"

Alice put her arms around Sybil and began to cry. After shedding a few tears of her own, Sybil sat down and looked at Alice,

"My therapist thinks the deep need to control my own destiny gives me strength, but is also responsible for burying the trauma so deeply. So I guess it's six of one, half a dozen of the other blessing-wise. However, and this may sound really crazy, I think I remembered some of what happened from a spiritual experience."

"Really, what spiritual experience, what did you learn?"

Sybil leaned back in her chair. "It wasn't something I could use in a court of law, but I had a sort of dream or half-dream in which I interacted with the person who committed the carjacking. I saw him, his face and some other features I had obviously blocked out. He also said something to me I heard very clearly. Believe it or not, Rocco has helped us use this knowledge to help the police identify the carjacker, but the police don't know the memories came through an alternative path."

"They caught the carjacker? That's great news. I hope he gets the punishment he deserves!"

"Yes, but he's a kid and they haven't caught the people he was working for yet. I think at least one of them has been identified, a woman I was meeting with that day. If the kid is telling the truth, she fingered me when we walked out to the parking lot together."

"Why would she do that?"

"I honestly don't know. We were talking about sharing information about the illegal activities of a real estate agency we've both been fighting over racial discrimination issues. I thought we were in agreement, that our two organizations were on the same page. I walked out believing we would work together to stop them. They have been so clever at getting away with things."

"Who are they?"

"A family owned real estate business called Farrow Holdings. You might remember their son. Rocco and Gail said they owned the apartment building you all lived in during the famous summer of 1973. They said the son, Teddy, was a royal pain to everyone."

Alice felt a familiar pit in her stomach that always came with the mention of Teddy Farrow's name. She didn't know if she would ever get over feeling guilty for bringing him into Daphne's life and for being the cause of her debilitating injuries and early death. How could she tell Sybil? Alice spoke slowly, "Oh yes, Teddy Farrow. Rocco mentioned that you suspect he may have played a role in the carjacking. That wouldn't surprise me at all. Even back when we were young, he was a slimy character and obviously very racist. I will always feel guilty for including him in our group. He was horrible to both Rocco and Gail but I think we put up with him, in part, because we had a sweet deal subletting the apartments and none of us expected to stay there much beyond the summer. That summer, I learned some things about Rocco and Gail I hadn't known before. They had both experienced racial prejudice and handled it with such grace. I think Teddy Farrow hated them even more for ignoring him."

Rocco, Gail and Rick, who had taken a walk to give the two women some privacy to reminisce, entered the apartment just as Alice mentioned their names. Catching the tail end of Alice's comments, Gail laughed bitterly,

"He was disgusting, and it wasn't just racist, it was totally sexist with me. He always found ways to stare at my chest and brush against me. Then he would sneer that horrid sneer."

Sybil nodded, "I've had the same experience with him. I think he's a misogynist. Makes me wonder how any woman would voluntarily have anything to do with him." Looking up at Rocco, Sybil continued, "I hope it's okay to talk about this. The only words I heard from the carjacker, that I heard in my dream state, were 'Teddy sent me'."

Alice sat up straight. "Did the carjacker identify Teddy by name?"

"No, that was all he said in the dream. However, at the police station after he was caught, he admitted someone told him to say those words."

"Someone?"

"I don't know if he was telling the truth, but he claimed he never met the person who hired them to do the carjacking and didn't know who Teddy is."

Alice looked closely at Sybil, "Do you think Teddy Farrow was behind the carjacking?"

"I don't know. I think he's a real piece of work who will do just about anything to save his own skin, and move his racist agenda forward. I have a hard time getting inside the head of a person who would do something like that, something that could result in permanent injury or even death." Sybil shuddered. "I know he hates me. From the get-go, he has always singled me out in hostile ways. We've all wondered why, I mean I'm not a particularly threatening person physically, and certainly have very little power. And our staff at Sussex Advocacy is very diverse. I'm not the only African-American who works there. I admit, I've been a thorn in his side for the past year, but he was awful to me even before. But murder? I just don't know."

Rocco interrupted. "I know we haven't talked about the court case my firm is working on that I had to come back for, Alice. This is a civil class action case to stop the Farrows and their cronies from going any further. We're hoping to win a major financial award on behalf of the people who've been illegally stripped of their homes and their legal rights by these overtly racist actions."

Looking around the room, which now included Carlos and Pablo, Rocco continued, "I invite you all, and everyone at Sussex Advocacy, to sit in the gallery. The trial is next week, Tuesday May 28th at 10a.m."

Taking this all in, Alice made a decision on the spot. "I will definitely be there, Rocco, but first, I want to tell you all something I've never shared with anyone. It's about Teddy."

She had everyone's attention.

"I have to start by apologizing to you, Gail and Rocco, for not listening when you asked me to push Teddy out of our happenings group. I'm ashamed that I was more interested in experimenting with human behavior. I was a kid, but that's no excuse. I had this idea that all people could be redeemed through art. I was very naive, and I was very thoughtless."

Gail spoke for everyone, "That was a long time ago, Alice."

"Nonetheless, it caused harm to my closest friends, and in the end, serious damage to an innocent person."

Now she really had everyone's attention.

"I believe Teddy was responsible for Daphne's accident, and ultimately for her early death."

Seeing Sybil's face go white, Rick crossed the room and took her hand. Everyone watched silently, waiting to hear his words. Once settled next to Sybil, Rick turned to Alice and said softly, "Please tell us the rest."

Alice went on to relate the whole story about Teddy following Daphne into the woods and scaring her with his threatening words. She told them how he had left Daphne's broken body on the ground.

Sybil broke in, "We, my family, never knew why she climbed the rocks and why she fell. Daphne would never talk about it. All we knew was that you had been afraid she was lost and went in search and found her lying on the ground. You saved her life."

Alice began to cry, "Oh Sybil, I truly loved Daphne and became very fond of your whole family, but I can't be painted as a saint. It was my fault that this tragedy took place. It was my fault for allowing Teddy to be part of what we were doing. I will never forgive myself for that. Now, hearing what he may have done to you Sybil, I feel like history's repeating itself, and with Daphne's niece. We can't let him get away with it again. The behavior's exactly the same, he continues to be a total coward, he continues to be motivated by racial hatred and disrespect, and he keeps getting away with it. No, I will not let that happen again."

Rocco and Gail were thinking the same thing. *That was what it was all about the day the three of us went our separate ways and we missed out on having one another all those years.*

Rocco said, "I don't know exactly what I'm going to do with this information, but I will figure it out. If we can get him on criminal as well as civil charges, we can prevent him from going forward with his destructive behavior. I've heard rumors about him running for public office. If we can get him convicted on criminal charges, attempted murder is a felony. Even if he never serves a day in prison, he'd be prevented from holding a public office. We have to try. Alice, I'm assuming Daphne told you what happened that day?"

"Yes, it came out in dribs and drabs but in the end we decided to keep it quiet because his family was so powerful. It was her word against his. She was afraid he would harm her family. I went along because I agreed with her that there was a huge power gap, and there were no eye witnesses."

Rocco nodded, "I'm thinking we have a better chance of getting him on the current carjacking/attempted murder charge and use the earlier crime to show pattern. That was a long time ago, but I suspect there have been other incidents over the years. Once we tap that vein, it's possible we'll hear other stories. I know it's all circumstantial, but a lot of circumstantial evidence can be convincing to a jury. We just have to do the research. Meanwhile, the carjacker remains in jail. I'm pretty sure he knows more and is the key to resolving this case."

The implications of what they had just heard began to seep in and everyone in the room sat silently while they absorbed it. Pablo was the first to speak up. The rest of the group could hear the wheels turning in his head as he looked at Rocco and said, "I will definitely be there to support your efforts, but is there anything I can do to help you prepare? Carlos and I have also suffered from discriminatory actions promoted by the Farrows, both for being Hispanic, and for being gay."

"Let me think about it. This case is very specific, but it can't hurt to demonstrate illegal discriminatory business patterns in general. These folks are extremely slick and extremely cocky about their ability to get away with things. We're quite convinced they're aligned with a variety of powerful like-minded special interest groups, including the mob."

Gail watched as Rocco went into lawyer mode. She was beginning to read his various moods, and enjoying every one of them. She particularly liked his laser focus and determination to right wrongs.

Alice had noted the comfort between Rocco and Gail. She was also remembering how seamless the three of them had been with each another throughout most of the summer of 1973, until they began drifting apart. It made her happy to think Gail and Rocco might be a couple.

Unaware of the two women's silent thoughts, Rocco continued musing about moving forward with the criminal case against Teddy Farrow.

"I think we've identified two witnesses who can probably point that finger. It was pretty obvious to me that the carjacker,

Joreth, knows more than he's told the police. But as long as they have him in custody, we can get more information from him. He's a kid and as tough as he tries to bluff, I think he's scared. He has yet to identify the other gang member who collaborated in the carjacking."

Sybil was curious. "Besides the other carjacker, who could very well be hidden away somewhere by now, who's the second witness?"

"This may come as a surprise to you, but I believe the Farrow's defense witness list includes your friend Angela Park."

Sybil sighed, "I'm not surprised. As soon as I heard she had fingered me, I learned that Angela has another agenda. But it's still shocking. She's supposed to be an advocate for people who are being discriminated against. I can't help wondering why she would do any of this."

Rocco continued, "Murder of any stripe is a whole other ballgame. I'm thinking out loud now. Of course we'll do what we can to get them on the civil discrimination charge, but I'm increasingly convinced we can put together a criminal case against Teddy Farrow as well. Do you think your mother would be willing to talk with me about Daphne? I'm sure there are things we don't know about what went down with Teddy."

Alice cleared her throat to release the lump that was forming there, "You know, I never connected those dots, but I do know that Daphne was adamant that we not tell anyone in her family about Teddy's role in what happened. I suspect Melissa never knew, but she was also a victim, wasn't she?"

Gail said, "If I recall, Alice, Melissa complained to you about Teddy's behavior a couple of weeks before our last happening. I think she stopped coming after that and we were surprised to see Daphne show up by herself that last time."

Sybil answered Rocco's first question. "I never heard any of this when I was growing up, but I know my mother shared everyone's negative opinion of Teddy. I think she said something about him when I called to tell her about meeting Rocco and Gail. Maybe you can ask her if there was a specific reason why she complained about him. Of course I can give you her number, Rocco. I'm sure she would be willing to help. I've always had the feeling she feels guilty for what happened to Daphne because she wasn't there to protect her."

Chapter 46

Teddy Farrow was sitting in the courtroom surrounded by a large team of lawyers. As Rocco and his colleagues courteously shook hands with the lawyers they knew, Teddy smirked at Rocco who gave him a big smile in return. Shortly thereafter, the plaintiff's side of the room began to fill up. Teddy glanced over to see what "losers" they had brought in to testify against him. He was shocked to see a number of people he hadn't seen in many years, and wondered loudly what they were doing there.

Stacy, Les and Ed, along with some of Angela Park's colleagues at Jaffe Anti-Racism filed into the courtroom and sat in the row behind the lawyers. They were followed by Pablo, Carlos, and Rick, along with four women Teddy had hoped never to see again. It was bad enough to see older versions of Alice and Gail, but when they all sat down and stared directly at him, he was looking at the mulatto bitch, Sybil Morgenstern, and an older woman who looked just like her. Then it hit him, she was one of the teenagers, one of the dancers in the park he had had so much fun with that summer.

Rocco was amused to see Teddy's face blanch as he clearly began to recognize each individual and started talking loudly to one of his lawyers, demanding,

"These people have nothing to do with our case. We need to remove them from the courtroom. You need to tell the judge, they are only here to intimidate me."

Surprised at the fear in Teddy's voice, the lawyer looked to where he was pointing.

"I'm not sure we can do that, Teddy, I don't know some of them, but at least half are from Sussex Advocacy and Jaffe Anti-Racist. They have a legitimate interest in this case. Let it go, man, we know we can beat them. Besides, we have one of them testifying that it's all lies."

As the courtroom began to fill with spectators, Rocco turned to his friends.

"I've been told that Angela Park will be their first witness. It's actually surprising she hasn't shown up yet. Anyway, the police said no to Joreth being in the courtroom so I'm going to have to find another way to show him her picture. By the way, try not to get too angry hearing how the Farrows talk about the people whose lives they've ruined. As you can see, the courtroom is filling up with them. This will be front page news one way or the other."

Sybil looked back at the courtroom entrance,

"Oh, there's Angela. It's so crowded here. How interesting, it looks like some of the people who've come to see this show, know her. I wonder if they're her clients. Won't they be surprised when they hear her defend the Farrows?"

Angela Park made it through the crowd and found a seat behind Teddy. Everyone on the other side of the aisle watched as Teddy greeted her and pointed at them. Instead of looking, Angela turned away and looked at the floor. Sybil couldn't help thinking there was something beyond strange going on with Angela. She did not look happy, and why would she be? Here she was actively undermining the people, her clients and colleagues, who had worked so hard to get to this place in their fight against racism and discrimination.

Then, the most extraordinary thing happened. Angela jumped out of her seat and began running up the aisle, pushing the throngs of people who were still trying to get into the courtroom aside. She was closely followed by Teddy Farrow, who was yelling at her to get back into the courtroom, the case was about to be opened and she was their star witness. She yelled back that she couldn't do it. They had the whole court's attention, so when Angela went through the doors into the corridor, followed by Teddy, they were greeted by a slew of reporters with both video and digital cameras.

Although they were pursued by members of the press, Angela managed to get away from Teddy, who was none too happy when he returned to the courtroom. His lawyers calmed him down by convincing him that Farrow Holdings had a clear legal right, according to state law, to choose who could live and work in their buildings and they did not need Angela's testimony to prove it. However, they asked the judge to postpone the beginning of the trial so they could readjust the order of witnesses, and were granted their request.

Rocco was happy with the delay. Not only did Angela back out of the case, he now had the time to seek out a reporter, any reporter, who had videotaped Angela as she left the courtroom.

As it turned out, he didn't have to beg a reporter for the video. More than one local news station had been broadcasting live and the Angela-Teddy drama had been one of the few bits they thought would brighten up a dull news day. Rocco rushed to the police department to ask if Joreth was allowed to watch television and discovered he was actually sitting in front of one at that very moment.

After he told Detective Costa that the woman they suspected of colluding on the carjacking could be seen on the news, the detective consented to go into the rec room and switch the station so he could observe Joreth. They wanted it to be as casual as possible, so the detective announced that he just wanted to catch a minute or two of the news. Moans and groans from the inmates followed and Joreth asked if he could use the rest room.

The detective took his time while Rocco settled in behind a two-way mirror. Then he addressed Joreth,

"In a few minutes, Joreth, I don't want to miss this."

As they tuned in, the news reporter was talking about the trial and the strange turn it had taken.

"The highly anticipated trial pitting disenfranchised minority renters against real estate companies that have thrown them out of their homes without due process, was abruptly paused this morning. In fact, it never actually got started as the lawyers defending Farrow Holdings asked to postpone due to a sudden change in their witness roster. Although no-one is talking details, as far as we can tell, a representative of the Jaffe Anti-Racism Society, a Newark based advocacy organization, Angela Park, was scheduled to be the first witness. She was seen entering the courtroom, which by that time was filling with throngs of people who felt they had been wronged by the defendants. As she entered the room, she had brief conversations with some of those people, then walked to the front and sat down behind the Farrow Holdings representatives and lawyers. Shortly thereafter, she left the courtroom followed by Teddy Farrow, who was obviously attempting to keep her from leaving. Although it happened suddenly, our reporters managed to catch some of their animated interaction as they pushed their way through the hall and out of the courthouse. It is not known where Ms. Park went, but Mr. Farrow returned five minutes later and spoke angrily to anyone who would listen, blaming the media and the crowds who had by that time gathered outside of the courthouse and filled its corridors."

As the reporter said these words, the broadcast repeatedly showed a short video of Angela Park and Teddy Farrow pushing their way through the crowd. While Rocco watched carefully to see if Joreth would indicate that he recognized Angela, Detective Costa wanted to be careful not to influence Joreth's reaction in any way.

The detective and Rocco were both discouraged as it was clear that Joreth had no interest in the news. Instead, with a bored expression, he amused himself by kicking a wad of paper he found on the floor. Then, he looked briefly at the television screen and began to complain that it was getting on his nerves. He stopped mid-whine as the video showed Angela trying to push away from Teddy and said in a soft voice,

"Ha Ha, there's The Sniffer, what an asshole!"

At that point Joreth began to watch the video with interest, but said nothing else.

Detective Costa looked casually at the two-way mirror, then turned back to Joreth who was trying to get his attention.

"Hey man, Mr. Policeman, I really need to go to the head. Can you take me?"

Detective Costa was pleased. This meant Joreth had something to say to him he couldn't say in front of the other inmates. However, the detective stayed in character as he turned to the rec room monitor and said, "You can switch the channel back to whatever garbage was on before. I'll take Joreth to the little boy's room and drop him back here before heading to my office."

There was a titter of laughter as Joreth and Detective Costa left the room, but neither of them paid much attention. Both were anticipating getting something they wanted, and both were focused on figuring out the best way to do that.

Detective Costa had been correct. Once he recognized "The Sniffer," Joreth had paid close attention as he heard the newscaster describe who "The Sniffer" was and that he was part of a family of multi-millionaires. This was a big big fish and Joreth could bring him down. His only regret was that he was inside now and couldn't directly blackmail him. But he could possibly cut a deal with the cops for a lighter sentence, or even probation. Deep down he was terrified of being in a real prison where he was vulnerable to prison rape and other shit he couldn't imagine. Yes, he had to negotiate zero prison time.

By the time they reached the bathroom, Joreth actually needed to go. His nerves were on edge and he needed to plan his next moves carefully, but he also feared this was his only chance. It was now or never. So when he walked out of the room, he addressed the detective with a clear voice.

"Can we talk?"

"Talk about what, Joreth? Seems to me you don't remember anything that helps us solve this. You say you were hired to steal the car, but don't know who hired you; you say you were signaled by someone at the parking lot; but you don't know who that was; you say you were with another gangbanger, but you've never given his name and he seems to have disappeared off the face of the earth. So what can you tell me I don't already know?"

"Can we go into one of those interview rooms? I don't want to talk in the hallway."

Detective Costa growled, but led Joreth into an empty interview room saying. "This better be good."

"If I help you, can I get out of jail?"

"That depends, Joreth. It would have to be really big."

"I think it's really big."

"Should we include your lawyer in this conversation?"

"What for, he's never done nothing for me."

"Okay, but before you talk, we need to bring someone else in here to be a witness. I don't want this to come back to bite me."

Detective Costa walked out to the hall where he ran into Rocco. He told him it sounded like Joreth was going to do some talking and he was going to his office to ask someone to act as stenographer. Rocco was still in shock about what he had observed from behind the two way mirror.

"He recognized Teddy! Wow, I didn't know they had ever met. In fact, I've been under the impression that he was strictly kept from knowing who had hired him to do the carjacking."

The detective nodded, "I actually don't know what he's about to tell me, but I do know he thinks it will help his case. He says it's very big."

By the time Costa returned to the room with the stenographer, Joreth was ready to burst.

The detective sat down and looked straight into Joreth's eyes. "You've already been read your rights, you understand them?"

"Yes"

"What do you want to tell me?"

"That guy on the news, the one they said was a multi-millionaire. He's one of my clients."

"What do you mean, your client?"

"I mean he's a junkie who buys my shit on the street corner. We call him "The Sniffer" because he sounds like he's got a runny nose twenty-four seven. I know a lot of sniffers, but this guy is extreme. He's always sniffing."

"Did you hear him sniffing on the newscast? Is that how you knew it was him?"

"Nah, it was the hair. No one has hair as weird as this dude. It's like he has clumps on a bald head that he combs over to cover the bald spots, then he dyes it an odd pinkish color. No-one else looks like him. I only had to see him for a second."

"When he was your 'client,' what did you call him? Did you ever hear his name?"

"Nope, he just showed up. He knew my hours and he always bought the same stuff, the powder mix I specialized in, and paid cash." Joreth hesitated for a moment. "But I heard his name on the TV it was Farrow, something Farrow."

"His name is Teddy Farrow, Joreth. Have you ever heard that name before?"

"I don't know. I mean I know the name Teddy. That's the name I was supposed to tell the lady in the car. Wait, are these things connected?"

Joreth stared at Detective Costa while his mind buzzed.

"The dope in the car, I was supposed to leave a bag in the glove compartment but I forgot. That's the blend The Sniffer uses. Could The Sniffer have been the one who hired us to do the carjack? That junkie! Shit! He set me up!"

Chapter 47

June 2002
Newark NJ

Angela Park never returned to the courtroom and apparently left for parts unknown. Even her colleagues at Jaffe were shocked when she stopped showing up for work without explanation and wondered what had motivated her to consider testifying on the Farrow's behalf. Without her testimony, Farrow Holdings failed to convince the judge they had the right to discriminate against Muslim families with no criminal history simply because "they were potential terrorists." In addition to proving that such discrimination violated the law, Rocco and his team were successful in demonstrating that the Farrows had a history of racial discrimination in their rental business and housing sales, a history that long preceded 9-11.

Sybil, Rick, Alice, Melissa, Gail, Carlos, Pablo, Stacy, Les, and Ed, attended every day of the trial. Each day, Rocco smiled benignly at Teddy as Teddy returned his signature smirk. Despite his attempts to appear unaffected by the fact that all these people faithfully attended to watch him lose the case, Teddy wanted to make it clear that he considered them to be the losers, that he was never the loser. He would rise to beat them next time around. Even when the judge announced her verdict, requiring Farrow Holdings to pay the aggrieved parties huge amounts of money and to allow them to return to the homes they had been evicted from, he continued to smirk as he looked straight ahead and said nothing.

However, he couldn't control his need to be disrespectful towards Rocco, and as they were all getting up to leave, walked over to him and said, "I should never have allowed you to sublet in my building back in 1973. We had to fumigate the apartment after you left."

Rocco laughed out loud. "And I thought you've ignored me all these years because you forgot about that summer."

By this time, the rest of the group was paying attention. Staring directly at Melissa and Sybil as if to challenge their ability to speak out, Teddy said, "I only remember it because it was the last time I wasted being with so many losers, with your stupid happenings in the park and your ridiculous walks through magic walls."

Sniffing loudly, Teddy began to walk away without noticing he was being followed by Detective Costa. Not surprisingly, the detective had taken an interest in the court case and attended the last few days of the trial. Rocco and his friends and colleagues took comfort knowing this was the first day of the rest of what they hoped would be Teddy's miserable life, beginning with a series of criminal cases resulting in his serving time in prison.

Everyone agreed this was a moment to celebrate the outcome of the court case and what they saw as a good beginning to stopping the Farrows, at least for the moment. They also recognized the road ahead would undoubtedly include failures as well as successes.

As they watched Teddy leave the courtroom, Alice surprised her friends by bringing up Watergate. "I know it's different now, but I can't help thinking that, if nothing else, a criminal record will prevent Teddy from being elected to public office. We dodged a bullet with Nixon, but came really close to losing our democracy to a mentally unstable leader."

Sybil smiled, "I know Teddy has delusions of grandeur, but he's so obviously crazy, there's no way he could win an election."

Alice said, "I hope you're right. Hey, is anyone interested in taking a walk in Central Park?"

Melissa walked over to Sybil and took her hand, "I think I'm finally ready to put the bad memories away where they belong. Are you up for dancing with me and Daphne around the magic tree?"

Rocco threw his arms over Gail and Alice's shoulders. Then he said, "Wait a minute, I almost forgot," and pulled out a small wooden frog from his pocket. "What do you say, Gail? Are you ready to take this trip down memory lane?"

EPILOGUE

Epilogue

With the new information from Joreth, the police, led by Detective Costa, began digging into what they were learning about Teddy Farrow and his personal history. The more they dug, the more they learned how much he had gotten away with over the years, that there was a clear pattern of amoral, sometimes criminal, behavior that almost always began with him feeling that some "loser" was preventing him from getting what he wanted. More often than not, the "loser" was a non-white female. Yet, he always got away with this behavior because he used other people to do the actual dirty work when it approached criminality and his crude behavior was excused as "a boy being a boy."

After hearing what Teddy had done to Melissa and Daphne, Detective Costa became dedicated to bringing together a criminal case for the attempted murder of Sybil Morgenstern. While the evidence was circumstantial, Costa thought he had a good chance of proving culpability. Even if the Farrow mob connections kept Teddy out of prison, he would never be able to run for public office as was being rumored. Detective Costa felt that he could at least provide this public service.

Once he realized how he had been used, Joreth told the police what he knew. In addition, although he had only seen her from a distance, Joreth identified Angela Park from photographs and news footage. This gave the police enough to get into her cellphone records, which, in turn, provided what they needed to connect her with the carjacking, and get a handle on her relationship with Teddy Farrow.

It was now in the hands of a Grand Jury.

Acknowledgements

So Much for Walls was originally created to re-imagine the outcome of a personal carjacking experience. Equally important, and totally unrelated, was a strong desire to write about two very dear friends, William "Gil" Gilmore and Gail Lee Cooper. They both had fascinating life stories and left us way too soon. While these were the seeds, as usual, the story and characters evolved and left reality in its wake. A complete work of fiction, this is neither the story of Gil nor Gail's life, nor the actual outcome of the carjacking, but writing it gave me an opportunity to create a more satisfying alternative reality in all three cases.

None of this would have been possible without the encouragement I have received from the many friends who enjoyed my first book and urged me to continue writing fiction. I cannot begin to describe how important their encouragement and feedback have been to my work. I specifically want to thank the following people who were kind enough to read and share their thoughts about early draft materials: Irene Angel, Diane Woodworth Liebert, Liz Smith, Bonnyeclaire Smith Stewart, Jean Woodley, and my fellow members of the Germantown-Mt.Airy Writer's Group, Patricia Beynen, Conrad Person, Emily Peña Murphey and Anthony Webb. Special thanks to super editor Donna Ursillo, who read the manuscript many times and patiently urged me to review my habitual overuse of certain phrases and semi-colons. Last, but never least, I thank my husband, Ray Basanta, for his support throughout this process. As usual he played an active role in helping me think about the characters and story development.

Publication of this book would not have been possible without the technical assistance I received from experts. I am very grateful to Nick Caya and Krizia Thompson of Word-2-Kindle for their assistance with final formatting and preparation of the manuscript, and to Rob Schmidt and Jim Deluzio of Blue Line Marketing LLC for the design and creation of the book's cover. Katharina Woodworth and photographer Mark LeNord generously shared the beautiful cover photograph he took of her standing on the shore of the Arctic Ocean in Alaska, an image that speaks to me as a metaphor for ways to think about walls, a central theme of the story.

Finally, I wish to thank Michael Albany for the back cover author's photograph.

About the Author

Lynn Woodworth Gregory was born in 1947 in New Rochelle, NY; lived in Buenos Aires, Argentina between the ages of one and six during the post-World War II dictatorship of Juan Perón; and spent the remainder of her childhood in Norwalk Connecticut. Her father was an international businessman who worked in the export-import shipping field and their home was often visited by people from around the world. A "Child of the Sixties," she traveled extensively throughout the United States, attending four different universities (in Cleveland, Boston, Long Beach, and Philadelphia) and ended up with college degrees in Social and Cultural Anthropology and Education and a professional career that revolved around research designed to learn about different cultures and ways to bridge gaps in cross-cultural communication. Throughout her forty-year career, Dr. Gregory met and heard the stories of a variety of interesting people, many of whom, along with her own life experiences have inspired the creation of the fictional characters and stories. She retired from her position as Executive Director of Partnerships for Creative Action in 2015, took a few years off to relax, then began writing fiction for fun. Her first novel, *The Other Side of a Tapestry* was published in 2020. *So Much for Walls* is her second completed work of fiction. She currently lives in Philadelphia PA with her husband, Raymond Basanta.

www.ingramcontent.com/pod-product-compliance
Lightning Source LLC
Chambersburg PA
CBHW020636260626
47157CB00008B/2778